Burial

Burial

Neil Cross

A Tom Doherty Associates Book

New York

BURIAL

First published in Great Britain by Simon & Schuster UK Ltd, 2009

A Forge Book
Published by Tom Doherty Associates, LLC
175 Fifth Avenue
New York, NY 10010

www.tor-forge.com

Forge® is a registered trademark of Tom Doherty Associates, LLC.

ISBN 978-0-7653-2587-7

First U.S. Edition: March 2010

Printed in the United States of America

0 9 8 7 6 5 4 3 2 1

This story is for Nadya, Ethan and Finn, for holding my hand and making me happy. It's for Jack the dog, too, if he promises to stop running away, and eating my macaroons.

Burial

1

The doorbell rang.

Nathan had a feeling – but he dismissed it, muted the TV and went to the door. There stood Bob; hunched over, grinning in the darkness and rain. Saying: 'Hello, mate.'

Nathan said, 'How did you find me?'

'I looked.'

Nathan tried to slam the door, but Bob put out a big hand, stopping it. Then he removed the hand and said, 'They're digging up the woods.'

'They're what?'

'Digging up the woods.'

'Why?'

'Does it matter? They're building a housing estate.'

'Of course it doesn't matter. What kind of housing estate?'

'The kind people live in. Are you actually listening?'

'Yes. Yeah, of course.'

Nathan glanced backwards, as if somebody was standing at his shoulder. But nobody was; it was Tuesday night. That meant Holly would be back late.

He said, 'Look. Give me a call. Phone me at work.'

'I'm here. Right now.'

'You can't come in. I'll meet you somewhere. Tomorrow.'

'I'll be gone in two minutes.'

'My wife will be home.'

But Bob just stood there, waiting in the rain. So Nathan gathered his breath and moved aside. Bob stepped over the threshold and stood dripping on the wooden floor.

He'd noticed the many framed photographs that hung in the hallway.

Nathan waited while Bob took a squinting step forward, examining the photographs more closely. A baby girl, naked on a towel. A gap-toothed girl with a pageboy haircut. The fringe was blunt and a bit crooked – obviously trimmed by her mother. A holiday photograph in which the girl was a very young teenager, her hair short and bleached and spiky. She stood on the deck of a boat, wearing an orange life jacket. She was holding up a long, silver mackerel. In that photograph, she was laughing.

Bob looked at the photographs for a long time.

When he turned to Nathan, his voice had gone.

'What the fuck is *this*?'

'I told you not to come in.'

Using the wall for balance, Bob lowered himself. He sat on the stripped Victorian floorboards. He looked wrong, like an optical illusion, like a drawing where the perspective and the scale have been altered.

Fingertips brushed the hair on Nathan's nape.

In the living room, the TV flickered – and it seemed to Nathan that the lights dimmed, and flickered, then rose again.

2

Nathan and Bob had met fifteen years before, in the summer of 1993.

Nathan was renting a small room in a house on Maple Road. A year after leaving university, he was claiming benefit and waiting to be awarded a job on the city's biweekly listings magazine. The magazine had yet to bother rejecting his unsolicited job applications, or any of his unsolicited gig, film and record reviews. Nathan was encouraged by this lack of explicit rejection: his plan was to sit around and keep applying.

Because all the rooms in 30 Maple Road were rented out, there was no communal space in which to gather. So Nathan and his house-mates spent the dole days drifting from bedroom to bedroom, drinking lots of Happy Shopper tea.

That afternoon, Pete's room was pretty quiet: from it there emerged only the earthquake throb of an E-string fed through a large amplifier and a digital delay pedal.

Nathan lay in bed, listening to it. Then he swung his legs over the edge of the bed, put on his trousers and a washed-out band T-shirt, and wandered across the mangy hallway.

Because Pete had lived in the house the longest, he'd graduated to the biggest room. In it, an old mattress doubled as a sofa. The sofa had been rescued from a skip outside next-door's house. Propped against the wall was a monumental, patched-together stereo – assembled from gaffer-taped components joined by coloured leads and soldered interconnects.

Pete always had people in his room. Often, they were members of what was still called *the convoy* – patchouli-ripe crusties who told endless dull tales of the Battle of the Beanfield. There were Goths, too, and sometimes ravers, a youth culture for which Nathan didn't much care. There were oblique Rastafarians, a benevolent hippie called Fuzzy Rob, a speed-dealing biker called Carnie Frank, a morbidly obese West Indian truck driver called Reds. There were dangerous-looking, sarcastic men in baggy old jeans and prison tattoos.

But this afternoon, there was just a big, scruffy, feline man lolling on one of the old sofas. He wore an ivory shirt, a navy-blue suit threadbare at the cuffs and long, knotty hair that might have been backcombed since last being washed.

Nathan nodded hello and sat on the floor, hugging his bony knees. The stranger put a Bic flame to the end of a John Player Special. When it was lit, he leaned forward to offer Nathan his hand.

'Bob.'

Nathan shook the hand. It was very big. Shaking hands made Nathan self-conscious, like a kid playing grown-ups.

Pete sat cross-legged beneath the monstrous, teetering stereo. He wore a matted red dressing gown and dirty white socks.

Bob had a leather briefcase with him; scuffed at the seams, perhaps a lucky find in a charity shop. From it, he withdrew a Dictaphone, which he put on the floor in front of Pete, saying: 'Shall we get on?'

Nathan said, 'So, what's this all about?'

Bob was producing a spiral-bound reporter's notebook and a chewed-up Bic. 'A friend of a friend put me in contact with Pete. He's agreed to be interviewed.'

'For what?'

'My research.'

'Cool. Are you a journalist?'

'No. It's just research.'

'For . . .?'

'My PhD.'

Nathan looked from one to the other and back again; at big-handed, cumbersome Bob – and Pete in his tatty scarlet dressing gown.

He said, 'Really?'

'Really.'

'What are you researching? Music?'

Music was Pete's only interest – music and a girl called Emma, who'd dumped him eighteen months ago.

Bob gave Nathan an imperious look, and Pete stepped in: 'He wants to know about my brother.'

'Mate, I didn't even know you had a brother.'

'That's the point.'

'So, what? Is he inside or something? Like, all black sheep and shit.'

Bob said, 'If you would,' meaning *Shut the fuck up, please*. He turned to Pete. 'Would you prefer to be alone for this?'

'Nah. Nathan can sit in. If he's into it.'

Nathan was into it.

Bob told him, 'If you stay, please don't interrupt. Please don't ask any questions.'

'All right. Whatever. Jesus.'

Bob leaned a little towards the Dictaphone and said, 'July 4th, 1993. 1.30 p.m. The subject is Pete King, aged . . .'

'Twenty-four.'

'Pete King. Aged twenty-four.'

For a moment, Nathan thought Pete was about to start giggling. But instead he sat up – cross-legged and straight-backed – and began to talk.

Bob: So, when are we talking about?

Pete: Summer, 1981. June or July or something. I think it was June.

And your older brother?

David, his name was. We lived out in the country – our dad had a farm. When I was little, I used to follow our David round. He showed me all these secret places. He called me a limpet; but he didn't mind, not really – not even when I went off alone to have a gander at his jazz mags.

[Laughter]

There was all these knackered old *Men Onlys* and *Razzles* and *Clubs*. He had them stashed in an old box between the roots of this massive old yew tree, right on the edge of our dad's land, down by the river. It must've been five hundred years old, that tree, and our David used it to stash dirty magazines.

And how old were you – when David died?

Twelve, I suppose. Twelve, going on thirteen.

What happened?

It was stupid, really. He was helping our dad fix the bailer. It was Friday afternoon and he was in too much of a hurry. He got his arm caught, then it was ripped out of the socket. Our dad was with him. He ran off to call the ambulance, but by the time it gets there, our David's dead.

And how did you feel about that?

I don't know how I felt about it, really. It was all a bit weird. Shock, or whatever. Our mum was crying and our dad was drinking, and all these aunties and uncles and neighbours and Granddad and Grandma were round. It was sort of like I wasn't there.

What happened next?

Well, they buried him.

Did you attend the funeral?

Yeah. But I didn't think that much of it. I'm sitting on this bloody pew in a suit, all tight round the collar. And nobody's said two proper words to me about him. It's a really hot day. You remember that summer – they had all the riots, St Paul's, Toxteth, Brixton and wherever.

So anyway. On the way home in the car, I'm not speaking. I don't cry or nothing; I just don't speak. And as soon as the car pulls up outside the farm, I run inside. Our mum's got this big spread laid out. Sandwiches and that – pork pies, this massive ham.

Our dad comes up to me and says, Don't do this to your mother, not today of all days.

So I start crying and run upstairs. I'm so pissed off, I don't know what to do. So I start looking round for something to smash. I want to break something – something I really care about. Does that make sense?

It's very common.

Anyway. I'm standing in the middle of my bedroom, fists all clenched, and I think: the Specials.

Our David had been to see them – in Bristol, at the Locarno, in

1980. He'd hung round outside and got the album signed. Not Terry Hall – but Neville had his name on there, and Roddy Radiation. It was David's most treasured thing, and I'd always wanted it. I used to nick it, hide it among my records. I only had about five – *Top of the Pops* and Disney songs and that – so he always found it, easy. So anyway. I go to David's bedroom and I kneel down, and there it is – the most precious thing in his world, the first Specials album, signed by Neville Staple and Roddy Radiation.

I had it in my hands – I was going to snap it – when I see something in the wardrobe mirror. I look up, thinking it must be our dad and I'm in deep shit. But it's not our dad. It's our David.

Your brother David?

My dead brother David, yeah.

What was he doing?

Just sort of sitting there. Smiling at me.

Did he speak?

He didn't need to. It was the kindest smile I ever saw. Like he knew exactly what I was doing, and why I was doing it. The funny thing is, the first thing I thought to do was to put the record back where it belongs. So I do that, and when I look up, our David's gone.

What happened next?

I sit there on the edge of the bed, next to where David had been. Then go down to the wake and say sorry to our mum and dad. They were all right about it.

Did you mention seeing David?

No need.

Had anything like this happened to you before?

No.

And since?

No.

One last question. What was David wearing?

[Pause]

I don't know. I can't even remember. How weird is that?

Bob sat back on the sofa, pocketing the Dictaphone.

Pete relit the skinny joint he'd allowed to go out.

Nathan said, 'Blimey.'

Pete puffed and exhaled, saying, 'Freaky or what?'

The door creaked loudly and Nathan's heart exploded in his chest. He looked over his shoulder, at the door, saying, 'Christ. I'm getting the fear.'

Bob told him, 'Sometimes, telling these stories acts as a kind of evocation.'

'Evocation of what?'

'I don't know. Whatever.'

Nathan's feet were cold. The worn carpet was bitty on his soles. He said, 'What are you talking about?'

'I'm doing ghosts.'

'Doing ghosts.'

'Studying them.'

'Yeah, right.'

'Absolutely. I'm two years into a PhD. Psychology.'

'But there's no such thing as ghosts.' He cast a quick, guilty glance at Pete. 'Sorry, mate.'

Pete shrugged, unbothered.

Bob began to pack up his briefcase, saying: 'So, is Pete lying?'

'Of course he's not.'

'Is he mad?'

'No.'

'Was he seeing things?'

'No.'

'Then what happened?'

'I don't know.'

'Nor do I. That's why I'm studying it.'

Bob stayed a little while longer. They drank a cup of tea and Pete played his band's demo. Bob nodded along and seemed to approve; he promised to come to Pete's next gig. They all knew he wouldn't. Then he thanked Pete and told Nathan it had been good to meet him.

Bob said, 'See you later, then.'

Nathan thought: *Not if I see you first*. But he said: 'You must have an idea – you must have an opinion.'

'On what?'

'On what they are. Ghosts.'

'They're any number of things. Illusion, delusion, hallucination. Electromagnetic phenomena dicking around with the temporal lobe. Infra-sound. All of the above, and more. Not many people know this, but most ghosts are spectres of the living. The ghost of a living person is called a fetch.'

'A fetch.'

'A fetch.'

'Yeah, right.'

'It's true,' said Bob, with the briefcase in his hand.

He said goodbye, and they heard him stomp down the stairs – then the creak and slam of the front door.

'Fuck me,' said Nathan. 'Where did you find *him*?'
They laughed.
On the bass, Pete banged out the riff from *Ghostbusters*.
Nathan said, 'Is it true? What you told him?'

He didn't see Bob again for four and a half years.

3

That September, Maple Road's tolerant old landlord died, leaving the house to his daughter, who put it straight on the market. Unprotected by tenancy agreements, the housemates drifted off and away.

After Pete's band, Odorono, split up, he moved to a squat in London. A couple of years later, Nathan saw a small picture of him in *Melody Maker*: Odorono had become the Odorons. They released one independent album before succumbing to musical differences. Nathan was one of the few who bought the CD; it was called *The Malibu Stacey Sessions*. Nathan played it three times, and tried each time to like it but never could. He filed *The Malibu Stacey Sessions* at the back of his collection, where it couldn't shame him with his indifference.

Now it was Christmas, 1997.

For three years, Nathan had been employed as a researcher on a late-night local talk-back programme called *The Mark Derbyshire Solution*. The presenter, Mark Derbyshire, was paunchy and balding – with a neatly shaped beard which failed to obscure his close physical resemblance to a beaver. He wore satin shirts in primary colours, open to the third button.

Usually, *The Mark Derbyshire Solution*'s lonesome audience could be relied upon to trumpet their opinion on the day's news stories. When those stories weren't conducive to late-night chat, Nathan had to dig up some current issue that involved paedophilia, satanism, immigration, child murder, miracle cancer cures, political correctness gone mad, or European integration. This was called research. Mostly, it consisted of reading the *Daily Mail*.

When this think-tank of the lonely was in proper, eye-rolling form, Mark Derbyshire and the show's producer (a louche and florid ex-Fleet Street hack called Howard) kept Nathan around simply to have someone to humiliate.

A great deal of Nathan's job, therefore, involved popping out to the local twenty-four-hour garage or supermarket to buy tampons, extra-strength condoms, laxatives, or K-Y Jelly. Sometimes all four. Sometimes, if Mark was feeling especially beneficent, Nathan might be sent to get the Jag washed instead. Sometimes, he was sent out with a pocket stuffed full of five-pound notes; in the early hours of the morning, he was required to approach strangers – in the street, on late-night garage forecourts and in taxi queues – whereupon he would ask them for that evening's code word, which had been decided by Mark: it might be simply *big brassieres*, or it might be *Nuke Saddam*, or it might be *Mark Derbyshire is a Sex Donkey*!

Slowly, this occasional item became a semi-regular feature. Eventually it was given a name: *A Fistful of Fivers, in Association with Infinity Motors, Ltd*. Mark would send Nathan on to the street at 2 a.m. with £2,000 in his pocket, cash. Nathan would hang around waiting to encounter some lucky member of Derby's Crew, which is what Mark called his listeners.

It didn't take Nathan very long to learn how to distribute the cash safely and quickly. Mostly, he handed wads of it to minicab drivers filling up at the twenty-four-hour garage round the corner – it was not terribly far from the police station.

Many of the cab drivers were regular listeners to *The Mark Derbyshire Solution* – although many of them, being immigrants, were also part of *The Mark Derbyshire Problem*.

Nathan was twenty-seven and at the fag end of a relationship with a girl called Sara, with whom he had once, not very long ago, believed himself to be in love. Now the sight of her nettled and demoralized him.

Sara didn't much like Nathan, either – so probably it was fortunate they barely saw one another. *The Mark Derbyshire Solution* was broadcast from midnight, which meant Nathan left for work shortly after 9 p.m. Sara worked in an office and didn't get home until 7.30. This left about ninety minutes for them to get through.

Nathan was pretty sure that Sara was sleeping with her boss, who was called Alex and looked like that kind of man.

There were hints. She'd taken to showering when she got home, as well as when she got up. She no longer wore her slightly tattier, more practical underwear to the office and her lingerie at the weekends; that behaviour pattern had suddenly (and neatly) reversed itself.

Nathan sometimes saw the flickerings of deceit in her face: the sidelong glance, the secret smile for a private allusion.

'Are you okay?' he would say.

'Fine,' she'd say – and smile that dreamy, knowing smile.

Nathan felt bad for her.

Now he'd decided the time had come to finish it with Sara; one of them had to do it. This is why he'd accepted that year's invitation to Mark Derbyshire's Christmas party. It was to be a kind of parting gift, and a kind of unspoken apology.

Sara didn't listen to *The Mark Derbyshire Solution* – it was on too late – but she'd always been impressed that Nathan worked for Mark Derbyshire, who had once been famous. And she'd always wanted to go to his party. But every year Nathan found an excuse not to.

The Christmas party had been written into Mark's contract when he still meant something, which was a very long time ago indeed. But the radio station still paid for the drinks, the canapés and a miserable local wedding DJ to play some Boney M. records. Most of the senior management and a number of the station DJs and newsreaders felt compelled to attend. Many of the junior staff actively looked forward to it and so, apparently, did the communities local to Mark's house.

Before leaving for work on Wednesday evening, Nathan told Sara, 'So. We've been invited again.'

'To Mark's party?'

'To Mark's party.'

She froze, like a fawn in woodland.

Nathan was putting on his plaid jacket, the one he wore to work during the winter. He said, 'It's probably best if we don't go. There'll be a lot of drugs around, I expect.'

Ordinarily, Sara disapproved of drugs. But now exasperation flickered round the edges of her face. This was Mark Derbyshire's Christmas party, and the presence or absence of drugs was of no interest to her.

She grew demure. 'But I'd really *like* to.'

She said this every Christmas. And every Christmas, Nathan said, 'Maybe next year.'

Now she simpered a little, half playing, half meaning it, stroking his upper arm with the back of her fingernails, saying, 'Pretty please?'

And Nathan said, 'Okay, then. Why not?'

She screamed and kissed him – smacking him on the cheek and on the forehead.

Even as recently as a few months ago, they'd probably have had quick, celebratory sex. But Nathan and Sara no longer had sex. Neither of them had mentioned it; it made them too sad, too awkward and too embarrassed.

Now, Sara got so childishly excited – running and whooping – that she had to run to the bathroom.

At first, this pleased him; it had been a while since she was so happy in his company. Then he began to wonder when, exactly, she'd begun closing the bathroom door when she needed to pee.

It seemed to him that he really should know something like that – if only so he could identify it as the moment he knew for sure that it was really over.

But he hadn't noticed, and the moment he knew for sure it was really over was right now, right this second.

After the moment had passed, he called out, 'I'm late, I have to run!' and opened the door.

From the bathroom, she yelled, 'See you, babes!' and he smiled.

He caught the bus to work.

Saturday was the night of the party. Nathan slept late and woke, unusually, to the sound of Sara going about the house, singing. It was a sunny, late-winter afternoon, and from the flat the traffic noise was reduced to a monotonous hiss.

He got up and pulled on an old and faded band T-shirt. (*Utterly Bastard Groovy*, it read, green on black. Utterly bastard groovy was exactly what Nathan never felt, not any more.) In this and a pair of Calvins, he slapped barefoot to the compact living room.

Sara was sitting at the table, one hand round a mug of coffee, reading the *Guardian* Review. Nathan was struck by the reality of her. He saw how pretty she was, and how young; with her face cleansed and scrubbed of make-up, he could see the tiny imperfections and freckles on her nose and cheeks, and her eyes looked naked and vulnerable. She was bare-legged, wearing only one of his T-shirts. It fitted her like a minidress. This is how she'd dressed on those far-off Saturday mornings when he first knew her; those days when it would have seemed impossible that he could ever grow to dislike her, or she him. Or that they could ever stop having sex.

In the afternoon they snuggled chastely on the sofa, watching a black and white film as the winter sun dipped in the west.

At 5.30, they began to get ready. Nathan took a shower and shaved. He had a couple of good suits hanging in the wardrobe – he'd bought them with his first credit card when he and Sara were first together and he was light-headed with the idea of being in love, and being loved by this lovely girl. There were some good shirts, too (also yet to be paid for), and several good ties. Nathan never wore ties; he had the wrong kind of job. But Sara kept buying them, and with each tie he unwrapped from tissue paper, he sensed her disdain for his lack of ambition ratchet up another notch. The ties hung on a rack in his wardrobe, a Technicolor indictment.

When, in a rolling cloud of scented steam, Sara finally emerged from the bathroom, wrapped in a white towel, Nathan was dressed and ready, laying out his wallet and keys on the kitchen table. He wore a charcoal-grey suit over a black T-shirt.

He sat on the bed and watched her. There was no prevarication; she'd been planning her outfit for days now. She blow-dried her short hair with brisk, staggering efficiency, so the asymmetrical fringe fell over one eye. She applied her make-up with a few, quick, practised strokes (but in a manner he knew required years of diligent practice, like elite sportsmanship). Towel off: knickers on. Bra. Pull-up stockings. Spritz of perfume. Dress. Slip on heels. Suddenly remember to apply roll-on deodorant. Examine self in mirror from several difficult angles, smoothing down creases with an alluring little shimmy. Open handbag. Double-check keys, address book, mobile phone, whatever other mysteries the bag contained. Lean in to mirror. Fiddle with fringe, minutely calibrating it. Add mascara.

She ordered a taxi and mixed them a gin and tonic. The plan was to sit listening to music – Sara's choice – until the taxi arrived. Nathan hated the Cranberries.

He walked to the bathroom, locking the door behind him. Faintly embarrassed by his own nervousness, he ran the taps just to make a noise. Then he removed from his pocket a little Ziploc bag containing four grammes of cocaine in four paper wraps. He'd cleaned out his savings account to buy it. The supplier was Howard, the grey-haired ex-hack who produced *The Mark Derbyshire Solution*.

Nathan racked up two fat lines on the cistern, then took the little pewter snorting spoon he'd bought from a now-closed head shop in Cornwall one good summer that seemed a million years ago, and he snorted back, crisply and efficiently. Then he stood straight, looking at the ceiling, sniffing. His snot tasted chemical. He smiled with joy at the memory of it and knew it was working already.

He tucked the spoon into one pocket and the wraps into another, opened the bathroom door and walked out, sniffing.

In her party dress, Sara stood alone in the centre of the room, one hand cupping an elbow, the other holding a long glass of gin and tonic. As if she were the host and waiting for the party to begin.

At the railway station, they queued for tickets. There were twenty minutes to kill. They stopped for a drink at the generic railway bar. Nathan visited the lavatory. Then they hurried to catch the train. It sat on a wintry platform. They boarded and sat without speaking, Sara staring – apparently sombre – at her blank-eyed reflection in the train window, and through it to the passengers on the platform who passed spectrally by.

Nathan said, 'Christ. I'd kill for a cigarette.'

She gave him the look.

'Come on,' he said. 'Just one night. It's party nerves.'

She allowed herself an expression of benevolent radiance. 'Go on. It's only one night.'

It's only cancer, he thought, producing a packet of Marlboro Lights from his coat pocket; one of four he'd bought to last him a long evening.

He stood between the carriages of the juddering train, blowing smoke out the window.

Half an hour later, they pulled up to Sutton Parkway. It was little more than a dark, astringently cold concrete platform.

Nathan gathered himself, saddened a little to know the best part of Sara's evening, the anticipation, was nearly over. Almost certainly, from now on, the evening would only get worse.

Outside the station, they caught a minicab.

4

Nathan paid the driver and the minicab pulled away, its tail lights smudged and indistinct in the billowing white exhaust.

Their party shoes scratched on the cold gravel of the long driveway. From inside the big house came a faint, muffled, repetitive boom; the windows vibrated with it.

Mark Derbyshire had built this mansion in the late seventies, when he could still afford it. At the rear was a helicopter landing pad, long since overgrown.

Nathan offered Sara his elbow and together they approached the door. It was answered by a balding man dressed as a butler; Nathan hoped he'd been hired for the evening.

Sara removed her coat, shrugging it from her narrow white shoulders in a way that made him remember, for a moment, why he'd once believed himself to be in love with her.

The magnolia hall was hung with gold and silver discs from forgotten bands and singers whose records Mark Derbyshire had once helped to climb the charts. And there were many framed eight by tens. In them a younger and thinner Mark Derbyshire – but with the same neatly trimmed beard, the same look of jovial malice – placed his arm round the shoulder of one squirming celebrity or other: a young Madonna was there, and David Bowie showed his David Bowie teeth. Elton John looked frumpy and unhappy in a straw boater and comedy spectacles. The photographs made Nathan melancholy.

Sara said, 'Shall we?' and – feeling for a moment like Cary Grant – he led her inside the double door into the ballroom.

At the far end, the wedding DJ stood at his mixing desk. A few guests, mostly young local girls, were dancing.

Sara tugged his elbow.

'What?'

'Celebrity count?'

'It's early days. It's not even nine.'

She looked at him, trustingly. They pushed and 'excuse-me'd and danced round the loose crowd to get to the drinks table. It was a long trestle, behind which stood six young men in burgundy shirts, pouring drinks.

Nathan surveyed the party, holding a gin and tonic. He barely knew anyone – certainly nobody to whom he felt inclined to introduce Sara. He wondered what on earth they could find to talk about until it was time for her to go home disappointed.

They stared at the party and into their drinks. Nathan tried not to look at the senior managers – whom he regarded with contempt for their black suits and their big, old-man ears and their stupid fucking cigars.

He made an effort to point out colleagues whose names he might have mentioned in passing, but Sara wasn't really interested; she wanted to see, and be introduced to, celebrities. But no real celebrity had stepped over Mark Derbyshire's threshold since Margaret Thatcher was in power.

Eventually, Howard strolled past. Although to Nathan he was obviously fucked out of his mind, he carried a certain louche charm, with his curly grey-white hair, his unlatched bow-tie. Nathan grabbed his elbow.

'Howard! Mate! Have you met Sara?'

Howard had not met Sara.

Shaking her hand, he glanced at her creamy décolletage with an expression that resembled sorrow. Then he locked eyes with her. Howard had pale Icelandic eyes and they shone like a missile-guidance system.

Nathan said, 'Tell her about some of the people you've worked with.'

'I'm sure she's got better things to do than listen to my war stories.'

'The Rolling Stones,' said Nathan, not without desperation. 'The Beatles. Spandau Ballet.'

'Spandau Ballet!' said Sara.

And that was it. She was happy.

Nathan hung around for a while, but soon it became clear he was no longer required. He wandered off to get another drink, then followed the chlorine tang towards the indoor swimming pool.

The atmosphere round the pool was excitingly muted and full of potential. Nathan leaned against the damp wall and stared through the steamy glass ceiling at the pin-sharp December sky. He recognized none of the constellations and for a moment fantasized that he'd entered a deeply foreign country. He felt good.

In the corner was Mark Derbyshire. He was engaged in restrained conversation with a big, shambling, shaggy-haired man in crumpled dinner jacket and an Hawaiian shirt. The shambling man seemed to be controlling the conversation: Mark Derbyshire looked diminished, clutching his glass of wine in one hairy-backed hand, nodding along, glancing left and right.

Mark spotted Nathan and rolled his eyes with relief, beckoning Nathan over.

'Nathan. You have to meet this guy.'

The shambling man turned. And for the second time in his life, Nathan reached out to shake Bob's hand.

'Mate,' he said, recognizing Nathan. 'Good to see you.'

Mark said, 'You know this guy?'

Nathan said, 'Kind of.'

Bob said, 'From way back. How are you? You're looking a bit more prosperous.'

Nathan looked down at his suit, still unpaid for. 'Well. Y'know.'

He caught Mark Derbyshire's confused, malevolent little eyes.

Bob explained to Mark, 'He was a bit of a hippie when I knew him.'

And Nathan protested: 'I don't know about *that*.'

'Bit of a new age traveller,' said Bob. 'All patchouli and ganja.'

'That's great,' said Mark, who at least knew what ganja was; he'd heard it mentioned in a comedy reggae song. 'It's great that you two know each other. I can make you Bob's liaison, Nathan.'

'Great,' said Nathan, not knowing what Mark was talking about.

'We're going to have Bob on the show,' said Mark.

'As an experiment,' said Bob.

'What he means is, for a trial period. Thursday night, 12.30, for six weeks.'

'It's part of the research,' said Bob. 'I'm compiling stories for a book.'

'Still working on the PhD?'

'Inter alia.'

'Nathan, boy,' said Mark. 'Do us a favour – go and get us a drink.'

It was at once a jovial and venomous reminder of who was boss. Bob caught Nathan's eye and winced in sympathy. Nathan set down his drink and walked quickly to the trestle table, ordered the drinks, looked for Sara, saw that she was still enchanted by Howard, then went back to the pool. He handed Mark Derbyshire his whisky and Bob his vodka tonic.

They said *cheers* and clinked glasses. Then a doddering, silver-haired guest took Mark's elbow. Unsure whether to address Nathan or Bob, he alternated between them. 'Do you mind if I borrow the host?'

'Not at all,' said Bob, and lifted his vodka tonic in silent salute. The guest led Mark Derbyshire back to the party.

Bob watched him go.

'Christ,' he said.

Nathan smiled, not without guilt.

'I mean really. What a cocksucker.'

Nathan laughed, but he was uncomfortable.

Bob changed the subject. He said, 'So. Do you have any drugs?'

They stopped off at the bar. Sara was still in conversation with Howard, but they'd been joined by a number of other partygoers. She looked like she was enjoying herself. Making friends. Wherever she went, she made friends.

Clutching a bottle of gin in one hand and three wine glasses in the other – one glass full of ice – Bob sidled alongside Nathan.

'She with you?'

'Yeah. Well, nominally.'

'Lucky man.'

Nathan ignored that – it hardly mattered to him any more that Sara was good-looking.

And, actually, Nathan got the impression that Bob had disliked Sara on sight. Not many men did that, and Bob kind of went up in his estimation because of it. In some strange way, it made him an ally.

They hurried up the main stairwell. On the first-floor landing, they turned down a half-lit, door-lined hallway.

Nathan said, 'Have you been here before?'

'Nah. I'm following the vibe.'

'Right.'

'I know it sounds like bollocks. But you attend as many hauntings as I do, you learn how to read a house.'

He tried a door handle, moved on. Tested another; the door opened. He groped in the darkness and a light came on. They stepped into the room and Nathan closed the door.

It was a guest bedroom, impersonal as a Holiday Inn. A double bed, a bedside table, a mirrored wardrobe.

Nathan turned on a standard lamp that stood in one corner; it shed a more pleasing glow, so he killed the overhead light.

He said, 'You really believe that stuff?'

'Yep.'

Nathan took from the wall a square mirror, about the size of an LP, and lay it mirror-side up on the quilted bed. Then he kneeled and laid out four lines of cocaine, a cat's claw gash across his reflection.

Bob went hunting in his thick, greasy wallet. He produced a ten-pound note. Two lines each.

Then they were sitting on the floor with their backs to the bed, sniffing.

'So,' said Nathan. 'Have you ever actually seen a ghost?'

'Not as such.'

'What does that mean, not as such?'

'It means, I've seen their effects.'

'Effects like what?'

'Anomalies in haunted houses. Electrical disturbances. Cold spots. Poltergeist phenomena.'

'No *way*.'

'Yes way.'

'As in, you've seen a ghost that throws stuff around?'

'People used to think it was that. But we're pretty convinced it's some kind of geothermic reaction – like an intense, very localized electrical field. It sort of charges things up – and yeah, throws stuff around.'

'No shit?'

'No shit. A professor I know in Copenhagen, he built a poltergeist machine. Honest to God. He built a room inside a kind of electro-magnetic chamber. He filled it with everyday stuff – chairs, furniture, newspapers, mugs. Then he runs a charge through it, a really powerful charge. And guess what? He reproduces poltergeist phenomena, right there in the lab: things levitate, fly across the room. All that.'

'You've seen it?'

'Seen it.'

'What's it *like*?'

'Creepy as shit.'

Nathan was enthusiastic. 'So you think that's what it is, the super-natural? Just natural phenomena.'

'Pretty much, yeah. Ninety-nine per cent of it.'

'And the other per cent?'

'It's the other per cent that really interests me. Probably a good ninety-nine per cent of that last one per cent is explicable. We just don't know *how* yet. But the remaining one per cent of the one per cent?'

He pinched his nostrils and closed his eyes.

'Jesus. Do you have a cigarette?'

Nathan could feel each cell of his body vibrating.

After hoovering the last of the cocaine, then wetting their finger-tips with spit and rubbing the bitter residue into their gums, Nathan refilled the wine glasses with ice and Bombay Sapphire.

Bob sat rigid on the bed, holding his glass by the stem.

'Fucking hell,' he said.

Nathan told him, 'I stopped taking this stuff two years ago. Can you imagine?'

Bob said he couldn't imagine.

They went quiet.

The quality of the light seemed to change.

Bob said, 'What's wrong?'

'Nothing.'

'Something's wrong. You've got something on your mind.'

Nathan thought about it.

Eventually, he said, 'So, yeah. I've got this problem.'

'What problem?'

'I was going to finish it with Sara.'

'Like, dump her?'

'That's a very strong word for it. We've kind of, y'know. Drifted apart and whatever. Somebody has to say something. One of us.'

'Won't it cause a scene?'

'Not tonight. I'm too wired. Are you wired?'

'Yes.'

'Me too.'

'So, if not tonight – when?'

'Tomorrow. Over lunch, a late breakfast.'

'Why?'

'She's having an affair.'

'With?'

'Her boss.'

'Okay. So where's the problem?'

'Second thoughts. Am I doing the right thing? Should I be, like, fighting for her?'

'If you loved her, you would.'

'Would I?'

'Yeah. Nathan, mate. The decision's already made. This is just anxiety talking.'

'And booze.'

'And booze.'

'And coke.'

'And that.' Bob leaned over and, with an index finger, he tapped Nathan's head. 'But in here, you know what to do. You've already decided.'

'You reckon?'

'I reckon.'

'I'm not sure I do.'

Bob seemed to be thinking very hard. He said, 'Do you love her?'

'I don't think so. But when I think of us not being together any more, it makes me a bit sad.'

'That's natural. But that's not love, it's regret. It's the end of love.'

'The end of love,' said Nathan, awed by the concept. 'Blimey. The end of love.'

Bob slapped his thigh and stood. He wavered a bit. His knees clicked.

He said, 'Let's consult the oracle!'

Nathan blinked up at him.

Bob said, 'Go to the bathroom. Bring back a plastic lid, like from a can of deodorant or something. Air freshener. Whatever.'

Excited – and too wired to question what he'd been asked – Nathan hurried down the corridor to the bathroom, which had long since passed its best days. The shower and bath and sink were limescaled. The sinks wanted plugs. The taps dripped. Nathan rooted in the cupboards and found a can of shaving foam, from which he removed the plastic lid.

Back in the guest room, Bob was writing letters of the alphabet on sequential pages of a pocket notebook. Finally, he ripped the pages from the notebook, one by one, and lay them on the back of the mirror – forming a rough circle. He placed the word YES at twelve o'clock, followed by the letters A through to M. At six o'clock, he placed the word NO, followed by the letters N through Z.

Nathan looked at the makeshift Ouija board and laughed.

'Come on. Look at the state of it. There's not even a *pointer*.'

'*Planchette*,' said Bob, and nodded at the plastic lid in Nathan's hand.

'You're joking.'

'Give it a try.'

Nathan giggled as they sat cross-legged before the board. Bob placed the planchette in the centre of it.

Nathan said, 'What do I do?'

'You rest your index finger – very lightly, lightly as you can – on the planchette. Then wait.'

'How does it work?'

'Something called the *ideomotor* effect: tiny involuntary muscle movements. It'll help you find out what you're really thinking.'

'I'm not sure I want to know what I'm really thinking.'

But Nathan did as instructed. They waited, in the loaded silence. And then the planchette seemed slowly to rotate beneath their fingertips.

Bob closed his eyes and licked his lips. 'Okay. Have we got anyone?'

They waited again. Until, with a dry creak on the mirror's surface, the planchette slid to the word YES.

Nathan took his finger from it.

'Fuck off. You're moving it. I can feel you.'

'Afraid not. Now, come on. You don't want to piss them off.'

'Piss who off?'

Bob looked at the ceiling. 'Them.'

Nathan said, 'Christ. You're giving me the horrors.'

Bob implored him with impatient eyes. So Nathan touched the planchette again.

Bob asked the air: 'Do you have a name?'

The planchette slid to the letter D. Then the letter A.

David

'Do you know us, David?'

no

'Then why have you come through?'

can you hear

'Yes. Do you have a message?'

die cunt

'Is that your message?'

die cunt die cu –

'Then goodbye.'

Bob took his finger from the planchette, saying, 'Mate. You're shaking.'

'Fuck me. Tell me you were doing that on purpose.'

'Were *you*?'

'No.'

'Me neither. Shall we try again?'

Nathan shook his head; no way.

Bob told him, 'Look. It's nothing. It's coming from inside your head.'

'Or yours.'

'Or mine, yes. Possibly. Now come on.'

Once again – Nathan much more tentatively – they placed their fingers on the planchette.

'Now,' said Bob. 'Do we have someone?'

yes

'Who do we have?'

sunny

'Have we met, Sunny?'

hot here

Nathan removed his finger.

'Fuck that.'

Bob's face had darkened. 'Put your finger back.'

Nathan did.

Then Bob relaxed himself and once again spoke to the air, 'Why are you here, Sunny?'

fuks him

'Who fucks who?'

fuks him

fuks him

fuks him

Nathan stood up.

'Really,' he said. 'Fuck that. I mean really. Fuck it.'

He looked down at the mirror. Then he hit the main light switch. He was dazzled by the sudden, whiter glare. With his foot, he scattered the letters of the Ouija board across the carpet.

Bob was standing up, too. 'What are you *doing*?'

'And fuck you, too.'

'Do you know how *dangerous* that is?'

'You're cracked in the head, mate.'

Nathan picked up his cigarettes and left the guest bedroom. Outside, in the dim hallway, he looked at his watch. His eyes wouldn't focus. He leaned against the wall.

Then he strode downstairs, where it was hotter than ever. The bodies and the noise pressed down upon him. He squeezed into the ballroom.

He looked at his watch. An impossible amount of time had passed. Sara was on the dance floor. 'Crocodile Rock' was ending. It was followed by 'He's the Greatest Dancer (That I've Ever Seen)'. Sara was dancing with Mark Derbyshire. Mark had discarded his jacket. Nathan watched them; Mark was grinding his hips, all but dry-humping her, and Sara was laughing. Mark's shirt was soaked under the armpits and between the shoulder blades.

The dance floor was packed and the music was fast and everyone seemed to be enjoying themselves.

Nathan snatched a bottle of Chardonnay from the trestle table, then went to collect his coat and walked out the front door.

5

The cold and quiet hit him, the skin contracting like cling film across his skull. He clenched his teeth and sat in the spilled light on the stone doorstep, the muffled sounds of the party behind him, and wondered what to do. The big house mocked him. So he went for a walk in the darkness, clasping the bottle by the neck.

Beyond the east wing was a small copse of leafless trees. On the other side was a tennis court. Around the tennis court were arranged some benches. On one of these benches huddled a dark mass. As Nathan approached, the dark mass seemed to bloom, sprouting a white head. It resolved into a girl. Her short hair was glossy black in the starlight. She was bundled up beneath a man's overcoat.

She said, 'Hello.'

'Hello,' said Nathan. 'So what are you doing out here?'

'Getting some air. Y'know.'

He laughed, once. Too loud: a bird erupted from the dark trees behind them. She looked over his shoulder and up, tracking its progress.

'What's that? An owl?'

He squinted into the darkness. The Milky Way spread like a distended contrail across the sky.

'I don't know. I think it was maybe a crow.'

'Whatever. You didn't impress it much.'

'So, how do you know Mark?'

'I don't. Not really. He's a friend of my dad's. Which is lucky, if you think about it.'

'Please explain.'

'Because Mark respects my dad, he technically can't make a pass at me.'

'That is lucky.'

'I did say "technically".'

'Oh my God. He didn't.'

'No, but he was working up to it. Mum, Dad and my sister had already gone home. So I sneaked out, to get away from him. Let him find someone else to lech over.'

Nathan sat down next to her and, in unconscious imitation, drew his knees up to his chest and hugged them.

He passed her the wine. She took it.

He said, 'I think you're safe. Right now he's dancing with my soon-to-be ex-girlfriend.'

'Ugh.'

'You should see him.'

'I'd rather not. I've seen it. I've felt it. He shoves his hard-on into you, kind of grinds it around. Like you won't notice.'

He shuddered.

The girl said, 'So what makes her your soon-to-be ex? The danc-ing thing?'

'Nah. It's a long story.'

'Who's in a rush?'

'Long story short, she's seeing someone else.'

'Behind your back?'

'Pretty much.'

She ruffled his hair.

'Poor puppy.'

Something passed between them. The night had magic in it.

They sat for a few minutes, watching the slowly circling sky – until Nathan said, 'I'm freezing.'

'Me too.'

'Would you like to sneak inside and maybe have some drugs?'

'What would your girlfriend say?'

'I don't think she's my girlfriend any more.'

'Just checking.'

'Ha.'

'What've you got?'

'A little bit of coke. There's a room. Up the main stairs, take the dark corridor, the little offshoot.'

'To the guest bedrooms?'

'You've been here before.'

'Every Christmas since I was nine.'

'Cool. Third door on the right. I'll meet you in there.'

'I'll go first. See you in five minutes?'

'Five minutes.'

He consulted his watch. Not yet midnight.

The girl scurried off, lost in the big black overcoat.

He waited on the bench, watching the sky. It was so clear. He saw a satellite, a quick-winking light passing too high and too fast to be an aircraft.

Then he retraced his steps to the house. By now he was beginning to wonder if the girl had been real. He paused on the stoop and remembered how the darkness of the leafy copse had swallowed her up like ink spreading on a drawing. He remembered the cold touch of her hand on his brow.

He walked back inside and was received by a burst of warmth, party chatter, and 'La Isla Bonita'. He re-checked his coat, then cautiously popped his head into the ballroom. Sara was in the corner, talking to somebody, a woman.

He hurried up the stairs and ducked down the twilit hallway. He went to the third door on the right, paused for a moment, and tried the handle.

The door was open and the light was on and the girl was in there. She'd thrown her overcoat down on the bed. She wore a short skirt and a tight T-shirt with some kind of ironic legend on it. Adidas trainers. In her hand she held several scraps of paper. He saw the word YES. She said, 'What's all this about?'

'You don't want to know.'

'Were you doing a Ouija board in here? Jesus, what are you, twelve?'

Once again, he took the mirror from the wall (in the lamplight, he could see the looped, dried snail-trails of his and Bob's wetted fingers) and laid it on the bed.

He passed her the little pewter tube. He hadn't been able to share it with Bob – to see Bob shove it up his hairy ectoplasmic nostrils. But the girl's nostrils were of an altogether different order. The girl had pretty nostrils, and up them she snorted two of the lines he'd laid out for them.

She sat on the bed and let it begin to work.

She glanced at him. Then she glanced away. Then – very carefully and very precisely – she patted the mattress next to her.

'Come and sit next to me.'

He went and sat next to her.

They sat there like that. Their knees were touching. They talked for a bit.

He put his arm round her. She felt tiny. She turned to face him. He moved to meet her. Their lips touched. Her tongue darted between his lips. She tasted of cocaine and cigarettes and wine. He slid a hand beneath the hem of her T-shirt. Her flesh was warm and soft and firm. He pushed her back. Her hands were laced at the nape of his neck. He could feel her ribs. He cupped her breast and squeezed; he felt her nipple harden in the palm of his hand. She arched her back.

The door opened and Bob walked in.

Nathan sat up and said, 'Jesus fucking *Christ*, Bob.'

He saw that Bob wore an earnest, worried expression. It infuriated him: it made him want to rip Bob's ears off. He said, '*Fuck off*, Bob. Please, just fuck off.'

But Bob didn't fuck off. Instead, he said, 'Sara's looking for you. She's on the warpath, mate.'

Nathan groaned.

'I was introduced to her downstairs,' Bob said. 'She's wondering where the hell you've got to.'

Nathan was bored and angered by the thought of Sara's disapproval; he imagined her tapping her foot and crossing her arms, pouting, flicking back that precisely calibrated fringe.

While he pictured it, Bob turned to the girl and said, 'I'm Bob, by the way. Friend of Nathan's.'

The girl was smoothing down her T-shirt, saying, 'Elise.'

Nathan peeped at her sideways, as if properly to say hello. She peeped back. Nathan's triumphant erection was wilting away. He moaned, 'Sara's the last person I need to see.'

'So let's keep hiding,' said Bob.

'She'll find us.'

At which, Elise nervously checked the door and straightened the hem of her T-shirt again.

Bob wasn't in the mood to give up. He said, 'So let's run away.'

Nathan thought about it for a moment – not too long, because he wanted to look decisive in Elise's eyes.

He said, 'That may be a good idea.'

He unlatched the bedroom window and wrenched it open – then stuck out his head, to see how far it was to the ground.

6

Nathan told Elise to wait for him while he shinned down the drain-pipe, in case he should slip and tumble to his destruction. But once he'd wormed his way out of the window, the descent proved straight-forward; he dropped the last two metres with some elan, pleased Elise was there to witness it.

Then she followed him, clambering down with the dexterity of a spider monkey.

Nathan was embarrassed.

They ran for the bushes, the distant thud of disco behind them. They stayed in the shadows, following the gravel drive towards the main gate. Here, they squatted in a slough of darkness so black and cold it clung to them like viscous liquid.

After a few minutes, Bob pulled up. He was at the wheel of an old white Volvo estate.

Nathan and Elise clambered on to the back seat, keeping low, and Bob pulled away with too much wheelspin. They passed through the gates, all three laughing.

'Now,' said Bob, at the wheel. 'We need somewhere *dark*.'

Elise said, 'I know the place,' and put her hand on Nathan's thigh. He kissed her.

Out of nowhere, he felt like he was having the best night of his life.

Elise directed Bob through the small town of Socombe, past some farmland, through a village called Sutton Down, then along a road that ran parallel with a managed forest – an oak woodland. She tapped Bob's shoulder.

'Turn left back there.'

'Back where?'

All he could see was trees. But he reversed until Elise told him to stop. Before them, the headlights showed a place where the entrance to a narrow lane had been occulted by the overgrowth. Bob executed a five-point turn to get the car down there – a tunnel of darkness with a hummocked asphalt surface, just wide enough for a single vehicle. Soon they were swallowed by it, following the headlamps.

Nathan said, 'How do you know this place?'

'All the local kids know it. You know about it way before you get to come down here. It's like lovers' lane or something. In the summer, anyway.'

'Cool,' said Bob. 'So, you've been here before?'

'Once or twice.' She glanced at Nathan. 'Except the big kids, they tell the younger ones that, you know, it's haunted. By a lady in white.'

Bob grinned in the rear-view mirror. 'Is there a river close by?'

'There's kind of a stream. A brook or something.'

'There's always running water. Near haunted lanes. Supposedly haunted.'

'Why's that?'

'Who knows? Geothermic forces or whatever.'

Nathan said, 'Don't get him started.'

Bob pulled the car to the side of the road. Its nearside tyres were caked in leaf mould and humus. He turned on the CD player. Charlie Parker.

Nathan fished out the remaining cocaine. Bob turned on the interior light. They were bathed in its sickly, intimate glow. Nathan cut out some squat, fat lines on the CD case. He snorted first and passed the CD case to Elise. As she brought it to her nose, Bob and Nathan looked at her, then at each other. She passed the CD case to Bob, who propped it on the steering wheel.

Elise wiped at her nose. The action caused her T-shirt to lift above her navel. She'd left the overcoat back at the party.

Bob pressed himself deep into the driver's seat.

'Christ.'

He turned off the interior light. For a few seconds the darkness was absolute. A voice in the blackness, Elise said, 'I like nights like this. When you don't plan anything, but it all seems to happen.'

Bob swivelled in the driving seat, to face them. He said, 'Look. You two. I feel bad. I feel like I'm ruining the night for you – walking in on you. Y'know. The way I did.'

Elise made a slapping motion at him and said, 'No, your timing wasn't great.' Then she drawled his name in a bad American accent: *Bahb*.

Nathan tried to laugh, and Bob grinned, resting his big jaw on the headrest.

'So why don't you go ahead and finish what you started?'

Elise slapped at him again. 'What are you *like*?'

Bob met her eyes and held them.

'If it was possible, I'd go for a walk. But the lane is dark and cold and, I have to say, a bit creepy. And even if I were to go out there, you'd be so tense about me coming back at the wrong time, you wouldn't relax. But you might never see each other again. It seems such a shame. So listen. I'll sit back and close my eyes and I'll turn up the music. And you two can . . . you know.'

She laughed again, loud in the darkness, and said, 'You're sick.'

Elise looked at Nathan. Then she looked at Bob.

'You'd *watch*.'

'I'll try not to.'

'You'll *listen*.'

'Then keep the noise down.'

'I *can't*.'

'Can't? Or won't? Are you having bourgeois reservations?'

She went to speak, but then she guffawed and slapped Bob's shoulder again. She turned to Nathan. 'Do you want to?'

'Do *you*?'

'Do *you*? Do you have a problem with it?'

'With what?'

'With Bob. Being here.'

'No.'

Suddenly nobody was smiling.

Elise took off her T-shirt.

'Bob, you're looking.'

'I'll stop in a moment.'

'You'd better.'

Nathan leaned forward. Her tongue was slower this time. She seemed very aroused. He knew it was the booze and cocaine and the evening's sense of adventure. She tasted of wine and cigarettes. Her hand tugged at his shirt, found flesh. He kissed her long neck. He struggled from his jacket. She kissed his throat, his chest, helped him from his shirt. In his rush, he lost a couple of buttons. She fumbled at his fly. His cock, when she freed it, was springy as a cosh but cold to the core. She popped it into her mouth. The warmth was so abrupt that he jerked back, as if about to fall. Then he forced himself away from her and fumbled with her skirt. She lifted her arse to help him, wriggling at the waist, and when she muttered 'Bob, you're still watching' there was no real protest left in it.

Nathan was transfixed by the imprint of elastic in her bare flesh, and the shadow cast by her sharp hips, by the movement of her small, white breasts as she prepared herself for him. She bit his shoulder when he entered, and gasped. She pressed her feet, still in Adidas trainers, against the back of the front passenger seat. She was so warm. She wrapped her ankles around him and murmured something in his ear, he didn't know what. Her eyes were open.

It didn't last long. When Nathan tensed in orgasm, teeth gritted and neck corded, she hissed a single word through her teeth.

Bob's gaze, solemn and amused, was heavy on Nathan's back as Elise eased him from inside her. Nathan flopped, gasping, on the seat next to her. He was naked from the waist up and his trousers were gathered round his ankles. He was beginning to detumesce. Naked except for her Adidas, Elise sat laughing and gasping. Beads of Nathan's jism glinted on her pubic hair.

She said 'Oh, God' and brushed at her naked thighs as if they itched.

She and Nathan made eye contact. She squeezed his softening dick with affectionate good humour.

He said, 'I know. I'm sorry. Give me a minute.'

'But first – more drugs, I think.'

'But what about Bob?' said Bob.

Elise leaned forward and slapped his shoulder again.

'Don't be such an old perv.'

'But I'm very aroused.'

'Bob,' she said.

On her knees, leaning on the front seats, she brushed back her fringe.

'Look, I like you. I really do. But I can't.'

'Can't? Won't?'

'*Don't.*'

'Aha. Don't. *Don't* implies that class values are struggling with more basic desires. Did you come, just now?'

Elise laughed at Bob's audacity.

'No.'

'Would you like to?'

Quick as a fish, Bob's hand darted between her legs. He slipped two fingers inside her. Elise flinched.

'You cheeky bastard.'

She said it three times. Each time it sounded more like a compliment. She moved her narrow hips in a figure of eight.

Nathan met Bob's eye. Bob's eyes were blank.

'Nathan won't mind, will you, Nathan?'

Nathan was becoming aroused again. But he pulled up his trousers and said, 'Of course not.'

Bob said, 'Mate. I think we'd better swap places.'

Elise lay back in the seat.

'I'm going to regret this in the morning.'

'I promise you,' said Bob. 'You won't.'

Nathan gathered his clothes, his jacket and shirt. They were damp.

Big and intent, Bob began to climb on to the back seat. Nathan opened the door and edged out, his shirt and jacket bundled in his arms.

Elise reached out for him as he left. She grabbed his wrist and squeezed, as one might at the apex of a rollercoaster. He squeezed back, he hoped encouragingly, and let go.

There was a blast of cold, December air. Nathan hurried into his clothes. His hands fumbled at the buttons.

Inside the car, Elise said, 'Oh my God.'

The Volvo lurched on its springs.

Nathan decided to get in the front seat and watch. But first he needed to piss. He walked behind the car. It was difficult to piss in the freezing cold, especially with a growing erection – and the noises she made, the grunts and yelps. It took a long time and when it came, the wind whipped at the pale stream and scattered it over the rear wind-screen of the Volvo.

Accompanying the car's increasingly violent movement, he could hear muffled, profane voices. Elise's voice rising in pitch and urgency, calling alternately on God and Jesus. A kind of bitten-back scream. Nathan wanted to make her scream like that. Bob's voice was lower and insistent. Nathan wondered what she looked like, locking her white legs around his broad back. He stopped pissing and zipped himself up, not without difficulty. He opened the front passenger door and got inside. It was warm, and musky like a bedroom, under-cut with cigarettes and leather upholstery.

By then, the car must have stopped rocking on its springs. Because when Nathan slammed the door and turned in his seat, Elise was already dead.

7

Nathan never seen a dead person before, but he knew it immediately. Something had left her – whatever it was that a few moments before had made this fresh cadaver a girl named Elise.

A flock of starlings erupted in Nathan's chest.

Bob was sitting on the back seat – shirt-tails askew, naked from the waist down. His horse's cock hung thick and wet and glinting. Elise lay naked and almost face down, her feet on his lap.

Nathan stared at her.

There was only the sound of Bob's breathing. Elise's feet twitched.

An old joke, filthy, rose unbidden and popped on the surface of Nathan's mind – *Now* you're fucked. He shook it away.

He said: 'What the fuck have you *done*?'

His voice was girlish, and hearing it – hearing the rise of panic – made him still more afraid.

Elise's Adidas quivered at Bob's thigh. Bob stared at it, then shoved her legs from his naked lap. She let out an extended exhalation, like a post-coital sigh.

Nathan's sphincter loosened.

Bob said, 'She cramped. Down there. You know. I couldn't. I couldn't get it out.'

Nathan vomited into his mouth. He threw open the passenger door and let the vomit slap on to the road. He hacked up for a long time.

Then he ran away.

He ran and ran. His arms pumped. He felt no friction or resistance. His breath came in hot and cold rasps. There were only the slow-shifting trees to the side of him, twisted oak and silvery ash, the twinkling sky above him, the pounding of his feet, a white cloud of breath.

He slowed to a wavering jog and then to a halt. The exertion caught him and he vomited again. He stood holding his knees. Branches shifted in his peripheral vision. He leaned against a tree. He spat.

He didn't know if he'd run towards the road or away from it. But now he imagined himself, breathless and drunk and hopelessly wired – mad-eyed, unkempt – somehow managing to flag down a passing car. What would he say?

What would he say to Sara?

He stood there, getting his breath back. Then he trudged back towards Bob's car.

It took a while. He began to wonder if Bob had gone. Perhaps he'd dumped Elise by the side of the lane and had left Nathan alone with her, here in the woods. Then the white Volvo began to emerge from the night.

Nathan walked up to it. He opened the door and sat down.

Bob was still there, on the back seat. He didn't seem to have moved, except to have pulled his trousers up. His belt lay unbuckled in his lap and his flies were unzipped.

He said, 'I think she had a fit.'

Nathan wanted to kill him: to cave in his skull with a tyre lever. Then he'd make his way back to the party. He'd find Sara: he'd tell her everything was all right, and they'd go home. And in the pearly grey, late-winter dawn he'd immerse himself in the cotton-fresh duvet and wake late in the bright December morning and he'd go and get the newspapers, and a bacon sandwich for them both. And they'd eat the sandwiches and read the newspapers and drink tea and watch the *EastEnders* omnibus, and everything would be all right. He wished so ferociously never to have come to this dark lane with this man and this girl, that it seemed impossible the wish would not come true.

He said, 'We have to call an ambulance. Right now. Or they'll think—'

Bob pushed aside the hair which overhung his bloated cherub's face. 'They'll think what?'

'Christ. Surely not. She had a *fit*.'

'While I was fucking her. I don't know what happened. Maybe she had a weak heart. Maybe it was the cocaine.'

Nathan gagged, and this time brought up only stomach acid. 'I can't believe this is happening.'

'We weren't to know.'

'But it wasn't my fault.'

'We don't know that. Not for sure. What if it was the drugs? What if you supplied her with the drugs that killed her?'

'Oh, Christ. What are we going to do?'

'We put her in the boot. Then we go back to the party.'

Nathan put his head in his hands and began to groan.

'I'll say I found you,' said Bob, looking up now. 'I'll say I found you by the side of the road. You'd seen Sara dancing with what's his name, Mark. Flirting with him, whatever. You were drunk and pissed off. You were trying to walk into the village, to catch a minicab home. You didn't realize how far it was, or how cold. I'm on my way home. I see you, I pull over. We're parked at the side of the road, talking about Sara, love and the meaning of life. All right? I talk you into going back, saying sorry to her. So now we go back. We stay at the party for half an hour, and then you have to make sure — absolutely make sure — that you have an argument with Sara, because you're going to storm out and everyone is going to see you. I'll follow on. I'll say I'm driving you home. And then we'll drive back here. And get rid of her.'

Nathan rode a swell of panic, a surge like surf, and he rode it down again.

'I can't do that.'

'You have to.'

'I can't.'

'Do you have any better ideas?'

'I'm not thinking straight. I'm fucked. I've had too much coke.'

'You haven't got time to think straight. We have to get back to the party. We have to confuse the timeline.'

'What timeline?'

'What time we were at the party, and what time she was. Nobody saw you go in there together, nobody saw her leave with you. So we need to be back at that party. And we need to be seen at that party. Everybody has to see us. Acting normal.'

Things were shifting in Nathan's peripheral vision. He was scared to look.

He couldn't remember a time before this hateful old Volvo, a time before Charlie Parker on the CD player, a time before Elise.

'I can't come back here.'

'We have to. Because only a local would know it.'

All this time, they hadn't made eye contact. Now Nathan swivelled in his seat.

'We're going to get caught.'

'No, we're not. We just have to get through the next few hours. There will never be a time as bad as right now. I promise you that. This is the worst of it.'

Bob opened the door and squeezed himself out into the cold night air. He stood there for a while, his breath steaming, looking at the stars.

Soon, Nathan had joined him.

8

Nathan expected Mark Derbyshire's house to have changed. It would be antiqued, as if an age had passed. The guests would be slumbering and ivy-wrapped, ready to stir when he located Sara and woke her with a chaste kiss.

But the house had not changed and time had not slipped. The same party was taking place, with the same people in it.

Bob parked the Volvo on the gravel drive and they walked to the front door. The same hired butler took their coats. Nathan felt soiled, as if his clothes and hair and eyes and ears were caked with mud and shit and blood and semen – but he looked merely dishevelled and blank-eyed, as if he'd fallen asleep on the back seat.

Passing his car coat to the doorman, he caught a whiff of Elise's perfume; something young and clean, the smell of sleepy sunny afternoons, the smell of laughing on English seafronts.

Bob followed him to the ballroom, where Nathan expected the guests to form a slow, chanting ring around him. But no mob formed. They were too busy dancing to 'Waterloo'.

He got himself a drink. He had to order it three times; his voice had gone. He drained the glass and asked for another. No tonic this time.

He followed the bleach stink to the swimming pool. Several girls were in there, all of them wearing swimming costumes and bikinis, having come prepared to be spontaneous. There were several men in there, too – in Speedo trunks and board shorts, their underwater bellies pale and rippling, their tuber-pale legs diminishing to points. There was some modest screaming and splashing.

Wearied by the din of the main room, many guests had retreated to gather round the edges of the pool; they stood in discreet, sedate clumps. In one of those clumps stood Sara. Her group was comprised of several women and a few men. Among the men were Mark Derbyshire and Howard.

Sara was as flawless as the retreating cliffs of Dover, her purity a trick of distance and light. Nathan joined the group, which grew quiet in a way that implied he'd been the topic of conversation. Pretending not to look at him, everyone looked at him.

Sara said, 'And where have *you* been?'

He had no name for it.

'I'm sorry. I had too much to drink. I went for a walk. To clear my head.'

'You went for a walk where?'

'I don't know.'

'Because there's not really anywhere to go, is there?'

'Well, obviously I know that now.'

'I don't know what's wrong with you.'

This was quite enough for the other members of the group, each of whom had now found somewhere else to look. 'Waterloo' ended.

'Ant Music' came on. Screeching and splashing in the pool behind him. Perfume on his lapel. Semen in his underwear. And Bob behind him, casting a violet shadow.

Mark Derbyshire was grimacing, perhaps trying not to smirk. Howard was staring into the depths of his drink, a grey lock fallen across his brow.

'Look,' said Nathan, 'I had too much to drink. I'm sorry.'

'You had too much of *something*.'

'Too much of you.'

He had a little time to wonder where *that* had come from –

– before Mark Derbyshire grabbed his elbow and said, 'Right, sunshine.'

Nathan struggled, but Mark Derbyshire's hairy grip was absurdly powerful.

A flush rose from between Sara's breasts and spread over her sternum.

Nathan pulled at Mark Derbyshire's hand, shouting, 'Fuck *off*!'

Mark Derbyshire was implacable. 'Mate, you had *way* too much of whatever you've had. Now let's all calm down a bit.'

Nathan tried to punch him. But he drew his fist back too far, too fast, and lost his balance. He fell. The ground slammed the wind from him. He struck his head on the wet edge of the swimming pool.

He lay there on his back, in the wet, trying to breathe. Mark Derbyshire and Sara and Howard and Bob were looking down on him.

Behind them, steam and accumulated human exhalation on the glass ceiling had erased the crisp night sky. There was only a shifting, grey obfuscation that seemed about to clear, but never did.

As Nathan got to his feet, he was aware of a great quiet. The guests

in the pool stood like statues on a half-drowned island while he
brushed the worst of the water from his sopping arse.

Sara's lip twisted, and soon the rest of her face followed. She spat,
very slowly: 'Just piss off, Nathan.'

He thought of a dozen replies. Instead, he put his hands in his
sodden pockets and said 'What's the point?' before marching away
from the swimming pool and past the ballroom and once more – the
final time – to the balding man at the coat check.

All this time, Bob loped at Nathan's heel like a faithful
Newfoundland.

'That wasn't half an hour,' said Bob, outside. 'But it was pretty
fucking committed, I'll give you that.'

They buried Elise face down, by the river. The grave was shallow,
dug in the cold earth with their raw hands and the edge of chalky
boulders. They covered her with rocks and gravel, upon which they
sprinkled moss and twigs and leaf mould. They stuffed her clothes
and shoes into a knotted carrier bag, rooted from some corner of the
Volvo's boot, and buried that alongside her.

In the car on the way home they rehearsed again and again their
simple story, until Nathan half-believed it to be true.

When Bob pulled up outside Nathan's front door, it was still dark.
They were filthy.

Bob said, 'We shouldn't see each other again.'

'No.'

'But you can always trust me. I need you to know that.'

'I know that.'

'And can I trust you?'

'Yes.'

Nathan opened the car door. He wavered, and then said, 'Just as long as I never see you again, Bob. I mean, not ever.'

Bob nodded.

And Nathan climbed out, on to the pavement. Soil caked his clothes and his shoes and his hair and his eyelashes. His nails were split and black with it.

He went to the main door and fumbled at the lock. Then he rushed through the door and ran upstairs and into his flat. In the December dawn, he removed his shoes and socks and shirt, his suit and his underwear, and he threw them all in the washing machine.

Then he went to take a shower. He watched the water run brown, then grey, then clear. He stared at the bar of soap in his hand, a translucent lozenge of Pears, the cleanest smell he knew, and he began to cry.

9

What little remained of Nathan was wiped out by the sunrise.

Through the plasterboard walls he could hear the flush, the kettle boiling, the muffled radio: the neighbours, waking and stirring. He thought them hallucinations.

Sara came home in the afternoon, but only to leave him.

He was lying in bed and didn't speak as she packed three suitcases, ready to cram them violently into the boot of her old Golf. She was going to stay with her friend Michelle until next Saturday, by which time she expected Nathan to have found somewhere else to live.

He got out of bed. There were colourful detonations across his field of vision. He stood there, swaying.

'Look, I'm sorry.'

'What? That you thought I was flirting with that beardy little turd? Or that you left me all alone and then embarrassed me at a party where I didn't even *know* anybody?'

She looked at him with tired and angry eyes. Her hair was still damp, showing the tines of a comb, fragrant with shampoo.

'Fine,' said Nathan. 'Whatever.'

When she'd gone, he stood staring at the door. By the time he'd snapped out of it, he was standing there in the dark.

There was movement behind him – a furtive rustling, as if somebody was lurking there, in a dark corner. His hackles rose like a dog's and he moved quickly round the flat, turning on the lights.

When that was done, he sat staring at the yellow bulb, anxious in case it should blow while he slept, letting the inhabited darkness creep up on him.

He woke with a spasm of panic. Somebody was in bed with him. Nose to nose, she was observing the juddering of his dreaming eyes. All the bulbs had blown. The flat was in darkness.

It took him a long time to breathe. But it wasn't dark: it was morning. Monday morning, his second full day in this new world. The sunlight swam in and out of focus. He ran to the toilet and vomited. He hadn't eaten since Saturday afternoon; there was nothing left to throw up.

Rinsing away the yellow acid taste, he was too frightened to look in the mirror. But there was nothing behind him, except the bathroom. His pale reflection resembled the survivor of some disaster, a train crash or perhaps a bomb; one who is filmed hunkered at the roadside in a grey blanket, their forehead cobwebbed with blood.

He wondered what he could do.

There was nothing. It had happened. He couldn't make it unhappen.

At this impossible thought, he grabbed the edges of the sink.

There followed a moment of strange elation. Something within him seemed softly to illuminate, then to swell until it was passing through the confines of his skin. It left his body, and he was floating in the high corner of the bathroom, looking down on himself, double-imaged in the mirror. Then whatever it was began to contract, to fold about itself like a pair of wings; to draw back into his body. When it had gone, this fleeting, illogical rapture, he could not say what he'd felt, or what he'd become when, briefly, he had broken away from himself.

He showered in a hurry because he stank, but he didn't shave. He found a pair of jeans, another band T-shirt, and a plaid, fleece-lined jacket. He bundled his ruined suit and his shoes and his cashmere pea coat into a carrier bag, and hunted round for his house keys. Then he went outside for the first time since becoming whatever he had become. He had to wait in the hallway until the panic had gone.

The noise and the air of Monday morning. He huddled in his jacket. Outside the flat were buses and cars and people. He passed through them. He walked half a mile. His hands were very cold, red-knuckled and raw. He passed the twenty-four-hour garage and the corner shops. Then he turned into the local high street. He went into the charity shop next to the dry cleaners and handed over the carrier bag which contained the clothes he'd worn on Saturday night. Then he went to the newsagent next door.

The woman behind the counter was nervy and thin and tall. She suffered some mild form of mental illness – Nathan had stopped buying his newspapers there because sometimes she ranted at him, accusing the Council or the Royal Family or the police of having her under surveillance and controlling her thoughts. But she didn't scare him now.

He bought *The Times*, the *Guardian*, a *Daily Mirror*, the *Sun* and forty cigarettes. He folded the newspapers beneath his arm, left the shop and walked to the Moonshine Cafe.

An adult education college was being built across the road, and the cafe was full of builders in dirty jeans and work boots with exposed steel toecaps. Nathan ordered a cup of tea and a full English breakfast.

He took an empty Formica table and opened the *Mirror*. He skipped through, looking for mention of Elise. Girls were missing, but none of them was her. He opened the *Guardian*, and skipped through that too. And the *Sun* and *The Times*.

Breakfast arrived. He pushed it around the plate and forced himself to take a mouthful of scrambled egg, which had the consistency of seafood. His body wouldn't accept it; he placed the fork on the edge of the plate. He sipped tea and tried to read the paper, but his eyes skipped over the words. He left two papers for the builders and stuffed the other two in the book-sized pocket of his jacket. He lit a cigarette. The nicotine nauseated him and made him giddy. He walked home.

The door to the flat looked blankly at him. He felt like a burglar. This was Sara's place. He wondered what he'd do about finding another place to live.

At 3 p.m., when the sun grew low in the sky and dazzling, he scuttled round the flat turning on the lights. He turned on the television and watched it without seeing until it was time to go to work.

He took a second shower, more hurried than the first. He left the shower curtain open, fearing whoever might be standing there, waiting, when he opened it again.

When he'd dried himself, he didn't feel clean. He could smell his own breath, the smell of truffle, or tumour. He tried to clean his teeth and retched until luminous fish darted and wriggled in his peripheral vision. He dressed in his work clothes and the plaid jacket. He found his beanie and his wallet. From habit, he put a paperback book in his pocket. And then, as he did every weekday at the same time, he stepped out and caught the bus to work.

As he signed in at the desk, the security guard gave him a strange look.

He caught the lift to the second floor and walked to the studio. Howard was making a cup of tea in the narrow kitchen; there were cold, squashed teabags dotted all over the glittery Formica.

Mark Derbyshire was in the tiny, shared office. Most of the lights were off. Mark's screen saver scrolled unread across his monitor, its beige casing smeared with inky fingerprints.

Stubble sprouted in the normally contoured beard that Mark believed made him look a bit less like a beaver. He was sitting at his desk, looking down into his cup of tea; his cuffs were loose, exposing his hairy forearms and gold identity bracelet.

Nathan rapped on the door. Mark looked up.

'You've got some fucking nerve, sunshine.'

'Are you going to sack me?'

'Oh, fuck. I don't know. Probably. Whatever.'

'Mark. What's wrong?'

'A friend of mine. Graham. He lost his daughter.'

Nathan wanted to sit down. He shifted his weight so it was borne by the doorway.

'What?'

Mark's scalp was naked, but for some baby-like fluff that sometimes caught the light and made him look simple and surprised, like a gigantic duckling.

'My friend, Graham. His girl. Elise. She's gone.'

'Gone where?'

'That's the thing, mate. Nobody knows. She was at the party.'

'What – *your* party?'

'Yes – *my* party. Then . . .' He made a fluttering, bird-like motion with his hand. 'She was gone.'

Nathan pulled up a moulded plastic chair. He hoped the gesture looked intimate and concerned. He could no longer stand.

'Where'd she *go*?'

'Nobody *knows*. That's the point.'

Howard arrived.

'Kettle's boiled.'

'Yeah,' said Nathan. 'Cheers. Has somebody called the police?'

'Graham's got friends on the force,' said Mark. 'They're already on it. None of this "missing for twenty-four hours" bollocks. They were round my place by Sunday evening. I was still in bed.'

'Well. That's great. That's good news.'

Mark knuckled at his raw eyes. 'You really are a little prick, aren't you?'

Nathan looked at Howard. Howard raised an eyebrow and shrugged.

Mark said, 'Unless she turns up, and soon, the show's fucked. I've already been interviewed by the police. How long do you think it'll be before the *tabloids* get hold of that?'

'I see,' said Nathan. 'Right.'

'Right.'

There was no show that evening – they'd be playing a 'best of' compilation, one of several they kept behind for illness and other emergencies. Howard and Mark had turned up simply from habit, to sit in the half-lit offices, drinking coffee. Neither was married. Not any more.

Nathan said, 'I'm sorry. For Saturday night. Trying to hit you and that.'

Mark waved it away. They could hear the late-night traffic outside.

Nathan felt insubstantial.

He said, 'I thought she was going to sleep with you.'

'Who? Your bird?'

'Yeah. Sara.'

'Fat fucking chance. All she did was jabber about you. Rabbit fucking rabbit.'

Nathan's head twitched.

'I'm sorry?'

'All she did was talk about you. How brilliant you are. How I could use you better. Blah blah blah.'

Nathan smiled at his lap.

'Right,' he said.

'The funny thing is, I was sort of starting to believe her.'

Nobody spoke until Nathan said, 'Fuck it. Shall we go for a drink?'

The only place they could find was a cheesy nightclub. The music was too loud for conversation – so they just sat round a table and drank, and got drunk, and caught taxis home.

The next morning, a smiling snapshot of Elise Fox was on the front page of the *Daily Mirror*. But the main photograph was of Mark Derbyshire. He looked unshaven and haunted, snapped getting into his BMW. He wore a polo shirt that was too small for him, and a leather jacket that was too young for him, jeans that were too baggy, and a baseball cap and sunglasses that did not suit him.

The headline read FEARS GROW FOR PARTY GIRL, 19. The sub-heading was *Elise 'Not Seen' Since Disgraced DJ's Showbiz Party.*

In the snapshot, Elise was smiling. Nathan stared at it. He couldn't connect the face to the dead girl they had lain face down and naked in the soil.

The full story was on pages 9–13, and Nathan looked it up. But all he saw was a rehearsal of Mark Derbyshire's previous, disastrous run-in with the tabloid press – and a sneering list of the Z-list celebrities 'rumoured' to have been in attendance at his party.

In the evening, Nathan turned up for work as usual. But again, Mark Derbyshire didn't.

The deep scores in Howard's face were deeper. Tonight there was no 'best of' tape. Instead, the station had pulled Dave Huckabee, a retired breakfast DJ from a chair on the local television news. Dave had agreed to host the show until Mark Derbyshire returned.

Mark Derbyshire had been accused of no crime, but from the moment another man slipped on his headphones and sat before his microphone, that became a technicality. So did Mark's acquittal, fully thirteen years before. All that mattered to the press was the past accusation and the humiliation that followed it: Mark's 'fall from grace'.

Nathan looked at the newspaper photograph of Mark and was moved to a terrified pity. But he knew he'd let Mark go to prison forever before he allowed himself to be implicated in Elise Fox's disappearance.

He thought of his own face in the newspapers, and felt the world spinning out of control.

The next afternoon, two police officers came to his door.

10

The man – who was compact, with reddish hair – introduced himself as DS William Holloway. With him was PC Jacki Hadley.

Nathan invited them in.

Holloway asked if he might have a glass of water, then went to the kitchenette and took a mug from the drainer. The mug had been sitting there so long its base was filmed with dust.

The woman, Hadley, stood by the window. A double-decker bus went past. Hadley was watching it. Nathan understood. There was something surreal and fascinating about it: an upper deck of oblivious strangers, sailing directly past your living-room window.

Holloway drained the water.

'Do you mind if I sit?'

'Please.'

He took a dining chair, the first person to sit in it since Sara, in just a T-shirt, reading the *Guardian* Review.

Hadley stayed by the window, hands clasped at the small of her back, watching the intermittent buses go past.

Nathan sat on the sofa and crossed his legs, offering Holloway a cigarette. Holloway said, 'Not since New Year's Eve, 1989,' and took a biro from his jacket. 'So, Mr Redmond.'

'Nathan.'

'So, Nathan. I expect you'll have gathered why we're here.'

'Pretty much. Mark's party.'

Holloway pointed the biro at him, as if to say *Well done!*, then said, 'What time did you arrive at the party?'

'I don't know. Nine, maybe. A bit later.'

'And what time did you leave?'

'That, I can't tell you.'

Holloway scrutinized him.

'Drinking,' said Nathan. 'Quite heavily. Quaffing.'

There was a patch of sweat between Nathan's shoulder blades.

Holloway said, 'And while you were there – quaffing – did you see, or speak to Elise Fox?'

'Not that I know of.'

'Not that you know of.'

'I mean – there were like a million people there. So all night you're hello this and excuse me that. So I suppose I might have, whatever. Said hello or something.'

'There's no need to be so nervous. I'm not hungry.'

Nathan boggled at him.

Holloway said, 'I'm not going to eat you.'

'Oh. Ha ha. Yes.'

Holloway grinned, and from his pocket he took a packet of Chewits. He unwrapped four of them, placing the wrappers neatly back in his pocket. Then he popped the sweets into his mouth, four at once, and, chewing, said, 'Did you, to your knowledge – accepting the fact of your heavy drinking – did you see Elise Fox?'

'Not to my knowledge, no.'

'So, I understand you *left* the party – and then came back.'

'That's right.'

'You left at what time?'

'I'm not sure. Pretty late.'

'After midnight?'

'Before, I'd say. Just before. Quarter to? But I can't be sure. I was—'

'Drinking heavily, I know. So what happened?'

'How do you mean?'

'You left the party, why?'

'Oh. I had an argument.'

'With . . . ?'

'My girlfriend. You know how it is.'

Holloway's cool look implied that no, he didn't know how it was. And Nathan began to wonder if his apparent ennui might not be some kind of affectation.

'You argued about what?'

'Well, it wasn't an argument. Not at first.'

'Then what was it?'

'I saw her. Dancing with Mark.'

'Mark Derbyshire?'

'The one and only. Yes.'

'And . . .'

'And I got pissed off.'

'Because she was dancing with him?'

'Because of the way she was dancing.'

'How was she dancing?'

'I don't know. He was, like – he was practically goosing her.'

'And you didn't like that.'

'No, I didn't like that.'

'And you – what, stormed out?'

'I did. I stormed out.'

'With what intention?'

'I don't know, really. I just sort of went for a walk.'

'A walk to where? There isn't really anywhere to go.'

'That's what *she* said.'

'Who?'

'Sara. My girlfriend.' He ground out the cigarette. 'Ex-girlfriend.'

'Right. That'll be Sara Reed, of this address.'

'That's right.'

'And where is Sara now?'

'She's staying at her friend's. Michelle's. I'd need to look up the address.'

'No need. And how did you get back to the party?'

'A bloke called Bob came driving past.'

'Driving past.'

'He'd left the party. He was on his way home. But he stopped to pick me up.'

'Right. I assume we're talking about Robert Morrow here?'

'Probably. I mean, yes. I didn't know his surname.'

'He picked you up and took you back to the party.'

'That's right, yes.'

'And how long have you known Mr Morrow?'

'I don't really *know* him. Not really. We met once, a few years back. I hadn't seen him since. Tell the truth, he's a bit odd. He's into ghosts and what have you. Spends his time in haunted houses.'

'I know.'

'Oh. Right. I see.'

'It takes all sorts.'

'Apparently.'

'So. You and Mr Morrow were gone for some time.'

'Probably.'

'What were you doing? Ghost-hunting?'

'Ha. No. I'd stormed off. I was pissed off. Drunk. I had this idea, that I'd walk into the nearest town, village, whatever. Call a minicab.'

'Minicabs are thin on the ground, in that neck of the woods.'

'Well I know that now. The minute I started to sober up, I felt pretty stupid. It was really cold.'

'So Robert Morrow drives past . . .'

'Yeah. He sees me—'

'Limping along, thinks you're a spook . . .'

'Ha, yes. He stops. I get in. We have a chat.'

'About?'

'Love. Life. I tell him about the thing with Sara, her dancing with Mark. Bob convinces me to go back to the party. Talk to her.'

Holloway stared at him, chewing the sweets.

He said, 'Look, Nathan. There's probably not a great deal for you to be worrying about here. All I'm trying to do is establish a timeline. A big party like that, it's complicated. Life's not like *Inspector Morse*, right? People are drunk, people take drugs, people have sex with people they shouldn't be having sex with. People get confused about what happened when. People get embarrassed about the way they behaved, they don't want to talk. They lie, pretend to have blacked out. So accounts differ – what happened when, to who, at what time. It's the nature of these things. I don't care what you were doing in that car with Robert Morrow. I don't care if you two were taking drugs, making love—'

'Drugs,' said Nathan, quickly. 'Cocaine. We had a few toots of cocaine.'

'Good for you. I just need to know exactly when you were doing it—'

'For the timeline.'

'Spot on. So, you and Bob are in the car. Chatting. Love and life. You neck a bit of Bolivian.'

'Quite a lot, actually.'

'You neck quite a lot of Bolivian. Bob says, don't do this, don't walk out on the girl of your dreams. Or words to that effect, and—'

'And we go back to the party.'

'This is what time?'

'This is, I'm not sure. I was, y'know. My state of mind. But there were some people around when I tried to hit Mark, so—'

'Yes, there were.'

'Oh. Okay. So what time was it?'

'Shortly after 2 a.m.'

'Right. Ouch. A lot of people saw it, then.'

'Quite a few. Something like that – drunken bloke punches the host, misses, nearly falls into the swimming pool – it makes for a bit of a highlight. People remember it. So we use it, a kind of tent pole. To help establish the timeline.'

'I see. It wasn't a very good punch.'

'From what I hear, it was all a bit Charlie Chaplin.'

'Ah.'

'So, that's it? You left, round midnight. Bob picks you up. You get yourselves a bit fired up. Have a deep and meaningful chat. You go back to the party. Try to land one on your boss—'

'I embarrass myself horribly. Bob drives me home. I wake up, and I want to die. Merry Christmas.'

Holloway sat there for a few long moments, scrutinizing Nathan with mint-blue eyes. Then he sighed, glancing over at Hadley. She was still looking out the window, as if waiting for another bus to pass.

Holloway said, 'We may be in touch.'

'Okay. Do you think she's all right? The girl.'

'I don't know. I hope so.'

'But you think she'll turn up?'

'They usually do.'

'Good,' said Nathan. 'Good. This is awful. This is awful for every-one.'

Holloway gave him a courteous nod. Hadley gave him a mute glance. And they were gone, Nathan closing the door on them.

He sat down and put his head in his hands.

Then he went to the kitchen cupboard and removed a bottle of vodka.

He filled the mug from which Holloway had been drinking.

The vodka burned his gullet on the way down and sat like molten glass in his guts. He emptied the bottle. But it wasn't enough.

Sara called.

'Have you found somewhere to go?'

Nathan said, 'No.' And to her teeth-grinding silence he said: 'It's been a weird week. Have you seen the papers?'

Her voice was quiet when she said, 'What do you think? You know him. Is there, could there be anything in it?'

Mortally offended, he cut her short, 'The last thing Mark needs at the moment is his *friends* gossiping about him.'

Ashamed of herself, she gave Nathan another week in the flat. One more week, and that was that. If he wasn't gone, she'd have him thrown out.

She had brothers.

He told her thanks, he'd find somewhere as soon as he could.

He put down the phone.

It rang again, immediately.

He picked it up.

'What?'

It wasn't Sara. It was a tabloid journalist called Keith. Keith offered Nathan half his annual salary to talk about Mark Derbyshire.

Nathan looked at the receiver as if it was firm and warm and damp, like a semi-erect penis.

He said, 'How did you get my number?' and, without waiting for an answer, he slammed down the receiver.

He curled on the sofa and tried to sleep.

He woke to the twilight and went to work. They fired him.

He and Howard, both unemployed now, went for a drink.

'Jesus,' said Howard. 'What a week.'

Nathan chinked his glass.

'Fuck it,' he said.

Mark Derbyshire's landline had been disconnected. So in the early afternoon, Nathan called his new mobile. Only four people knew the number. Mark answered almost immediately.

'It's Nathan,' said Nathan.

He didn't know where Mark Derbyshire was speaking from. But he got the idea he was alone in a hotel room, watching Sky Sports and waiting for the phone to ring.

'What the fuck are you *doing*?' said Mark. 'I'm trying to keep this line clear, for Christ's sake.'

'They fired me.'

'I know that. It's still *my* fucking show. I know that.'

'It's your show. But I don't have a job on it any more. Neither does Howard.'

'Howard will be all right. He's probably got a job already.'

'I don't care about Howard.'

'As soon as I'm back on air,' said Mark, 'Howard will come back. He'll be all right.'

'I don't care about Howard.'

'Well you fucking *should*. He's worth a hundred of you. A thousand. A million.'

'Be that as it may. They didn't give me severance pay. I'm out without a penny in my pocket.'

'Because you were sacked for gross misconduct. You tried to hit me at my own party.'

Nathan sighed and said, 'Why are you *doing* this? Surely you need all the friends you can get?'

'You're not my friend. You *were* my employee. Now you're not even that. Right now, I need the station to love me. And if I can save them a few quid by firing you at no cost, and pulling in some work-experience fuck who'll work twice as hard for fuck all, then that's what I'll do.'

'You're unbelievable.'

'Yeah. Well. Wake up and smell the monkeys.'

'But I haven't got a pot to piss in. Or anywhere to live. What am I going to do for money?'

'Listen. Good luck. Really. But I need to keep this line clear, so I'm going to hang up now. Okay? So fuck the fuck off.'

But he didn't hang up. He was lost and alone and scared and desperate for somebody to talk to. Even Nathan.

Who said, 'But I need money.'

'Don't we all.'

'Listen, Mark. Just listen for one minute. Please?'

'One minute,' said Mark Derbyshire. 'Fifty-nine seconds. Fifty-eight seconds. Fifty-seven seconds.'

'I've been fired,' said Nathan. 'Not made redundant. Which means I can't even claim benefit for – I don't even know. Months. And I've got to leave my flat because I broke up with my girlfriend. And don't say I should kick her out, because it's her flat. Yesterday a tabloid journalist phoned me. I don't know how they got my name or my number, but they were willing to pay me – and I'm not kidding here – they were willing to pay me a lot of money.'

Mark Derbyshire stopped counting down.

'Pay you money to what?'

'Talk about you.'

There was another, longer silence before Mark said, 'Talk about me, how?'

'I'll say whatever they want to hear,' said Nathan. 'I can't afford not to.'

He didn't even feel empty. He felt like he didn't exist.

'Jesus Christ,' said Mark. 'How much do you want?'

'Thirty grand.'

'Fuck you. I haven't got it.'

'Sell something. They offered me fifty.'

'And if I pay? How do I know you won't go to the papers anyway?'

'Because I'm telling you I won't. You have to trust me.'

Three days later, £30,000 was credited to Nathan's bank account. The same morning, he stuffed some belongings into a black nylon holdall.

He paused to look at what he was leaving behind: his CDs, a few books, some videotapes. His television, his stereo, his sofa.

None of it meant anything. It seemed strange to think that it ever had.

He left the flat and checked into a seaside bed-and-breakfast hotel: the kind of place that shouldn't have existed since about 1975. It was a backdrop for repeated sitcoms, for laughter-tracks behind trapped lives in a bygone England.

But it was real. He dumped his bag on the single bed, and slept with the lights on.

Three weeks after Elise disappeared, Nathan endured the sight of her parents and her sister on the local television news, making a plea for her safe return. He stared at the screen.

The family knew Elise wasn't coming back. He could tell by the way they looked at the camera. By the way they looked through it, and directly at him.

In the early weeks of March 1998, it was leaked to the press that the police were interviewing Mark Derbyshire in connection with the case.

It got a lot of coverage. On television, Nathan saw it announced that an 'item relating to the case' had been found on Mark Derbyshire's property. This didn't sound remarkable to Nathan; everyone knew that Elise had been there. God knew what she might have dropped or left behind. But whatever the item was, it was enough for the police to take Mark in for questioning.

Once again, Mark Derbyshire's past was rehearsed in every newspaper and on every news report.

Mark was released after questioning: he was never charged. But the country knew he'd done it, even if nobody was legally allowed to say so. And so Mark Derbyshire's long career finally ended.

The police didn't find Elise's body, and nor did anyone else.

Nathan couldn't imagine why; he didn't think he and Bob had done such a terribly good job of burying her.

Perhaps the police were simply looking in the wrong place.

Every morning, he woke and immediately turned on the radio – expecting to hear an announcement that her body had been found.

But the announcement never came.

11

That spring, he bought a rucksack and a six-week European travel pass. But he took Elise with him.

He was too old to be sharing late-night trains with gap-year students. After six weeks, he found himself alone at 3 a.m., dangling bare, tanned legs over the dock on Icaria. He'd sat all night outside a restaurant, alone with a book he was pretending to read, half-hoping somebody might strike up a conversation. But nobody did.

Since leaving England, he'd barely spoken, except to order a drink, or dinner. His orbit was marked by something dark. People didn't come too close.

He pretended to himself that he wished he'd gone to America instead, that he'd chosen this cheap travel pass because he was trying to conserve money. But that wasn't true.

When Nathan was eighteen, he'd come to the Greek Islands with Chloe, his girlfriend. It was their first and only time away – and for its three weeks they were happy-sad, because they knew this trip was an extended goodbye. They were about to start at different universities, and they knew that what was to come would change them. There was no way to maintain their relationship – Chloe had seen her two brothers make that mistake, and it had brought them nothing but unhappiness.

Now – alone on the dock at Icaria – he saw that over the last few weeks he'd followed almost exactly the route he and Chloe had taken, when he was a child who thought himself nearly a man.

He spat into the dark and watched it loop and spin into the lapping, oily Mediterranean. Then he got up, brushing the grit from his arse and slinging the rucksack over his shoulder. He found an all-night bar and sat in the corner drinking Amstel until the sun came up. Then he slapped a pile of euros on the bar, didn't wait for his change, and walked out to greet the early morning ferry. His flip-flops slapped to the rhythm of his feet.

He watched the ferry dock. It was rusted and ponderous, weathered as a coastal rock.

At length, it discharged blinking, fuzzy-headed young backpackers, American and German and Dutch, British and Canadian and Australian, on to the dock. Some of their faces were still marked with the weave of the ferry's dirty carpet.

Nathan was one of three or four people to embark. He sat in a patch of ringing sunlight, cooled by the sea breeze, and stared past the corner of a lifeboat, into the ferry's frothing wake.

In Goa, he saw a Hindu funeral. The corpse, draped in white, garlanded with roses and jasmine and marigold, was carried on a stretcher to a riverside pyre. On the pyre, it was arranged with its bound white feet facing south – the direction of the dead.

The chief mourner walked round the pyre three times, sprinkling water. Then he put the pyre to flame.

Nathan watched the body burn. The perfumed smoke, billowing, diffusing against the sunset. The yellow flames. The brown river.

He grabbed his bag and walked away.

He flew from Delhi and walked wearily through UK customs.

He stood in the English airport, ridiculous in his gap-year student clothes – this man with no idea who he had become.

Before leaving Heathrow, Nathan called Sara at work. She answered on the fourth ring.

'Nathan?'

He swelled with a violent nostalgia. It took him a moment to speak. And then, all he could say was: 'Hi.'

'Where have you *been*?'

It seemed to her that losing his job, his girlfriend and his flat within a couple of weeks had worked something loose in Nathan's head. She'd told her friends (in a grave, not unhappy tone): *Nathan had a breakdown.*

He said, 'I'm okay.' It sounded true when he said it. Then he told her, 'I've been to Greece,' and it sounded like a lie. Before she could ask any more questions, he said, 'Look, I've no right to ask this. But I need a reference.'

'What kind of reference?'

'A landlord's reference. I need a place to live.'

'So what you're phoning to ask is: pretend we never went out, and write a letter saying what a fabulous tenant you were.'

'Pretty much. I know it's a shitty thing to ask.'

It *was* a shitty thing to ask. But she said 'Fine' because she pitied him.

He caught the train home and booked himself into a cheap hotel, then showered and shaved and went to buy a local newspaper.

The next afternoon, armed with Sara's reference, he paid the deposit and two months' rent in advance on a small, clean, one-bedroom flat.

It was on the top floor – into the eaves – of a big, Victorian building. On the ground floor was a day nursery; his little bedroom overlooked the playground.

Since it was summer and the nights were short, Nathan could afford to wait until the first comforting signs of dawn before trying to sleep – which meant that, often, he woke to the pleasant screams of young children at playtime. He lay in bed listening to them, just as he might lie in a sun-warmed tent, listening to a chattering brook.

The sound of the children made him happy. Their existence seemed so tremendously unlikely, he took comfort from it. He never watched them playing, because he thought that from their perspective his face – peering down from the small, high bedroom window – would look ghostly and lost, and he wanted to spare them that.

But even their tears and tantrums, from this high place, sounded good to him.

He lay there, listening to them, and wondered what he was going to do about getting a job.

It was easy.

He visited an employment agency, where his agent displayed contempt for his paltry CV, enquiring in a frigid tone why he'd left his 'previous employment'.

He took in a slow breath, held it for a moment and then told her: 'I was kind of made redundant.'

'Kind of. Was there a restructure?'

'Not really. Kind of.'

'Kind of.'

'The show I was working on – it was called *The Mark Derbyshire Solution*.'

After a moment, she said 'I see' in a manner that Nathan had learned to recognize; it was the way people chose to hide their sudden, incandescent interest in celebrity, even minor celebrity. She looked Nathan in the eye and said, 'It must have been terrible for you.'

'It wasn't good, no.'

'And if it's all right to ask – how is he?'

'How's who? Mark? I haven't spoken to him.'

'I see,' she said. 'Yes. That poor girl.'

So Nathan went on the books of the employment agency, and a week later, the agent called to let him know she'd lined up an exciting interview with a prestigious company he had never heard of.

Nathan no longer owned an interview suit or good shoes; they'd gone into the washing machine and then to a charity shop, scrunched up in a carrier bag. So that afternoon, he went shopping.

On Monday, he was interviewed for the position of sales executive at Hermes Cards, Ltd. The interview was conducted by two men and two women, who sat behind a long desk like the top table at a wedding.

Nathan told them he had no sales experience, and that he had no particular interest in greetings cards. Nor had he ever stopped to consider the profound part greetings cards had to play in observing British rites of passage – birth, marriage, illness and death.

'But I've certainly been thinking about it over the weekend,' he said, and the interviewers laughed. From one of the women there was even a little flirtatious pen-playing.

When the chuckles had died down, he said, 'The truth is, when times were good, working with Mark taught me about working under pressure. And when times were bad, it taught me a lot about loyalty.'

When he'd done talking about Mark Derbyshire, a certain gloom settled on the room.

They thanked Nathan for coming along. He shook their hands – one by one – and thanked them, and left, and went directly to the pub. He sat in the garden. The sun shone so bright he could barely read his newspaper.

Hermes Cards called back the next day: they wanted to see him again next Tuesday.

He bought a new tie, a raincoat and a folding umbrella, in case it was raining on the day. He wondered how the person who wore these clothes related to that lost man in Greece, in his Gap cargo shorts and Nike sandals; and how that man related to the wired madman in the Paul Smith suit, scrabbling with bleeding nails at the cold, wet earth. He could draw no line of connection between them. He was a series of disconnected dots, a Morse code.

The second interview took place in a different room. This time, they sat round a shiny oval table, and Nathan knew before anyone spoke that he'd got the job.

He was to start on the 1st of July, which gave him ten days of nervousness. He had no idea how to go about doing a proper job.

He went to the Business section of his local bookshop and spent seventy pounds on titles that promised to make him a more effective communicator – but none of these books seemed to tell him anything that was not already perfectly obvious.

During the sleepless nights he lay in his bed, clamped between the past and the future. In the morning he lay listening to the children play.

And then the day came, and he went to work.

At reception, he introduced himself, saying: 'I'm the new boy.'

The receptionist said, 'If you'd like to take a seat, Roy will be down in a moment.'

Nathan had no idea who Roy might be. He sat with his briefcase on his lap, and waited.

Behind the reception desk was a wall-to-wall, ceiling-high, hardwood bookcase. Ranked on it were hundreds of greetings cards. There were bawdy cartoons; floral tributes to the sick and the bereaved; congratulations for new parents and new graduates. Blank inside, they were rich with the passage of lives yet to be lived.

The receptionist saw him, scanning their ranks.

Nathan said, 'Is there a *Congratulations on your new job?*'

She swivelled in her chair. 'There must be one up there, somewhere.'

He smiled, then turned to the ping of an elevator door. A man he took to be Roy came striding towards him. Roy was trim and sprightly, not far from retirement; his handshake nearly pulverized Nathan's finger bones.

'You must be Nathan.'

Roy put an arm round Nathan's shoulder. Nathan had not been touched by another human being in many months; he tried to relax into Roy's paternal grip, as Roy said, 'I've heard a lot about you.'

'Okay,' said Nathan. 'Good.'

Roy led him to the lift. Nathan stared at his reflection as they whispered up two floors. Then Roy led him past what he described as the glass boardroom then through a set of double doors into the office building's working interior.

The floor was open-plan, lined with small, glass-fronted offices in which imprisoned executives and managers spoke into telephones or listened to telephones or hunched over laptop computers.

'This is sales and marketing,' said Roy. 'Welcome home. You'll soon get to know it.'

He wasn't wrong. When he wasn't on the road to Swindon or Edinburgh or Birmingham or Cardiff, the modern sales executive spent a great deal of time on the telephone and the computer.

The modern sales executive also spent most of his time engaged in pursuits which didn't involve selling anything to anybody: Nathan found himself attending weekly marketing meetings, and weekly pre-marketing meetings, and weekly post-marketing meetings which, with grim and affected professionalism, were called 'post-mortems'.

In addition, there were quarterly, half-yearly and annual sales performance review meetings. There were monthly sales projections meetings. There were bi-monthly regional and national sales meetings. There were two sales conferences. There were buyers to entertain. There were lunches and dinners and drinks without number. There was karaoke in Sheffield and go-karting in Swindon.

The sales department was structured in a way that Nathan didn't completely understand. There seemed to be four UK sales directors, three of whom were beaten and bitter men who reported to one, younger boss, whose job title was simply Director (UK Sales).

In addition, sales shared an arcane crossover of responsibility with marketing, which meant each department was in a position to blame the other when budgets were overspent or financial targets hadn't been met, which was always. Thus, the relationship between sales and marketing was alternately cordial and hypothermic.

At first, Nathan enjoyed the inanity of it. He was paid an initially modest but increasingly handsome salary, plus theoretical bonuses, to sit round a table for hours, pretending to care about the late delivery of 5,000 New Line Easter cards to a godforsaken warehouse in East Anglia.

As the weeks bled into months, then years, Nathan would some-times be struck by wonderment as he was cleaning his teeth in the morning – but by the time he was knotting his tie, the sense of affa-ble farce would have deserted him and he'd be worrying that Norfolk (as the warehouse was simply and ominously known) would be unable to clear the late delivery of 55,000 New Line Eclipse cards that had arrived late from the printers.

Getting into his car, an Omega, he would be anxious that the pro-posed New Lines for Christmas-after-next would not correlate with what marketing had identified as the post-Millennial Mood; or that a leading chain of high-street stationers would not after all decide to retail the new, cartoon-Jesus Easter cards which had been enthusi-astically endorsed, first by the board, then by every other department – and which would just as systematically be disowned if they failed.

He knew thinking about all this was a waste of time; but it was much, much better than thinking about anything else.

And then, during the Winter Sales Conference, 2001, he saw Elise's family on television. They were making an appeal for information that might lead to her return.

12

He'd spent a long, buttock-numbing day in an overheated hotel conference room, listening to inept presentations by senior management and non-executive members of the board.

Nathan was always frustrated by the Sales Conference; partly because he wasn't allowed to participate in the presentations, and partly because he was forced to share the complicit eye-rolls and watch-glances of the stultified sales reps, who weren't listening to a word of it.

The day's session ended at 4.45 p.m. In the foyer, there were coffee and biscuits for the delegates, who would then enjoy an hour or two of free time before reconvening in the Boleyn Bar for the formal dinner.

Overheated and itchy with boredom – except the senior management, each of whom glowed with the invigorating success of their talk on *Seasonality: A Picture of Shift? Or Opportunity for Growth?* – the delegates filed into the lobby where little clumps began to form, like matter after the big bang.

The muttered conversation centred on how bored everyone was, how *hot* it was in there – and who was sitting with whom at that evening's Formal Conference Dinner.

Among the marketing department's regular triumphs was a fastidious seating plan for the formal dinner. This seating plan tacitly acknowledged the company's deep structural enmities; those who loathed each other were seated at different tables – as were those who were sleeping together, and those who were no longer sleeping together. Those who'd been passed over for promotion weren't seated next to the successful candidate. Despised graduate *wunderkinder* weren't seated by strawberry-nosed alcoholics still stewing over the loss of Christmas bonuses long past.

Ten days before every conference, this piece of work – known with unfeigned reverence as the *Draft Seating Plan* – would be submitted to the CEO and other members of the main board. The CEO and the main board would then ignore the draft seating plan until ninety minutes before the formal dinner, at which point they would reject it.

This caused the marketing department – six women and two handsome, diffident male graduate trainees wondering what the hell they were doing here – to hunker down, as in a military command centre, and descend into logistical, chain-smoking chaos.

The result of which was: nobody got to sit next to somebody they liked – nobody except the marketing department, who placed themselves, the art department and a select number of the brightest and funniest reps on two tables in the farthest and most private corner, where they would get drunk and tell jokes about the CEO and the board of directors until 3 a.m.

Like everyone else, Nathan hated the formal dinner – it never failed to achieve the opposite of what was intended; one could sense the nexus of resentment, neurosis and outright hatred, festering like bad wiring.

And worse, there was never any way to predict if this time he was in favour with the marketing department, and therefore chosen to sit with them.

So, as everyone in the foyer gathered in murmuring clusters, Nathan decided to avoid the stress of discussing it.

He stopped, patting himself down as if confused – perhaps looking for the expensive lighter that should be right there, in his pocket. With a scowl of consternation, he walked off, still patting his pockets as if expecting the lighter to weirdly materialize. Then he ducked to the right, and into a lift, and pressed UP.

Nathan liked hotel rooms. In them, he could pretend that he really was the person he'd made himself into. He liked the tautness of the bedding and the bright sterility of the bathroom; he liked the constant hum of air conditioning. He liked the unquestioned might of the *Do Not Disturb* sign. He liked turning it to read *Please Make Up My Room* when he left in the morning, straightening his tie. And he liked the transgressive feeling of closing the door and loosening the tie, then removing his suit and lying in socks and boxer shorts on the bed with his rumpled clothes in a pile alongside him, flicking through the television channels.

Doing this, he fell into a doze with the remote control clasped in his hand. He woke with a jolt, glued to the bed by a line of spit that had dried to a fine, flaky crust on his chin.

He'd turned up the air conditioning too high: his legs were cold. He drew into himself. It was dark outside. He had no idea what time it was; he thumbed the volume on the remote control. The national six o'clock news was just beginning. So there was plenty of time to wake up properly, have a good shower and still be changed and ready for dinner.

He crawled under the covers and lay with his eyes closed, listening to the headlines, the usual catalogue of metropolitan calamity and international speculation. The thing in him that, long ago, had been moved and enraged and scared by the television news had long gone.

After the major headlines, he heard this: *And, almost four years after her disappearance, the family of missing Elise Fox launch a new appeal for information.*

Nathan sat up.

In this unhaunted hotel room, the blue television light flicked and lashed at his face and naked body. At 6.15, the headlines were rounded up. After this, the newsreader addressed the camera: *The family of Elise Fox, who disappeared almost four years ago after a party in Gloucestershire, have today relaunched an appeal for information which might help to find her.*

Nathan watched as, on screen, three people filed into a flashing room and took seats behind a desk. A trim, refined man. A woman in a wine-red suit. And a younger woman – a little older than Elise would have been, had she lived.

She was Elise's older sister.

They sat before a blown-up snapshot of Elise. She looked young and beautiful and careless. Nathan wouldn't have recognized her. His Elise was a flickering series of snapshots: the white-faced bundle by the tennis courts; her white breasts in the darkness of Bob's car; the shocking warmth inside her; the way her dead foot twitched on Bob's naked lap. A naked shape, face down in a scooped-out grave.

As the cameras flashed, the man spoke from a prepared statement.

'If somebody out there, anybody out there, knows what happened to Elise, or if someone out there knows where Elise might be, we beg you to please, please, get in contact.'

His voice broke on the word 'please' and his daughter reached up and touched his elbow, squeezing gently.

'We beg you,' she said. Elise's sister.

She was staring into the camera and through it.

Nathan jumped out of bed and turned on all the lights – the ceiling lights, the standard lamps, the bedside reading lights; the lights in the bathroom and in the wardrobe. Then he removed a miniature bottle of whisky from the minibar. His hands were shaking too badly to break the seal – he opened it with his teeth and tipped the bottle into his gullet.

The phone rang. Nathan snatched it up, not thinking.

'Hello?'

'Hello, mate,' said Justin, who was Nathan's boss. Justin thought himself an old school salesman: at conference dinners he drank whisky and loosened his tie and rolled his sleeves and smoked cigars into the early morning.

Justin and Nathan didn't trust one another. Because of this, they pretended to everyone – including each other – to be very close friends.

Justin said, 'Where are you?'

Nathan looked at his watch, then glanced at the TV. They'd moved on to another story now. Global warming or something.

'Sorry, mate. I must have fallen asleep.'

'You'd better get down here. The drinks have started.'

'When's dinner?'

'In forty minutes. But I need you down here, soon as poss.'

Nathan realized that he'd broken an arcane rule – that the sales reps should never be left to mingle and speak freely. Instead they should be vexed by someone from head office whom they did not like, and who had nothing to say to them.

Nathan hurried to the shower. He stood under the water and tested his fingers, to see if he could feel them. He shampooed his hair and washed himself with the expensive soap he'd brought along. He put on fresh boxer shorts and socks and shirt and a fresh suit, and shoes and cufflinks. Today's suit he hung from the shower rail, where the shower steam would ease the creases from it.

He saw himself in the mirrored wall of the elevator. Smart suit and perfect hair. Bloodless lips.

He went to the formal dinner.

Two weeks before, Nathan had argued with Amrita about the cost-effectiveness of an advert she'd placed in the *Oldie* magazine – Amrita had called him a pompous wanker. So Nathan's long-term favoured status had taken a setback. He didn't get to sit with the marketing department.

The Foxes were on television again that night, and in the morning they were in the newspapers.

Over the next two weeks, he became almost accustomed to seeing them on the news, or in magazines and newspapers: the father's fine-boned face, the mother's air of bewildered efficiency. And the clear-eyed directness of Elise's sister, who featured in many of the print interviews.

Her name was Holly.

Nathan read and reread these interviews until he'd memorized them.

He didn't know why he did this; familiarity with Elise's name in print didn't relieve the dread of seeing it again – or make it possible to sleep with the lights off.

But he connected with something in Holly Fox's clear-eyed gaze, and was greatly moved. It felt like a kind of love, forged in the same smithy.

He wished that things could be better for her – that Holly Fox could be happy.

Nathan wished that he could be happy, too.

Eventually, he wondered if their possible happiness, like the fact of their unhappiness, might not somehow be linked.

That's when he decided to find her.

13

He had to wait until after Christmas.

It was the worst time of year. Even when he came home drunk following some work-related function – work-related functions amounted to the whole of Nathan's social life – it was necessary to drink a bottle of wine and double-check all the lights before attempting to sleep. It was also necessary to check the spare long-life bulbs were stacked in a pyramid in the kitchen, next to the kettle.

Over the utilitarian mirror in the bathroom, he nightly secured a thick blue towel – hanging it firmly from nails hammered into the wall for the purpose, such that it was impossible for the towel to work its way loose during the night and fall. If it had – if Nathan heard that sudden, slithering noise behind the closed door in the empty flat – he would simply and immediately lose his mind. The second mirror, full length, he kept inside the wardrobe door – and he secured the wardrobe door with two simple sliding bolts, one at the top and one at the bottom. He would not risk it swinging open during the dark hours.

In each room he kept a 12-inch, aluminium-cased Maglite torch. Although these torches had never been used, he changed their batteries on the first Monday of every month, in addition to which he kept one pack of spares per torch secreted in each room. This unopened pack too was replaced, unopened, every six months. He sometimes woke, having dreamed of a power cut, reaching for the cool metal tube beneath his pillow. Sometimes he slept cupping a Maglite like a teddy bear.

At the foot of the bed he left folded a pile of emergency clothing: a sweater, jeans, slip-on trainers. This was in case he was required to dress and be gone from the flat in a hurry – if the towel in the bathroom should fall, say, or the wardrobe door should creak open. For the same reason he left his keys hanging inside the front-door lock.

Gradually, he'd learned to sleep with softer, indirect lighting – which made the possibility of a single blown bulb less catastrophic. There was a standard lamp in each corner of the bedroom, banishing troubling shadows, and a desktop lamp on the bedside table – to reach for, should the four standard lamps for any reason blow simultaneously.

He'd left the main light fitting empty because to accidentally switch on the overhead light, then to correct himself and switch it off again, would make the room appear, momentarily, to be a little darker – even with all four standard lamps on. No degree of darkness was permissible.

He'd experimented with an eye-mask, but it had proved impractical; if Nathan heard a noise – a click or a creak or a sigh – it was necessary to fumble inefficiently with the mask's edges and flip the whole thing inside out on his forehead. Instead, he slept on his back with a light pillow placed over his eyes.

In December the dawn was late and the night was long.

Although Christmas was Hermes' busiest retail period, there wasn't much for Nathan and his head office colleagues to do; it was down to the boys in the front line – which is how the field sales reps were described when business was brisk. As the month waxed, then waned, he could do little more than keep an eye on sales and stock levels, measuring their failure against performance targets.

As Christmas Day approached and the possibility of a performance-related bonus once more evaporated, head office slipped into languor. The silent resentment wasn't helped by the seasonal round of obligatory departmental lunches, nor the Christmas party.

On Christmas Eve, Nathan worked as late as he could – it was always possible to find something to do, even if it was filing or clearing out old paperwork. At 3.30, he wandered twice round the building, looking for somebody to have a drink with. But his colleagues were all gone; one by one, they'd bid cheery seasonal goodbyes and bundled themselves into overcoats, picking up their briefcases and handbags.

On the way home, Nathan stopped off to buy some food. Then he parked his car behind the nursery and approached home via the rear entrance. The nursery was in darkness; the children would soon be tucked up, enduring their own excited sleeplessness at the thought of a nocturnal visitation. But the darkness in the nursery didn't frighten Nathan. The walls were lined with painty splodges on cheap sugar paper. It wasn't conceivable that something wicked lurked in there.

But now he noticed the flats on the first floor were in darkness – and so was the attic flat that abutted his. He looked at his watch, as if it might suddenly have become three o'clock in the morning.

Frowning, half embarrassed, he walked to the front of the building to see that, except for his own flat – which he kept illuminated even in his absence, in case the uninhabited darkness should act as an invitation – there were no lights on. Not even in Flat A, on the first floor – where steadfast, boring Wendy and Dave lived. In an act of what felt to Nathan like calculated malice, they'd turned off the winking Christmas tree lights.

It hadn't occurred to Nathan that all of his neighbours might be away for the holiday. It hadn't happened before. The thought of all those empty rooms – of all that darkness, below him as he slept – dried his mouth and caused his scrotum to shrivel up.

His key rasped too loud in the latch. Stepping into the hallway, every movement seemed to echo. Having banged the timer switch firmly with the heel of his hand, he made it up the first two flights of stairs.

Then he stopped.

He hit the timer switch again and, still clutching his shopping, he turned and ran back downstairs and out the front door.

Eventually, he found a city-centre hotel that was not fully booked. The room was not cheap, and Nathan was not sufficiently composed to negotiate himself a last-minute best-price deal.

He returned to his flat in the drizzly light of Christmas morning, to pick up a few things: some clothes, some toiletries, a book, and some magazines for when he lost interest in it. He ate a room-service Christmas dinner while watching a repeat of *Only Fools and Horses*. He spent Christmas evening in the bar, defiantly reading and drinking. He didn't know how drunk he was until he stood to retire. The walls performed a trick of perspective, retreating from him, and the barmen looked wicked and malicious.

But New Year's Eve, at least, was tolerable. He watched television and, because the hotel was in the city centre, close to the renovated docklands, he could hear the cars hooting their horns and the girls screaming and laughing and groups repeating one verse of 'Auld Lang Syne', over and over again, and still not getting it right. He could watch it on television too: he could watch a celebrity count in another year, and that was good. That put another year between him and it.

January kicked off with a cold snap. Winds blew in unchecked from the Russian steppes. England descended into bedlam, the way it always did when faced with weather that to whatever modest degree actually resembled winter.

So he had to sit out January, too — because nobody went house-hunting when frost was hard-baked into the ground, making soil like hardwood and concrete brittle like seaside rock. Nobody in England, anyway.

It was not until February that he began to compile a list of local estate agents.

He made the calls from work, during his lunch hour. If the call should be traced, he need only claim to be house-hunting. In case this should ever be checked out (he well remembered Detective Holloway's cordial malice), he went to see his bank's mortgage adviser, who agreed on the spot to a mortgage in principle.

There were many more local estate agents than Nathan had antic-ipated. A single, large advert in the *Yellow Pages* might cover half a dozen local branches. Because of this, and because he didn't always get a lunch break, it was nearly three weeks before he called Morris Michael estate agents and said, 'Hi, can I speak to Holly Fox please?'

By now, he'd repeated this sentence so often that, somewhere along the line, it had lost its meaning. So the reply —

'I'm afraid she's out on a viewing right now, may I take a message?'

– was followed by a long silence, during which Nathan's salesman's throat tightened and let him down. He slammed the receiver into its cradle and hurried to the lavatory.

He fumbled at his belt and suffered a protracted bout of diarrhoea. Then he went to the car park behind the office and sat in his car, listening to loud music. He smoked seven cigarettes.

He watched motorcycle couriers with packages to deliver, and colleagues who'd nipped out for a smoke (there was a forlorn, stained patch of concrete designated for smokers: contrived to be as uninviting as possible, it deterred nobody). He turned down the music and pretended, ineptly, to be speaking into a mobile phone.

Back in his tiny, glass-fronted office, he wrote the estate agent's number on a Post-it note, and returned the *Yellow Pages* to Angela's desk.

It took him more than a week to call the number again. But he thought about little else; the idea had annexed a corner of his brain, like adolescent obsessions sometimes had. Whatever else he was doing, the greater part of him was rehearsing imaginary conversations with Holly Fox.

When he called a second time, the voice on the line asked him to wait. There was a basso rumbling as the receiver was set down. He hadn't been left on hold and he could hear the background sounds of somebody busy approaching the phone: muffled snippets of conversation, other noises rendered indecipherable; the rumbling of the phone as it was lifted from the desk; a hand cupped over the receiver.

Softly, 'Okay, I will. Later.'

Then:

'Hello, Holly speaking.'

Nathan stood up, as if someone had entered the room, saying: 'Hello?'

'This is Holly. How can I help you?'

'I'm looking for a house.'

'O-*kay*.'

He thought by the tone of her voice that she was searching her desk for a pen.

He told her his price range. She asked what he was looking for.

He said, 'Something nice.'

'Okay. That's a start. A flat? A house?'

'Can I afford a nice house on my budget?'

'You'd be surprised. If you pick the right area.'

'Okay. A house would be great. Obviously. Yes. A house.'

'Bedrooms?'

'Yes, please.'

'Got that. How many?'

'Oh. I see. Sorry. I don't know. Two?'

'Two bedrooms. And would you consider a three-bedroom if it fell within your price range?'

'Maybe. Should I?'

'Most Victorian properties have three bedrooms, you see.'

'Right. I see. Okay. Then yes.'

'One of them is usually quite small. A lot of people use them for home offices.'

'Okay.'

'They make good office space.'

'Right.'

'So. Let me have a look at what's available. Then it's probably a good idea if you come in and see me to have a chat. I don't want to show you something you're not interested in.'

'Okay.'

'Right. When is good for you?'

'Any day after five. Except usually Tuesdays and Thursdays.'

'Right. So that's Mondays, Wednesdays and Fridays.'

'Except the first Monday of every month.'

'Okay.'

She either consulted her diary or pretended to; he couldn't imagine that February was a very busy month when your business was selling houses.

'How about next Wednesday? Five o'clock?'

Today was Friday afternoon.

To hide a sudden rush of panic, Nathan pretended to consult his own diary.

In fact, he knew very well that he had a meeting on Wednesday afternoon at 5.15 p.m. It wasn't the kind of meeting he was able to cancel – the buyer of a small but potentially profitable chain of stationers wasn't happy with the service provided so far by Hermes. But he said, 'Wednesday would be great.'

'Great,' said Holly. 'I'll see you then, then.'

'Great.'

'Out of interest, how did you get my name?'

'I'm sorry?'

'You asked for me by name. Have we met?'

'No.'

'I didn't think so.'

'A friend recommended you. A client, actually.'

'I see. Well, that's always nice to know.'

'Right,' said Nathan. 'See you Wednesday.'

'See you Wednesday,' said Holly Fox, and hung up.

Nathan sat, staring at the telephone as if it might at any moment leap into the air like a frog and attack him. But it just sat there until it rang again, fully fifteen minutes later, and almost scared the shit out of him.

14

He coped well enough until Tuesday. But on Wednesday he couldn't go to work. He lay in bed as the sun curved and dipped across the sky. But when he eventually rose at 3 p.m. it still seemed too soon.

He couldn't even drive. He sat at the wheel of his BMW, holding the cold steering wheel. The last parents, ruddy-faced with cold, were collecting their children from the nursery: tottering bundles in big winter coats and hats and colourful wellingtons.

He called a minicab and waited in the cold, propped against the BMW, until it arrived at the gate. If he sat in the car or went back inside, he knew he would not be able to go through with it.

The minicab was ten minutes late. By then all the children had gone. Through the bright-lit, curtain-less bay windows he watched the nursery workers talking and laughing and tidying up.

The cab driver seemed to pick up on Nathan's mood and didn't talk. Nathan asked to be dropped at the top of Blackstock Road; he needed the walk. He paid the driver and lit a cigarette and buried his hands deep in the warm pockets of his overcoat. People huddled at bus stops.

It took him another ten minutes to get there.

The estate agent's interior was obscured by cards in the window advertising houses and flats for sale and rent.

He walked in to a blast of central-heating warmth. The office was subdued; young men and women in dark suits sat behind their computers. There was a waiting area: a low coffee table with property magazines scattered on it, a couple of cheese plants, a water cooler. Now and again the phones rang, trilling like distant birds.

Nathan opened a magazine and pretended to read.

Then a woman said his name and he looked up and there she was. She smiled and held out a hand.

'You must be Nathan.'

He'd forgotten how to move. He put down the magazine and coughed and offered his hand and smiled.

'Sorry I was late.'

Up close, she was unmistakably Elise's sister. There was something about the angle at which she held her head, slightly tilted. She was probably in her late twenties. Shorter than Elise, softer. Hair much longer; it was corkscrew curly and red and fell over her shoulders. She blew a strand of fringe from her brow. She wore a charcoal-grey suit and a crisp white shirt with a large collar, worn over the lapels of her jacket. She seemed harried, busy, happy, clever.

He followed her to her desk. Her screen saver read HOLLY FOX and gave her mobile phone number.

She offered him a cup of tea. He thanked her.

She had an assistant to make the tea. Nathan had reached a point in his life when there always seemed to be an assistant to make the tea. This particular assistant was an Indian kid in a suit and tie. He couldn't be older than eighteen.

Holly Fox asked Nathan some questions. He coughed into his fist before answering. His throat was so dry.

He croaked, 'I'm sorry.' And she waved, as if his cough was both a trifle and a pleasure. Nathan knew she did this because she was keen to get his details on to her customer database, after which she could sell him a house at the highest possible price. If her earnings were commission-based, she probably needed it.

Nathan wasn't paid on commission, but a proportion of the reps' salary was, and he knew well what kind of anxiety it could cause – especially in the slow, dead months after Christmas. (That's why the reps loved Valentine's Day, and were beginning to like Easter, too.)

The tea arrived. It came in a bone-china cup and saucer, which Nathan thought a nice touch, except the saucer was chipped.

Nathan felt it coming back – the ability to do this.

He smiled at her. The smile ignited something inside him, some kind of reserve.

Holly produced an A4 file. His name was clipped to it with a giant paper clip. It contained about thirty sheets of A4, which she flicked through. She removed one or two pages from the sheaf, frowning as if in profound concentration. Then she scrunched the pages into a ball and dumped them in the waste-paper basket.

By such demonstration of mental effort was created the sense of a 'fully bespoke service' as promised in the firm's advertisement.

She showed him the details of three Victorian houses, two flats in Victorian conversions and one loft-style apartment in an area of town he would have feared to visit, let alone live in. The asking price for each property was just slightly above the absolute maximum Nathan had given – this was a trick he hadn't anticipated but which in ret-rospect looked obvious.

He told her he wasn't really interested in loft style apartment living, and he told her that – although the brushed-metal door handles were very alluring – the flats did seem rather overpriced. That left the three houses. All of them were on different streets in the same estate, all of them were owned by the same property developer.

'Would you like to view them?'

'That would be great. If you don't mind.'

'Not at all. Excuse me, just for a moment.'

She came back with a butterscotch mac slung over her forearm and a small, expensive-looking handbag in her hand. She wore a ring on the third finger of her right hand (a solitaire diamond set in platinum) and a fine chain round her neck, but no other jewellery. She wore good perfume. Nathan thought of a department store.

He followed her through the back of the office, past the tiny, rather grubby kitchen where his tea had been made, and through a rear door that opened on to a muddy yard in which were parked a number of cars. Holly skipped along the edges of shallow puddles, making a disgusted face, saying, '*Ick.*'

Then she unlocked a black Volkswagen Golf and sat at the wheel. Nathan buckled himself in the front passenger seat, saying, 'Nice car.'

Holly was looking over her shoulder, reversing into the road.

Concentrating, she said, 'It's a bit of an estate agent's car, really.'

'Isn't that what you are?'

With a few aggressive manoeuvres, passing the wheel through her hands like a rally driver, she nudged and lurched and then sped into the traffic. She held up a practised, dismissively regal hand to thank the van driver who'd been forced on pain of sudden death to let her in.

She turned on the radio. Nathan seldom listened to the radio any more – being able to imagine the psychopathology of the DJ always spoiled it for him. Then Holly's mobile phone went and she took the call – which consisted mainly of her saying: *Yes. Yes. When? Not really. Okay. Well, see if you can* – while driving with one hand as speedily as the laws of physics, rather than the laws of the land, permitted.

Exactly as the details suggested, the first house fronted on to a 'quiet, tree-lined street'. But the details had neglected to mention that it stood next to an electricity substation that hummed in a feline and sinister fashion. Its garden backed, via a decrepit wooden fence, directly on to a railway line.

Holly led him through the front door. The house was dark. There was darkness at the top of the stairs, and darkness at the end of the hall. He pretended to examine the external door frame while she turned on the lights, saying: 'Those are new doors. Very solid. Very secure.'

'Right,' said Nathan, as if he cared, then stepped over the threshold.

The empty house echoed with their footsteps. She led him to the through-lounge: a back and front parlour knocked into one long room, and into the galley kitchen. Its UPVC window overlooked the rear garden, which the developer hadn't got around to cleaning up; there was a rusty old wheelbarrow parked by a pile of bricks; a pile of wet sand on the patio.

The kitchen was newly fitted with cheap materials: maple-look veneer on chipboard. He opened a few cupboards, looked inside the oven. (An instruction booklet, still wrapped in plastic, lay in the spotless grill pan.)

Even Nathan could tell this kitchen would begin to fall apart in a matter of months, if not weeks. But he stood and dusted sawdust from his trousers, saying, 'Yeah, I like it.'

He followed her upstairs.

The second house was similar but smaller; the 'office' was barely large enough to accommodate a small table and a laptop. But it stood on a nicer street, with better access to public transport and the local shops. The third house was the biggest of the three, but in spitting distance of a forbiddingly brutal-looking housing estate with whose reputation Nathan was well acquainted.

Outside the third house, they sat in her car. She put the heater on.

She said, 'No pressure. But what do you think? Are we on the right track?'

'Oh, definitely. You've definitely given me a lot to think about.'

'I'm sure Mr Hinsliffe would take an offer,' said Holly. Mr Hinsliffe was the developer. 'Things are quite slow at the moment.'

'Okay,' said Nathan. 'I'll bear that in mind. Let me think about it.'

'Okay. What I'll do is this – I'll give you a call when a property comes on the market that you might be interested in. Things are coming in and going out all the time – weekends, especially. Something good can come on at nine and be sold by lunchtime. Happens all the time. It's a solid market. But you're in a strong position to buy, mortgage agreed, no chain, so I can afford to give you priority treatment. How does that sound?'

He nodded, as if she had spoken with great wisdom and kindness and had not flatly contradicted her earlier claim that things were slow at the moment.

He thought, *I left your sister alone in the dark.*

He said, 'That sounds great.'

'Great.'

She dropped him off at the high street.

In no rush, he caught the bus home.

He got back to discover his flat had changed. The interior angles seemed more acute. The walls seemed to huddle over him.

He lay in bed and stared at the ceiling. In feverish half-dreams, it seemed the flat was two dimensional – a drawing on a scrap of paper that, with him still scribbled on it, was about to be squeezed into a ball by a giant hand, and thrown away.

15

Holly called him at home on Saturday morning. He knew as soon as the phone rang that it must be her; nobody ever called him at home unless there was a crisis at work – and if there was a crisis at work, he'd already know about it.

It had rained heavily that morning, but half an hour ago the sun had come out, to make mercury of the puddles in the empty nursery playground. He took the call from his bed, looking out the window. He was wearing socks and boxer shorts and a rumpled white T-shirt, the one he'd slept in.

'Hello?'

'Is that Nathan?'

'Yeah.'

'It's Holly. From Morris Michael estate agents?'

'I recognized your voice.'

There was a pause – perhaps she was a little taken aback by his familiarity. He thought he detected a note of pleasure in the silence, but he couldn't be sure. Perhaps she was simply consulting her notes, reminding herself who exactly she was talking to. Or perhaps a colleague had handed her a Post-it note with an important phone number on it.

He met her at yet another of Mr Hinsliffe's houses. He parked outside, the *A-Z* unfolded, spine broken, in his lap. Holly was inside, waiting for him. Pulling up, he saw her face in the window. She darted away, and he began to doubt that he'd seen her at all.

But she was waiting for him at the door, wearing a blue-grey belted coat and a scarf and high, suede boots. The house still smelled of wood glue.

He thought, *I'm really going to do this*, and closed the door softly behind him.

They stood in the empty front room. He told her, 'It certainly catches the light.'

'It's south facing.'

'I like it.'

He walked through to the kitchen; it was very similar to the others.

'I'm still not sure about these *kitchens*, though.'

She squatted heel to haunch and experimentally opened the cupboard beneath the sink, telling him: 'Developers' kitchens. They buy them cheap, in bulk.'

He was pleased that she seemed to trust him.

'I expect that's reflected in the price though,' he said. 'The crappy kitchens.'

'Exactly. They're not really designed to last. They're more like a – what do you call it? – a *serving suggestion*. Would you like to see upstairs?'

'Would you like to have lunch with me?'

There was an awkward moment. Holly looked at her suede boots and pursed her lips and he thought he'd blown it. No second chances. He couldn't go through this again.

Then she said, 'Where do you have in mind?'

'You're the estate agent. You know the local facilities.'

'Then let's go into town, shall we?'

There was a moment outside the house when neither was sure which car to take. In the end, they took hers.

Holly turned on the radio, saying, 'I love this song.'

She turned it up. It was Smokey Robinson.

Nathan said, 'I second that emotion.'

She sang under her breath and beat occasional time on the steering wheel. She did not seem sad.

She parked outside a primary school; in the car park, they were holding a car-boot sale to raise funds. Closing the car doors, they looked at the families gathered there. Nathan glanced at her, to see if there was anything in her eyes. But he saw nothing. He followed her round the corner, past a deli, a newsagent, an Algerian cafe. They walked into a tapas bar. Inside, she removed her coat. They sat and he offered her a cigarette.

'No. Thank you. But you go ahead.'

'Do you mind?'

'Not at all. Go ahead. I'll breathe it in if I can.'

He made as if to put the packet away and she told him: 'Really. I'd say if it was a problem.' Then, unwrapping her scarf, she said, 'To tell the truth, I'd love a cigarette. I only gave up at New Year.'

'I gave up once. For two years.'

'Two *years*? What made you start again?'

'Oh, y'know. Stress.'

'Tell me about it.'

'So, it's stressful, being an estate agent?'

'I'm not really an estate agent. I mean, it's not a vocation or any-thing.'

'So, how long have you been doing it?'

'Oh, I don't know. Two years? Three years.'

'And how'd you get into it?'

'It's just one of those things. Life just . . .' She made a bird-like flut-tering with one hand, then said, 'What about you? How long have you been . . .'

'A salesman.'

'That's right. And what is it you sell, again?'

'Greetings cards.'

'That's right.'

'It's not as boring as you might think.'

She crunched on a breadstick.

'All right,' he said. 'It's pretty boring.'

'How long have you been doing it?'

'Four years.'

Their coffees arrived. He took a sip, lit another cigarette. Holly said, 'So, are you one of these salesman-types who thrive on stress? All that coffee, all those cigarettes.'

'Not really. I'm not really, like, one of nature's salesmen. It's just what I do.'

'So – I'm not a natural estate agent and you're not a natural sales-man.'

'I think you're probably a very good estate agent.'

She laughed, sudden and loud and raucous. Then she cupped a

hand to her mouth as if amazed at herself and looked left and right.

'Sorry.'

'That's all right.'

She covered up the sudden flush by saying: 'So, if I'm that good, are you going to buy a house from me?'

'I might. If you play your cards right.'

'I think you're probably a very good salesman.'

The meals arrived. She dug in with a fork, in the American manner.

She leaned over, to steal one of his French fries and chomped on it, grinning.

Then she brushed hair from her eyes and grew quiet.

He said, 'Are you okay?'

She waited a long time without answering, prodding at her food, taking a small mouthful, dabbing with a napkin at the corners of her mouth.

He said, 'Holly. You don't have to feel guilty for laughing.'

Her long silence intensified. She lay down her cutlery and looked at him.

'Why do you say that?'

'I don't know.'

She kept looking at him, as if suspecting they knew each other from way back, from long ago.

Lunch overran by half an hour.

Outside, Nathan told her he'd get a taxi back to the house and pick up his car from there. She thanked him. She was flustered, searching in her handbag for her car keys. She dropped them on the pavement.

They paused at the door of her car. She unlocked it with a flick of the wrist; there was a little beep of confirmation.

Holly said, 'Well. Thanks for lunch.'

'Can we do it again? When you're less pressed. When you've got more time.'

'Usually I only get an hour for lunch. You know. It looks bad otherwise.'

'I'm not talking about lunch. Dinner?'

She considered it.

'Dinner would be great. My treat.'

'Fine. Whatever. Great.'

'Wednesday?'

'Wednesday would be great.'

'Give me a call.'

'I will.' He mimed it, feeling like a dick. 'I'll call you.'

Then he stood on the street and watched her pull away: jerky, impulsive, somewhat dangerous. He stood there while her car waited at the lights. And he stood there when the car had gone, simply watching the empty space she had recently occupied.

16

On Tuesday morning – just after the marketing meeting – Justin came into Nathan's office and perched on the edge of his desk.

Justin was tall and grossly overweight, in trousers that were always a little too short. He had a babyish face and curly hair and (when he chose) the entreating eyes of Bambi.

For several seconds, Nathan ignored him – concentrating on a printed memo about another increase in paper costs. Then he swivelled round in his office chair.

Justin said, 'Are you okay?'

'What do you mean?'

'Well. You were off your game during the marketing meeting.'

'Look, I didn't mean to contradict you.'

'That's not what I'm worried about. I think I got us out of it. I'm worried about *you*.'

But Justin hadn't got them out of it: he'd just made a bumbling, mendacious spectacle of himself. Justin was often doing that, and only Justin didn't know it.

Nathan hadn't been paying attention during the meeting, because he was thinking about Holly Fox and, unintentionally, he'd contradicted one of Justin's lies. The lie concerned a chain of newsagents based in the north-east of England. The chain was usually a reliable source of revenue, particularly for the meat-and-potatoes novelty range.

In fact, the large stock returns were a consequence of Justin's failure to complete a renewed terms negotiation with the customer's chief buyer.

The returns were slow-moving stock that, ordinarily, the retailer might have held on to or sold off cheaply. But, as a signal of intent, they had been returned, still shrink-wrapped, to the Norfolk warehouse – from which point, business between the two companies had been suspended. Justin was trying to keep all this from the board of directors.

The episode had nearly driven Justin to a nervous breakdown.

But now he was saying, 'I'm just worried about you, mate. It's not like you to drop the ball.'

'Really,' said Nathan. 'Don't worry about me.' Then he said, 'How are things with Georgia?'

Georgia was the buyer for the north-eastern chain. If negotiations with Hermes weren't restarted quickly, she'd allocate Hermes' shelf space to their bigger competitors. Getting it back would be humiliating and costly.

Justin said, 'Georgia will come on-line shortly.'

'I think you'd better drive up there to see her, mate. Have a face-to-face meeting.'

'I'll leave her for a few more days,' said Justin. 'To sweat.'

Nathan tried to hide his amusement by turning away and lifting a random sheet of paper from his desk; he pretended to scan it with a distracted frown. He said, 'I'll go up to see her, if you like. See if I can calm things down a bit.'

Unutterable panic flitted across Justin's big baby face.

Then he said, 'I can't let you do that. Not in your state.'

'In what state?'

'Look at you. You're on the edge.'

'I'm *fine*.'

'Why don't you *talk* to me about it?'

'There's nothing to talk about.'

'I can't let you see Georgia. Not in your present condition. There's too much at stake. She's an important customer.'

'Okay. Fine. Whatever.'

'Is it a woman?'

'Is what a woman?'

'It.'

'It's not a woman. It's not an anything. I'm *fine*.'

Justin said: 'What are you doing for lunch?'

This was the question Nathan dreaded above all others.

Justin took lunch in one of a number of local pubs. For the sake of appearances, he'd order a square of lasagne, then ignore it while he worked his way through six pints of lager and a packet of cigarettes. Often, lunch was followed by an afternoon 'meeting' or two, in the same venue.

He'd return to the office with his tie loose and his shirt untucked and his shoelaces untied.

'I'm sorry,' said Nathan. 'I'm really, really busy. Really busy.'

'Busy with what?'

'I have lunch with marketing.'

'The marketing lunch is tomorrow.'

'This is a pre-lunch lunch. We want to finesse the agenda for tomorrow's meeting.'

'Okay. Let's do that, then.'

Nathan gave up. He said, 'Give me five minutes', then hurried upstairs to the marketing department.

He found Amrita at her desk, eating a Pret a Manger sandwich and typing an email one-handed. Otherwise the floor was empty.

Nathan sat, telling her: 'I'm in trouble.'

Amrita turned on her swivel chair. 'God. I've been meaning to *call* you. I thought Justin was going to *die*. The fat lying bastard.'

'The fat lying bastard has invited himself to lunch.'

Amrita laughed, spitting a mouthful of damp breadcrumbs. She tutted and brushed them from her keyboard.

She said, 'That'll be nice for you.'

'Lunch with me and *you*. I used you as an excuse. Sorry.'

'I'm not having lunch with Justin. I have a sandwich.'

'Please.'

'Last time, he came back from the toilet with a wet patch on his trousers. I nearly threw *up*.'

'I know. Really.'

'And he touches my *knee*.'

'I *know*.'

'What did you think you were doing, saying yes?'

'He trapped me with his cunning.'

Amrita took another, pointed bite of BLT and said, 'You're not really on top form, are you?'

'What does *that* mean?'

'You sat through the meeting like this . . .'

She made a dreamy face and rolled her head round on a loose neck.

'. . . like you were somewhere else. You took about ten minutes to answer a question. And you called Justin a liar.'

'I didn't.'

'Good as.'

'He *is* a liar.'

Amrita crossed her legs, brushed crumbs away. 'Tough tits, I'm afraid. I'm busy.'

'Please.'

'No.'

'Please please.'

'No.'

'Pl—'

'No.'

She returned, sandwich in hand, to whatever she was typing.

Nathan wondered how long Justin would keep him this time. Two and a half hours was about average. But Justin was upset, so it would probably be longer.

On Wednesday night, he met Holly in a blue-lit cocktail bar for a pre-dinner drink.

Nathan hadn't known what to wear. In the end, he'd asked Amrita's advice and they'd sneaked out after the marketing meeting to buy him some new shoes and what she called a funky shirt.

Holly sat on a chrome bar stool, stirring a drink set down on the radiant glass bar. She was wearing a little black dress. He sat next to her.

'Hello.'

He wasn't sure if he was expected to kiss her cheek, or what? Helpfully, she glanced back into her drink and stirred it with a complimentary plastic swizzle stick.

Nathan said, 'Am I late?'

She said, 'Probably not,' and he knew something was wrong.

He set his coat, folded, on the empty stool next to him and ordered a margarita.

She said, 'I'm really sorry. I'm early for everything. I get it from my dad. He's got this punctuality thing.'

Nathan said, 'Are you okay? Or would you like another drink?'

'I'm okay. I'm fine for the moment. Thanks.'

He could tell this was not her first drink of the evening.

He said, 'Well, *this* is weird.'

She looked at him with an expression that Nathan should not have been able to understand. But he understood it, all right.

'What's weird?'

'I've never been for a drink with my estate agent before.'

She smiled, but there was something dutiful and tired about it.

They watched the barman prepare Nathan's drink. When it arrived, with an unnecessary flourish, he took a sip, then said:

'Are you sure you're okay? You seem a little—'

'I'm fine. Really.'

'Tough day?'

She reached out and, as if he had asked her a child's question, patted the back of his hand.

'It's not so much that.'

He took another sip. He wished he'd ordered a gin and tonic.

'You can tell me about it, if you like.'

'Can I have a cigarette?'

'Don't ask me that. You gave *up*.'

'Go on. Just one.'

He laid the pack on the bar.

'Take as many as you like. But I won't offer you one.'

She took a cigarette, brushed a trailing lock of hair behind her ear. She tipped her head sideways to light it and exhaled with great, grim satisfaction.

'Look . . .'

'What?'

'I don't really do this.'

'Do *what*?'

He grinned, as if he were exasperated. But really he was scared.

She said, 'I think you're a really nice man . . .'

'That's because you haven't got to know me yet.'

She chuckled, and then her eyes welled. She took another puff on the cigarette.

Nathan didn't know what to do with his hands. He laid them flat on the bar.

'It's just *difficult* at the moment,' she said. 'If the timing was better—'

'What? Are you *married* or something? Have you got a boyfriend?'

She brushed back her hair again.

'God, I kind of wish it was that. It would be great, if all I had was a boyfriend.'

She stubbed out the cigarette and Nathan said, 'Okay, you've got to help me out here. Just a little bit.'

'May I have another cigarette?'

He pushed the pack towards her with his fingertips. They each lit a fresh cigarette.

Holly said, 'Look. I don't know how to say this. It's a bit weird. Everyone I know already *knows*. So I've never actually had to *tell* anybody about it.'

Indecorously, she wiped her nose with the back of her hand and said, 'Okay. Say it. Four years ago. More than four years ago now, Jesus. Anyway. Four years ago, my sister . . .'

She couldn't bear to say the words, any more than Nathan could bear to hear them.

'Well, my sister sort of disappeared.'

It took strength to face her.

He said, 'Oh, Jesus. That's awful. I'm sorry.'

But she wasn't looking at him. He watched her profile. She wasn't seeing the bar any longer. She was seeing Mark Derbyshire's party.

'She went out one night. To a party. And she just never came home.'

'I don't know what to say.'

'The police searched for her. They even thought they knew who did it. But there wasn't enough evidence. And they never found her. There was no body or anything. So really, we still don't know.'

They sat in silence and watched the barman, a handsome young Australian with an easy smile, shake a cocktail then pour three drinks for a cackling hen party at the far end of the bar.

'Jesus,' said Nathan.

Holly drained her drink. 'I'm sorry to do this to you.'

'Oh my God, don't be *sorry*.'

She stopped him. 'I had a boyfriend, at the time. Well, I say boyfriend. Fiancé. We were supposed to get married. Three years ago, last June. Anyway. The strain was too much. You know, for the relationship.' She said this in an embarrassed, faux transatlantic accent and Nathan snorted in bitter complicity. 'It wasn't his fault, not really. I stopped being his girlfriend. All I could think about was Elise.'

'Well, what did he expect?'

She took his margarita and poured half into her own glass. Neither of them wanted to call back the Australian barman.

'It's easy to say that. But, you know, he's only human. And this thing, it sort of took over our lives: it was like there wasn't anything else in the world. It was impossible to do anything, to go anywhere, to, I don't know, have a *conversation* about something. It was like it was rude to be *happy*. So, anyway. We sold the house. I wanted to be close to Mum and Dad, so I left my job and moved back home.'

Nathan drained the last of the slush from his glass.

'I see.'

'I'm sorry to lay all this on you.'

'Not at all. Don't be stupid.'

'So. This is really the first time I've done anything since.'

'Gone out with somebody?'

'Gone out, period.'

He stared into his empty glass.

'Right.'

'Anyway. So I told Mum about it—'

'About tonight?'

'Yeah. This is a new dress.'

'It's lovely.'

'Ha. Thank you. Anyway. I told Mum I was going out. I had to. I came home with this new dress and these new shoes. And, I don't know, I was *excited*. And so was Mum. She had this look in her eyes.

And she asked me who you were, how we met. So I told her, and she asked where we were going and where I'd bought the dress and how much I'd paid for it . . .' She re-tucked the stray lock of hair behind her ear. 'And then we both began to cry.'

'Right,' said Nathan.

Holly laughed at herself as she wept, then took a big, long sniff, and wiped her nose again.

'So you see. I'm sorry.'

'I don't know what to say.'

'It's all right. Nobody ever does.'

The passing barman set down before them two chrome bowls of green olives and peanuts.

'Okay,' said Nathan. 'What do we do now?'

Through the corner of his eye, he could see her as she lifted her handbag from under her coat. She fossicked around inside and withdrew a tissue and blew her nose. Then she quickly withdrew a compact, flipped it open, examined her puffy eyes and smudged make-up in the small mirror, said 'God', closed the compact, put it back in her bag and slipped the bag beneath the coat again.

She stood up, saying: 'I'm sorry to do this to you.'

'It's okay. I understand.'

'Thanks for the cigarettes.'

It sounded like the most desolate thing he ever heard.

He said, 'I'll give you a call.'

She seemed to think for a moment. Then she shook her head and wrinkled her nose.

'Best not.'

She pulled her winter coat over her new dress, then belted it around her waist. She tested the clasp on her handbag, then slung it over her shoulder. She leaned in to kiss his cheek. She had to stand on tiptoes.

She squeezed his hand, and then she walked away.

He watched her go. Then he turned and signalled to the Australian barman to order a long, cold gin and tonic. The barman placed it on the bar with an impact like a gavel. Then he stood, his hands on his narrow hips and his bar towel stuffed into the belt of his smart barman's trousers.

'You all right there, mate?'

'Not really.'

Nathan drained the drink. Then he passed some cash across the bar and – without waiting either for his change or for the Australian to acknowledge the size of the tip – he too gathered his coat and left.

17

The next morning, Nathan parked across the street from the offices of Morris Michael estate agents. It was on a main road, so he parked on a double yellow, two wheels on the pavement, his bonnet nudging into a bus stop.

He didn't even know why he was doing it. Holly wouldn't come in via the front door: she'd drive her Golf Cabriolet round the back, via Merrily Road. Probably she'd make herself a cup of tea in the tiny kitchen at the back, and chat with a few colleagues before wandering through and turning on her computer. Somebody would raise the shutters and turn the lights on.

He wondered what she might do, if she wandered to the window and saw him out there, disconsolate at the wheel. He imagined there would be a moment — a jolt of surprise and fear, more appropriate than she could imagine — and he went weak with shame.

But, nevertheless, he waited until the lights came on.

Then he fumbled with the keys in the ignition and leapt headlong into the traffic.

He was an hour late for work.

That morning, he'd risen quickly. There was a raw patch of shaving rash round his throat. One sideburn was slightly longer than the other. He was not followed by a diffuse trail of Acqua Di Parma. He might as well have turned up naked but for a ragged blanket. Eyebrows were raised.

He closed the office door and set his briefcase on his tidy desk. Then he sat down and logged on.

He left it as long as he could stand it, a full working week, and then he phoned her at work. Deepak asked for his name. This was followed by a weighted pause. Deepak told Nathan that Holly was currently out of the office and could Tim maybe take his call?

Nathan thanked him and said, 'I'll call back later.'

But when he did, the same thing happened.

Sometimes it was difficult – even during meetings – to resist the urge simply to drive to her place of work and sit outside. He just wanted to see whatever she saw. This made him feel close to her.

He knew how dangerous this was. Holly's tolerance for peculiar behaviour from interested men was probably low. Given her occasional media profile – and the lack of success in solving Elise's disappearance – the police were likely to take any of her complaints seriously.

If she complained about Nathan, it wouldn't take the police long to learn that he had been a guest at Mark Derbyshire's Christmas party. If that happened, Nathan could be in serious trouble.

But he needed to be near her. Sometimes he fooled himself that a wry and apologetic smile would win her over; that she could not fail to see the benevolence of his intent.

But he feared she'd see the gargoyle's face that leered beneath his own – the beast whose eyes he sometimes glimpsed while shaving.

He lay in the soft glow of his bedroom, drawing patterns in the irregularities of the ceiling and thought about following her home.

He dismissed the idea as impractical.

Then he thought about it again.

Eventually, under bright electric lights, he slept. Every night came the same dream. In the dream, he was Bob. He stood in the dark corner of a room he knew to be Holly's. In the dream, she slept – a shape under the blankets that Nathan did not want to see.

That morning – as once more he cleaned his vomit from the bathroom floor – Nathan realized that he knew how to find her. He went to the chest of drawers and opened the lowest of them.

He removed the various work-related files and documents he'd brought home over the years, including some paperwork of Justin's that he'd surreptitiously lifted and photocopied, in an effort to protect himself legally from the ramifications of one fuck-up or other. Beneath all this were collected a number of newspaper clippings: the articles that had appeared around the fourth anniversary of Elise's disappearance.

Two of these articles featured similar sentences.

From the *Telegraph*:

The Elise Fox Trust, which June runs from their family home in Sutton Down . . .

And, from the local press:

The trust is run from a spare bedroom in the Sutton Down house where Elise was born . . .

Nathan stared at the clippings as if they were very old – antiques discovered behind a black-spotted mirror. Then he placed them carefully back inside their folder, and the folder back inside the drawer. He closed the drawer and, still not dressed or shaved, and once again running late for work, he found the phone book. It was stacked with a dusty *Yellow Pages* in the small cupboard which housed his electricity and gas meters.

There were a number of Foxes in the 2001 phone book, but none were listed in Sutton Down. He set the book aside.

The previous tenant's collection of telephone directories and *Yellow Pages* were stuffed, slightly damp and cobwebby, near the back of the cupboard. Nathan pulled one out. It was six years old: dated to a time before the Foxes had any reason he knew of to go ex-directory. He flicked through the pages. And there it was.

He went to get his phone. He entered the number and the address under H.

Then he replaced the phone books at the back of the cupboard. It seemed to him that every action associated with Holly Fox must be covered up.

He imagined Detective William Holloway, squatting to peer in this low, musty cupboard, finding the telephone directory, finding that its broken spine opened on her number; that Nathan's fingerprint was smudged in damp newsprint on Elise's address.

The thought made him giddy. He sat down and called in to work that once again, he'd be in late.

He gave no excuse, assuming that his normally perfect timekeeping and wasted holiday entitlements justified the occasional late morning. But Nathan had never experienced what it was to be the target of office gossip.

At work, as he stood gathering his morning's mail from the departmental pigeonhole, Justin affected to breeze past him, a zephyr of mint and whisky and Issey Miyake. He sidled up to Nathan and muttered, 'Did she keep you up all night?'

Nathan pulled himself upright and made as if to speak. But he could feel the entire department looking at him. Heads were raised at desks like deer at a waterhole.

He said, 'Oh, for fuck's sake, Justin,' and whirled on his heel and marched to his office. He paused on the threshold and then, very deliberately, slammed the door so that it trembled in its frame.

He booted up his computer, listening to its mysterious internal ticks and whirrs, then entered his password.

There was a rap at the door. It was Angela, the departmental administrator.

She said, 'You all right?'

'Yeah. Y'know.'

Apparently she did. She pressed a palm to her vertically extended fingertips.

'Tea?'

He smiled back, for her implicit English assurance that there was no problem in the world that a cup of tea could not, somehow, make better.

'Please,' he said.

Ten minutes later she brought it to him. She'd prepared it just as he liked it: strong white, one sugar. Alongside it on his desk she placed four jammy dodgers, Nathan's favourite biscuit. While the kettle was boiling, she'd nipped to the local shops to buy them for him.

Looking at the biscuits, a symbol of something lost, Nathan was overcome with the urge to weep.

And Angela stood there, nodding slightly, exactly as if she understood.

18

On Friday Nathan ordered flowers. He gave the florist his credit card details and told them price was not a problem – he wanted the flowers to be beautiful but not ostentatious. They must look, he said, exactly as if he'd spent a great deal of time discussing them with a florist. He picked them up on Saturday morning.

The shop was weirdly humid. The pale sunlight filtered through a glass ceiling and deep green foliage. The flagstones were damp beneath his feet.

The florists were a rotund Japanese woman and a lithe Scot with a coppery crewcut. They were excited to greet him and (having discussed him over coffee that morning – their best customer of the week) fussed around him like manservants. They told him what each of the flowers were, their significance, and why they had been chosen. They wrapped the bouquet in cellophane and brown paper and ribbon and handed it to him with no small degree of ceremony.

He left the shop carrying the flowers like a vast offering. He was aware of people looking at him, bundled up in a long coat, carrying such a big bunch of flowers. He knew what they were thinking and enjoyed the fact they were right. Eventually, he found the courage to return some of the glances, smiling complicity with a couple of pensioners in powder-blue macs and sensible shoes.

He lay the bouquet on the back seat of his car, which still smelled faintly chemical from the valeting. He turned on the radio and spread a map book on his lap. Gradually, the car filled with the thick scent of flowers.

He was distracted as he drove out of town.

Eventually, something caught his attention. He looked up to see he was driving past a field of forlorn cattle. He saw the name of the town, Sutton Down, written on a road sign.

He took a road through the forest where Elise Fox lay face down. He looked for the entrance to the dark unnamed lane, but didn't see it.

After passing the forest, he pulled over to the grassy side of the road until his heart had slowed. He wanted a drink and he wanted a cigarette. But he also wanted to smell clean. He wanted to look like he had stepped out of the shower, bright and handsome and confident.

He didn't recognize Sutton Down. The night he'd passed through, it had been indistinct shapes in the night. Now he saw that it centred on a long, oval village green. There was an ancient, low-ceilinged pub with a pagan sign.

He identified the correct house on the third circuit of the village green: it was three or four hundred years old, set back behind some twisted apple trees preparing to blossom. He parked the car by the grassy verge. He pulled his coat from the back seat, and put it on. It was speckled with dark spots where moisture had dripped from the bouquet he'd rested on it. There was a golden smear of pollen across the chest.

He hoiked the flowers gently under his arm and remote-locked the car with a wrist-flicking flourish, an over-compensation in case an onlooker should perceive his nervousness.

On the drive, an old, racing green MG was parked alongside a white Peugeot 205 gone rusty round the wheel rims. The door to the house was framed with ivy. Nathan stood on the stone doorstep. He was almost giggling with anxiety.

He rang the doorbell.

After a long minute, he heard some obscure shuffling in the hallway. Panic rose in him and he considered squatting down behind the Peugeot, to hide. But he couldn't imagine how he might explain himself, should he be seen. So he stayed where he was.

It wasn't Holly who answered the door; it was her father, a neat, narrow-shouldered man who wore pressed indigo jeans and a pastel shirt.

He said, 'Yes?'

'Mr Fox?'

'Yes?'

'I'm Nathan. A friend of Holly's.'

Holly's father eyed the flowers. Nathan almost presented them to him.

'I'm afraid Holly's not home.'

He had a clipped, old-fashioned diction that made Nathan think of war films, but it was not unkind.

'I see.'

'Have you come a long way?'

'Not far. Only from town.'

'Well, listen. She shouldn't be gone too long, she's just running an errand for her mother. Why don't you come in and wait?'

'I don't want to be any trouble.'

'No trouble at all. Glad of the company. There's scones if you like them.'

'That would be lovely,' said Nathan, who did not like scones.

'Come in, then.' Holly's father stepped aside and Nathan stepped over the threshold.

'I'm Graham. Holly's dad.'

Nathan shook his hand. It was slim and dry and strong.

'Nathan,' said Nathan.

'We thought you might be the press, you see. They still turn up on the doorstep every now and again.'

The house smelled of potpourri and old leather and perhaps the tinge of old cigars. Nathan followed Graham into the kitchen. A long, bright room, it dog-legged into a glass conservatory that overlooked the garden and a small orchard. All of it was wet and brown and black, the colours of English spring. Apparently dead, but waiting to grow.

There was a woman in the kitchen. She was a bit younger than Graham: dark hair, sensibly cut. Slacks and court shoes. Widening through the hips. She was doing something to a flower beneath the running tap water. At Nathan's entrance, she turned off the tap and dried her hands on a York Minster tea cloth.

'June, darling,' said Graham. 'This is Nathan.'

She set down the tea cloth and looked at the flowers. She said, 'Aren't those just lovely? Shall I put them in water?'

Nathan was relieved to be unburdened of them.

June smiled. It was surprising and strangely moving.

'Just until Holly gets back,' she said, and practically winked.

In a series of dazzlingly quick and efficient movements, she'd opened the top drawer, removed a pair of secateurs, and begun to snip at the wet, green stems.

Graham passed by with kettle in hand. June shifted to one side to accommodate him as he filled it with water.

Nathan couldn't believe what he'd done to these people.

He followed June to the conservatory. They sat round a coffee table, upon which was spread the previous week's *Sunday Telegraph*. Nathan hitched his trousers as he sat, as if June were about to interview him.

A fragile rattling behind them was Graham, following them through with a pot of tea on a tray. He laid it out on the coffee table, with cups and saucers and spoons, a bowl for sugar and a little jug for the milk.

Graham too hitched his trousers as he sat. Then he leaned forward, took the lid from the teapot, gave it a stir.

'Let's give it five minutes.'

June offered Nathan a plate on which were arranged some shortcake fingers. Nathan took one, unhungry but glad of the distraction. He used a cupped hand for a plate until June passed him a saucer.

June said, 'She shouldn't be long. She's getting Hetty seen to.'

'Hetty?'

'Our daughter's cat.'

He knew which daughter they meant.

Not Holly.

He said, 'Oh.'

Sorrow descended on them like weather. Then Graham made a

visible effort to brighten. Nathan wondered how many times a day such an effort was necessary.

'So,' said Graham, 'how do you know Holly?'

'Well.' Nathan's salesman's smile felt stretched and taut, insincere as an evangelist. 'I suppose you could say we met at work.'

June raised an enquiring eyebrow.

'I was looking to buy a house. We met that way.'

'Ah.'

Another silence fell; it was not strained but there was sadness in it. Nathan felt trapped by the weight of it.

He said, 'We went for a drink, a couple of weeks back.'

June raised that eyebrow again. Graham poured tea into a china cup, then added a dash of milk.

'It didn't go so well,' said Nathan. 'To tell you the absolute truth.'

'The thing is,' said Graham, 'I'm afraid that Holly's had rather a difficult time of it, lately.'

Nathan looked at his lap, brushing at a pollen stain, saying, 'I know. Well, I know something about it. I mean, Holly mentioned it.'

'I see.'

They sipped tea.

Nathan said, 'I'm afraid I don't know what to say.'

'That's very kind. But you're really not expected to say anything.'

Nathan nodded. He could feel Elise in the room with them. Staring at him. Dirt in her hair and nostrils.

A gust of wind blew through the small orchard that backed on to the garden.

Nathan said, 'You have a lovely place.'

'It belonged to my father,' said Graham.

June said, 'We didn't want to bring the girls up in the city.'

Nathan nodded.

June said, 'Holly has taken on a great deal over the last few years. But we don't want her to be scared of *life*.' She glanced meaningfully at the flowers, glorious in a crystal vase.

Nathan nodded that he understood. He drained his cup. Immediately, as in a Japanese tea ceremony, Graham refilled it.

'So we're glad you came,' said June. 'Because we think she deserves a little happiness. A little bit of *fun*.'

Later, he assumed the old, stone walls must have muffled the sound of the car in the drive – because when Holly's key went in the lock he was taken by surprise. In his shock, he went automatically to stand and nearly spilled the fresh cup of tea. Mortified, he looked to June. But June was waving him towards the flowers, hurrying him along.

From the hallway, Holly called out: 'Whose car's that at the end of the drive?'

Graham made a happy, complicit face and called out: 'Tea, darling?'

'Gasping.'

Nathan heard a rigmarole as she set something down, then removed and hung up her coat.

He stood there with the dripping wet flowers in his fist.

Holly walked into the kitchen. She wore no make-up and had pulled her hair into a hasty ponytail. She was flushed with cold. She wore a cable-knit sweater, old blue jeans and big, grey hiking socks. In her hand she carried a cat box.

She looked at Nathan as if unable, for the moment, to place him.

Then she said, 'Oh.'

Nathan smiled and handed her the flowers.

'To say sorry.'

She was still holding the cat box.

'Sorry for what?'

'Making a mess of things.'

'You didn't.'

'Okay. Then I'm sorry it didn't work out the way I'd hoped.'

'That's not your fault either.'

'It doesn't stop me being sorry.'

'How did you find out where I live?'

Nathan had made no provision for this.

'No, really,' she said, 'how did you find out where I live?'

'I looked you up. In the phone book.'

'We're not in the phone book.'

'An old one. I've got all these old phone books. Well, they're not mine. They're in the flat. In a cupboard. With the meters.'

'And how did you know which village to look for?'

'You mentioned.'

'I don't remember that. Usually I make a point of not mentioning.'

He shrugged, as if he was sorry. 'You mentioned.'

Her look of flinty wariness softened. She glanced over his shoulder, at her parents who stood there bursting with hope. She put her weight on one hip.

'Whatever. It was pretty resourceful.'

'What can I say?'

'Not to mention determined.'

June stepped between Nathan and Holly, taking the flowers from him and saying, 'Holly, why don't you show Nathan the garden?'

Holly regarded him with an equivocal expression.

'Wait there.'

He did. She came back wearing a pair of green wellington boots and carrying a second pair, which she passed to Nathan, saying, 'It's pretty wet out there.'

So he found himself sitting on the floor of the Foxs' kitchen, shoe-less, tugging on a pair of wellingtons that were half a size too small. He stood, and Holly passed his coat.

He followed her into the garden. June made herself busy at the sink. Periodically, he could feel her eyes sweep across them like the beam of a lighthouse.

Holly wore a Barbour jacket, Graham's he supposed, and a scarf that looked wiry and uncomfortable. She dug her hands deep into its pockets. It was bright and wet: the sun low on the horizon. He could hear their footfalls and their breath. Long grass, heavy with water, brushed at his legs. He heard distant cows, the harsh barking of crows.

They stopped at the teetering, half-rotten picket fence at the edge of the orchard. Holly sat down on a stile, knees pressed together, elbows on knees, chin cupped in her hands. She stared without seeing in the direction of the house. Nathan stared into the scratchy, leafless complexity of the orchard.

She said, 'I can't believe you did that.'

'Did what?'

'Came to meet my *parents*.'

'They're lovely. They made me tea.'

She removed the band from her ponytail. Her hair fell around her face. She twisted the band round her wrist. Strands of red hair were caught in it, picking up the sunlight.

'Don't be completely fooled. Dad can be fearsome, when he wants to be. He used to be in the navy.'

'He didn't seem all that fearsome to me.'

'He must have liked the look of you.'

Nathan turned away to lean on the fence.

Holly was still looking at the house, quizzically, like someone trying to remember a dream.

She said, 'It was a lovely thing to do. In a slightly scary way.'

There was a bird in the tree. He didn't know what kind. A starling perhaps. It watched him with a still, reptilian eye.

'I don't know about *that,*' he said.

'Liar,' she said.

Later, they wandered back to the house. They kept their hands firmly in their pockets and their heads down. They hadn't spoken much.

In the kitchen, they kicked off their boots, left them on the mat, then removed their jackets and, in wet socks and muddy trousers, tramped down the hallway to hang them up.

They sat down to lunch with Graham and June: parsnip soup, then cold ham and oven chips with salad. Holly's parents asked a number of questions, mostly about Nathan's career. Nathan wanted Graham and June to like him, and he wanted Holly to see them liking him. So he found himself emphasizing his achievements – including those achievements which, even to his ears, sounded faintly absurd.

During lunch, Holly said little. But she looked at him sometimes. Later, while she read the newspaper, Nathan helped June rinse the plates and load the dishwasher.

With the business section of the paper folded under his arm, Graham excused himself and went upstairs for his weekend nap. On his way, he once again offered Nathan his hand.

144

'Very nice to meet you.'

'And you.'

When the dishwasher was loaded and in its cycle, Nathan checked his watch and said he must be leaving. He retrieved his shoes and jacket.

Saying goodbye, June offered her cheek. When he kissed her, she squeezed his hand once.

It was left to Holly to see him off. Still in her hiking socks, arms crossed over her breasts, head down, she accompanied him down the hallway and on to the drive. As he looked for his keys, she rocked back and forth on her heels.

'I don't even know you.'

He leaned on the low roof of his car. 'This is weird for me too. Do you think I do this kind of thing all the time?'

'I don't know.'

'Well, I don't. Trust me.'

She met his eyes. Something bright and angry in her gaze.

'We'll see.'

He laughed, although she was not joking, and he got into his clean car and started the engine and pulled away, leaving her standing there, diminishing, her arms crossed and her thick, grey socks soaked by the wet grass.

He took the long way home, circumventing the forest.

When he got home, he realized what had bothered him about the house. On the wall were hung several paintings: reproductions, some watercolours. On the bookshelves were arranged brass and china knick-knacks.

But there were no photographs.

19

When Nathan got back from lunch on Thursday, Justin was dallying in the corner of his office, a draft report concertinaed in his fist. Probably, it was something important and overdue – something that Nathan would be required to take immediate and urgent care of, because Justin had filed it in the boot of his Mercedes for the last three months.

It took twenty minutes to convince Justin it wasn't necessary to discuss this emergency down the pub.

When, finally, Justin had stomped away, Nathan retrieved his voicemail. The first two calls were from irate customers chasing delivery of orders agreed at terms two months ago. The third was from Holly. Gently, Nathan closed the office door and listened to the message three times, looking for hidden significance.

Hi. It's me. I hate these things. Anyway, I was wondering – are you still there? – if you'd like to come for lunch on Sunday. And then. I don't know. Go out or something. Am I rambling? I'm no good at these things. Anyway. Give me a bell. Right. Bye. It's me, by the way. Did I say that? Bye.

He lay his forehead on the desk. He was smiling. He too went to pieces when leaving personal messages on answer machines.

Then he strutted through to Justin's office.

He said, 'It turns out, I'm not as busy as I thought. I'll look after the report. We should talk about it down the pub.'

Justin almost burst with happiness.

On Sunday, Nathan took the long route to Sutton Down.

Graham had cooked the Sunday roast. When Nathan had finished clearing the table and loading the dishwasher and leaving the roasting tin to soak, Holly slipped her arm through his.

There was the shock of first physical contact.

She said, 'Come on.'

'Where are we going?'

'Drink?'

Nathan looked at June as if to say *What can I do?* as he and Holly got their coats.

A morning fog had not quite cleared. The village was quiet.

They walked along the banks of the river. He tried to think only good thoughts.

She said, 'We're doing this backwards.'

'What do you mean?'

'My parents know you as well as I do.'

'I don't mind that.'

They walked for a minute.

Holly said, 'Thanks.'

'For what?'

'I don't know. Trying to understand what it must be like.'

They had arrived at a mossy stone arch that crossed the river. It looked a thousand years old. The mist was deeper here. It pooled in the roots of the trees. He could feel the cold rising from the water.

He said, 'This isn't about your sister.'

She let go of his arm and turned to face him. There was an anxious comma between her eyes. 'I know that. But everything *has* been. For a really long time.'

She stood on tiptoes and kissed him. Then she grabbed the lapels of his coat: 'Well, *say* something.'

But he didn't want to hear his voice – he wanted to be someone else, in this good moment.

He said, 'You already know what I want to say.'

She slipped an arm round his waist and hugged him as they walked across the river, towards the pub.

They got back to the house at 10 p.m. It was dark. Graham and June had gone to bed at 9.30.

Nathan and Holly were both a little drunk. For ten minutes they stood on the doorstep, kissing. Then Holly dug out her key and let them in.

In the hallway, she said nothing. He followed her carefully upstairs – where she showed him the spare bedroom. There was a small vanity unit in there. Clean towels, a tube of Aquafresh toothpaste. There was even a toothbrush, still boxed, laid out for him. Holly said goodnight and closed the door. Nathan kicked off his shoes and socks and shirt, and leaned over to clean his teeth and wash his face. The existence of the small vanity unit made him feel obligated to do so.

There was a stealthy rap on the bedroom door.

He whispered, 'Come in.'

Holly was barefoot in creamy silk pyjamas. He glanced at her and felt uncomfortable and glanced away.

She said, 'Are you okay?'

'Fine. I'm good.'

She made a comical face.

'Goodnight then.'

'Goodnight.'

She closed the door. He listened to her, sneaking like a burglar back to her childhood bedroom.

He lay down and closed his eyes.

He opened them again.

Perhaps this had been Elise's bedroom.

But he knew it wasn't. Of all the places he'd been since the night of Mark Derbyshire's Christmas party, this house was the one place that Elise Fox was not. Her absence from it was absolute.

Nathan turned off the bedside lamp. His eyes were startled by the unfamiliarity of the darkness. It took time for them to adjust to the moon-tinted edges of the room. But he must have slept, alone in that darkness, because he woke to the first hints of the dawn chorus.

He got up and got dressed. He removed the duvet from the bed and left it folded there, with his towels alongside it. He slipped out the front door.

Outside, it was cold and wet. He was tired and the engine, in the country stillness, made a loud and lonely sound.

He went home first, to shower and shave, and was not late for work.

20

Sometimes, in those early days, they weren't sure where to go. Trips to the theatre or the cinema seemed contrived – but there was tacit agreement that Nathan should not invite Holly back to his flat, not even for a video and a Chinese takeaway. The moment she crossed his threshold would be charged with too much significance.

So they met at lunchtimes and ate at a nearby brasserie, or they met after work and spent an hour or two talking in the corner of some quiet pub or wine bar. Gradually, Nathan's neurotic desire to provide her with novelty began to diminish, and one place became their regular venue – a stone-flagged bar in the basement of an Italian restaurant. Often, it was empty but for the skinny Russian waitresses, playing eighties pop on a cheap stereo. If it was empty, they sat in a corner anyway, and ordered something to eat and a bottle of wine. Holly would tell him about her day. He learned a great deal about the day-to-day operation of being an estate agent. And he learned that Holly wasn't happy at work.

She'd taken a Business Studies degree at Southampton. Graham and June would've preferred her to do something else, something useless like English – but Holly hadn't seen the point then and she didn't see the point now. She'd wanted to run her own business since she was fourteen years old.

Elise had changed all that. The job at the estate agency was supposed to be a temporary solution, something to bring in the money while their lives were off-kilter. But their lives were still off-kilter, and Holly was still an estate agent.

She didn't like her boss, a dick called Neil who had an eighties flick and a supercharged BMW. He was about twenty-two and still spotty round the chin – but he had four children and an ugly house about which he never stopped boasting.

Holly still intended to be her own boss. It wasn't even a question of capital: her parents would remortgage their house, if necessary, and she had some savings – after all, she hadn't been paying rent for quite some time. Plus, her social life had been non-existent.

Then she dipped her head, exactly as she always did during these moments, and drew her finger around the rim of her wine glass. 'But the *timing*, you know.'

She told him about her parents.

'Dad was in the navy. It always gave him, what would you call it, this self-confidence. Like a dignity thing. But Elise, that sucked all the confidence from him. He's housebound. He potters all day in the garden or in his study. He won't go further than the garden gate for weeks on end, not even to go to the pub.'

This was the pub across the green where, two or three times a week since Holly was young, Graham had met his cronies to play dominoes, and poker at Christmas. One of those cronies had been Mark Derbyshire, whose name was no longer mentioned in the village.

'The press conferences were terrible for him,' she said. 'He used to throw up before leaving the house. I had to help him out to the car, like he was an old man.'

'Does he talk about her?'

'He can't. He just acts as if you're not talking. It used to drive me up the wall.'

'But not any more?'

'Well sometimes, yeah. But there was this one Sunday morning, I heard him crying. He was sitting on the floor behind the door of his little office. Just saying "My God, my God" over and over again, muffled, like he was biting his fist and trying not to cry. Like it hurt, y'know, like he was in physical pain. This is, like, a week before Elise's twenty-first.'

Nathan rested his jaw on his hands, saying, 'Oof.' And then, not wanting to hear the answer, he said, 'Your mum?'

'Mum used to be a secretary – she's organized. After she got married, she did work for charities, action groups, whatever. PETA, the WWF, the Women's Institute, homeless charities. She'd do this thing for the WI – she'd go to dodgy estates and teach single mothers and families on benefit how to budget – how to do cheap, home-cooked meals.

'So she knew what to do, to help her cope. She set up the foundation . . .'

This was the Elise Fox Foundation.

In time, other families of lost children had pledged effort and capital; the Foundation expanded, growing to offer a counselling service to the violently bereaved and to those, like June, whose grief lacked an object.

June had never sought therapy – the Foundation was her therapy.

But it grew so large that she became oppressed by it. Now she was its chair. Fund-raising and day-to-day operations were handled by a woman called Ruby, who lost her daughter on a French campsite in 1991.

With Ruby, June was at liberty to discuss Elise as something other than a girl whose primary characteristic was absence. She became a daughter again: a new baby, a stumbling toddler, a gawky, bespectacled eleven-year-old. While Ruby was around, Elise and her disappearance were not the same thing.

Nathan said, 'And what about you?'

'What's to say? Families pull together, or they break apart. I didn't have much choice.'

'But it's like . . .'

He waved his hand around, fighting for the word.

'I'll tell you what it's like,' she said. 'It's like being in open prison. From the outside, it looks like I've got all the privileges: job, car, friends. Y'know. But all the freedom is gone. I'd always sort of assumed that Mum and Dad would become my responsibility, one day. But not so *soon*, you know? I had plans. Not big ones, necessarily. Just normal plans: good job, nice husband, house, kids. Blah blah. And suddenly, all that . . .'

Again, she fluttered her hand, following its progress like a departing bird.

Nathan leaned forward over the table.

'You're not even *thirty* yet.'

'Not yet. Ha. Okay, the thing is, I know I'll probably have all that. But not in a way that'll seem natural. I'll always have this thing that happened to me, and nobody will be able to understand it. How do I have children? How do I even send them to school in the morning, after what happened to Elise? How do I tell them there's no such thing as monsters? How do I tell them not to be scared of the dark?'

She was becoming frustrated. She could explain, but not make him feel, the scale of this loss – that, like an explosion, it expanded from a central point equally in all directions: that it stretched back in time, infecting the day of Elise's birth; and the night she was conceived – it was a ghost in the shadows of the evening June and Graham first met, first danced, first kissed. And it warped into the future, it coloured every breath Holly would ever take.

'And whatever I have,' she said. 'Whatever I get in the end, whatever kind of happiness I'm able to build, all of it will be stuff Elise was never able to have. How do I live with that? How am I supposed to have the husband and the kids and the house and the job and, I don't know, the three holidays a year in sodding Barbados when my sister went out one night – and just *stopped*?'

'I'm sure Elise wouldn't want you to be unhappy.'

'Of course she wouldn't. But just because the way you're feeling doesn't make sense, it doesn't stop you feeling it.'

'Are you seeing anyone?'

'What, like a counsellor?'

'Yeah.'

She laughed and slapped his wrist.

'What, do you think I'm mad?'

'Not a *psychiatrist*. Counsellors, they – I don't know. They help you explore your emotions, or whatever.'

'I'm joking. Of course I saw a counsellor. But it wasn't for me.'

He topped up their glasses.

'And what about Ian?'

Ian was Holly's ex-boyfriend.

'What about him?'

'Do you ever see him?'

'Would it matter?'

'Of course not. I just—'

'No,' she said. 'I don't see him.'

The candle guttered in its bottle and she went on: 'I don't know. In some ways, I think breaking up with Ian was probably a lucky escape.'

'What was he like?'

'Well, nothing like *you*.'

'I'm not sure how to take that.'

'As a compliment, probably.'

He took a sip of wine.

She said, 'Look, he was supposed to love me enough to spend the rest of his life with me, sickness and health and all that blah. But when it came down to it, he didn't even bother to be my *friend* – do you know what I mean? It was too much work, just to be my friend. As soon as something *bad* happened, he couldn't handle it. It was too difficult for him. Poor puppy.'

Nathan lit a cigarette.

'You,' said Holly. 'You don't even *know* me. But you've been a better friend to me than Ian ever was. Than anybody was, actually.'

She drained her glass and they sat there, with one empty bottle and two empty glasses between them.

She said, 'I don't even know what you get out of this.'

'Out of this what?'

'You know what I mean. Spending time with me.'

'That's what I get.'

She put her head to one side.

'Why are you doing this?'

He wished there was wine in his glass. He cupped its fragile stem in his fist.

'I want to make things better.'

'And do you think you can do that?'

'I can try.'

She touched the back of his hand.

He said, 'The thing I'd like to do – more than anything in the world, the thing I'd like to do is make things better.'

He couldn't look at her. For a while, he thought she hadn't reacted. A hot, shameful blush rose from his sternum.

Then Holly touched his cheek. He took her hand in his. Kissed her sharp little knuckles.

She said, 'I don't believe this is happening.'

Nathan said, 'Neither do I.'

At the end of April, Holly arranged to be absent when he arrived at Sutton Down. It was Saturday morning. In the boot of the car he had flowers and champagne.

He rang the doorbell. Graham answered. Now it was spring, he wore his pastel shirts short-sleeved.

Graham expressed pleasure to see him; he shook Nathan's hand and ushered him inside.

The front of the house was gloomy and cool. It was the kitchen and conservatory that caught the morning sun. Nathan walked towards the light, with Graham at his heel.

Outside, the orchard was in bloom. The kitchen windows were open to let in the crisp green air.

'Tea?' said Graham.

It had become the order of things that Graham would offer tea, which Nathan would then offer to make. But today that didn't seem right, so Nathan cleared his throat and said, 'Tea would be lovely.'

'Righto,' said Graham, and made for the kettle. He opened the window another notch and called out to June that Nathan was here. Nathan heard the tone but not the content of her reply.

She came in, dressed in jumbo cords, muddy at the knees, and an anorak whose cut and colour dated it to the 1970s. People like June never threw anything away. Nathan admired that. The secateurs were in her hand, ugly and surgical.

He kissed her cheek. 'What are you up to?'

'Breeding lilacs from the dead ground.'

She saw his face and said, 'Never mind,' then hung the anorak over the back of a chair. Then she removed her gardening gloves and laid them next to the sink, saying, 'Holly's in town, at the shops. She shouldn't be long. She's taking a skirt back or something.'

Nathan coughed and said, 'I know.'

Then, before he had time to think about it, he said, 'Actually, I'd quite like a word.'

Graham and June stood next to each other. Hesitantly, June reached out and took Graham's hand.

Nathan said, 'I know that we – Holly and I . . . I know that we haven't known each other very long. But the fact is, the fact is, this has been the happiest time of my life. I don't want you to think we're rushing into anything. And I don't want you to imagine I do this kind of thing often. Because I really don't. Not ever.'

'What are you trying to say?'

'That we'd like to – with your permission. We'd like to get married. If that's all right.'

Now it was said, he felt worn out and awkward.

He looked past them, at the blossoming orchard at the foot of the garden. It was so quiet in the kitchen. Just the ticking of the clock, the croaking of the birds outside.

Graham and June had not so much as exchanged a glance. But June was squeezing Graham's hand in hers.

Graham said, 'We would consider it an honour.'

Nathan shook the proffered hand with measured formality.

Holly arrived home an hour later. She opened the door on the latch and called out a speculative 'Hello?'

The champagne was already half drunk and June's flowers were in the vase.

Holly stepped into the kitchen. 'I see he's told you, then?'

June and Holly held each other's hands and sobbed, happy-sad. Graham stepped back, casting his eyes upon his shoes. When June had disengaged, he hugged his daughter. He kissed her cheek and whispered something. It made her squeeze his hand and screw up her eyes and nod.

Nathan stood in the corner of the conservatory, watching them, the sunlight streaming in behind him, casting a faint amber lozenge on the floor.

21

A week before Holly's thirtieth birthday, she organized a table at a Greek restaurant, so Nathan could meet her friends. He was late; he hurried upstairs, clutching the flowers he'd bought as a gift for Holly's best woman.

Five women and a man were seated round a long table. Holly was in the centre, with Nathan's seat empty beside her.

Breathless, Nathan presented the flowers in a general, speculative way to the people seated round the table, saying: 'These are for Jacki.'

By the way all the faces turned to face one person, he guessed that Jacki was the woman sitting opposite Holly. She turned to him and stood, smiling.

He recognized her at once as the police officer who'd come to his flat with Detective William Holloway. He remembered how she had stood silently, watching the passing buses.

She said, 'Nathan?'

He nodded.

'Come here and give me a hug.'

He and Jacki hugged. The table clapped and whooped and whistled. He handed her the bouquet, then crab-stepped round the table, saying hello to everyone. He sat next to Holly. She squeezed his knee.

'You okay?'

'Fine, fine.'

'You look pale.'

'Mad rush. Bad day at work. The traffic's insane. The taxi was late.'

'Anyway,' said Jacki. 'Aren't you going to *introduce* us?'

Holly pressed Nathan's hand flat to the table. 'This, everybody, is Nathan.'

He gave a fey half-wave like an ailing monarch. There was more hand clapping, more whooping.

Only Jacki was in focus. She was pretty short – shorter than he'd imagined police officers were allowed to be. Practical haircut: sleek and dark, tucked behind her ears.

She said, 'We've heard a lot about you.'

'Not all bad, I hope.'

'Not all of it,' said the man, Martin.

(Everyone laughed, as if he'd voiced a broad innuendo.)

Holly squeezed Nathan's hand. It was a question. He squeezed back a reply: *Really, I'm fine*.

He feared the light of recognition in Jacki's eyes. That she'd drop her fork, clattering on the edge of her white dinner plate, and the table would fall silent and heads would turn and that would be the end of it all.

Nathan forced down his starter, then bolted a glass of wine. Steph leaned over to top him up. He thanked her. He could feel the wine, cold in his guts. He wanted a cigarette, but nobody was smoking.

Finally, a waiter arrived to clear the first course. Jacki produced a pack of Silk Cut, dumping them on the table like a deck of cards. In relief, Nathan reached into his own pocket.

Jacki looked round the table. 'Nobody else smoking?'

She half stood, grabbing Nathan's hand.

'Then it's the perfect opportunity to give my warning speech to the groom.'

Nathan allowed himself to be dragged outside. Martin made a loud and witless joke about handcuffs and going quietly. Nathan looked pleadingly over his shoulder. The table laughed.

Outside, Nathan and Jacki stood beneath a lamp post. Drizzle swarmed like midges in its yellow light.

Jacki lit a Silk Cut, offered the pack to him. He thanked her, said no thanks, took one of his own.

She blew a long plume of smoke and said, 'She doesn't know, does she?'

A car went past. Nathan followed its progress.

'No.'

'What did you think you were *playing* at?'

'I didn't know.'

'Ha.'

'She never talked about it. And by the time she *did*, by the time she told me, it was too late.'

'You have to tell her.'

'Tell her what? That, along with about a million other people, I was at the same party as her sister?'

'The night she disappeared, yeah. And that you knew the suspect.'

'It was his party. I was employed by him. I hated his guts. And he was never even *charged*.'

They fell silent and stepped aside, allowing two lovers to pass – huddled together, heads down in the rain.

'She's got a right to know.'

'It would break her heart.'

Jacki glared at him, defiant.

'Look,' said Nathan. 'For Christ's sake, she's happy. What else matters?'

'Yeah,' said Jacki. 'Well.'

'I know you care for her.'

'I've known her since she was eleven. Don't talk to me about caring for her.'

'Okay. I haven't known her as long as you have. But Jesus. Please. Come on.'

'Jesus,' said Jacki, and shook her head.

'Come on,' said Nathan. 'Please.'

Jacki made a face. He thought she was about to spit. She threw down the stub of her cigarette and watched it bob in the gutter.

'I hadn't seen Holly for years. Not since we left school. But it was me she came to, when Elise didn't come home. It was me she came to, because we were friends. I made her a promise. Do you understand that?'

'Of course. Of course I do.'

'I won't let you hurt her.'

'I don't intend to.'

'If you're not on the level, I'll fucking have you. I'll cut your cock off.'

'But it's the last thing in the *world*—'

'It had better be. Is what I'm saying.'

He said, 'Trust me. Come on.'

Back inside, nobody seemed to notice how long they'd been gone. Nathan drank two glasses of wine in quick succession. He and Jacki avoided eye contact, like guilty lovers.

The friends around the table had known each other for many years; the anecdotes were polished smooth with use, the language full of private references and arcane in-jokes. Early attempts to include Nathan fell away with the drink – everybody, Holly included, grew weary of explaining everything to him.

He barely noticed. But when the evening ended and the bill was paid and the coffees were drunk and everyone was gathering their coats and bags and calling taxis, Jacki made a show of hugging him. She planted a kiss on his cheek and told him – perhaps too stridently – how pleased she was for both of them, that she wished them every happiness in the world. That nobody deserved it more than Holly.

He thanked her. She tottered downstairs, to her waiting taxi.

Nathan and Holly sat alone at the table. Holly looked flushed and happy. Nathan was drunk. Acid spit in his gut. Holly asked him for a cigarette, her first since their aborted date.

'Are you sure?'

She moved her hand like somebody winding up a poor comedian. He passed her a cigarette.

He said, 'Are you okay?'

Deep dimples at the corners of her mouth.

'I'm happy.'

'Good,' he said. 'That's all that matters.' And it was true.

*

They married in September, at the small Norman church in Sutton Down. Nathan invited a few guests, all of them colleagues. They were mixed in with Holly's apparently vast network of friends, relations and neighbours. Holly wore white. As she progressed down the aisle in satin heels, there were some tears from her cousins, her aunties, her old primary school teacher.

At the reception, having raised a toast to his daughter, Graham remained standing. He rode out the guests' slight befuddlement, waiting for them to sit and grow still. Then he said, 'Now, this isn't the normal order of things. And – as many of you gathered here will know – usually I'm a stickler for order.'

He paused for laughter – a fond ripple of it.

'But June and I wanted to take this opportunity to say that a few months ago – a *very* few months . . .'

More laughter.

'Nathan blew into our lives a bit like a whirlwind. And the truth is, as many of you will also know, perhaps we needed a little whirl-wind in our lives.'

And now there was no laughter. Just silence.

'This young man didn't just win my daughter's heart, but my heart, and June's heart too – for the life he brought into our home. And for that, we'd like to thank him. So: to Nathan.'

They drank a toast while Nathan sat proud and terrified at the top table.

When the time came to give his own speech, he paused to gather himself and for a while could not speak. There were more tears at that, and some laughter.

When Nathan sat, Holly gripped his hand and Jacki came round to hug him from behind. She crossed her arms across his chest and squeezed, hard.

Holly had insisted on one more toast. She stood, raising her glass, saying: 'We all know there's a guest missing today. Since we were tiny, Elise and I talked about this day. We talked about what we'd wear, which pop star we'd marry. She was pretty stuck on George Michael, I seem to remember. That is, when she agreed to marry a boy at *all*; she was mostly interested in the dress and walking down the aisle with her beloved dad. She thought having a boy there would spoil it.'

Graham was looking at the table, smiling.

'But Elise is here. I can tell she approves of the boy I decided to marry – even though he's not a pop star.' She had to pause. 'And I can feel her, being all impatient for the disco to start. By now, she'd want to get her kitten heels off and her Doc Martens on. So I'd like you please to stand, and charge your glasses. Please join me in toasting my dear sister – Elise.'

Two hundred people stood and raised their glasses. They said her name, and sounded like the ocean.

Their first dance was to Van Morrison – 'Brown Eyed Girl'.

Later, Nathan hoped that nobody heard him, sobbing in the toilets.

In a hotel room in Barbados, he undressed her for the first time. Nathan had been celibate for five years. He and Holly had never slept in the same bed.

He woke in the tropical night to find her propped on an elbow, looking down at him in the darkness, her eyes unreadable.

He said, 'What?'

'You know what.'

He kissed the softness of her belly.

'Me too.'

She twirled an index finger through his bed-addled hair.

He wrapped an arm around her warm and naked waist.

She closed her eyes and smiled, drifting to sleep.

They were away for fourteen days.

22

Naturally, it was Holly who found them a house.

She led him round a damp Victorian shell with leprous, floral wallpaper, telling him about its potential. He pretended he could imagine it – but he was worried about the previous occupant. The old man who lived in this house had died in a nursing home, but before that he had succumbed to a lonely kind of dementia; his neighbours had found him billeted in the back room, half starved. Nathan winced to think of it, but Holly laughed and slipped her arm through his and told him not to be so stupid – it was part of the reason the house was such a bargain.

He looked at the yellow ceiling and said, 'Are you *sure*?'

She was sure.

Holly employed the architect and Holly employed the builders and Holly employed the site manager. Nathan visited the unfinished house only two or three times. Each time, it seemed to be in worse condition, not better; full of ripped-up floorboards and skinny men in painty jeans, and cups of tea. He decided the house was way too much to worry about, and stopped going. Holly learned to tell him about setbacks and reversals only when they'd been put right.

Most of their furniture had gone into this house a week before the wedding. Nathan spent a strange, transitional week in the almost-empty flat above the nursery, sitting in his one remaining chair, watching television.

He'd wondered if perhaps a wisp of Elise – the wisp he'd trailed with him – might be trapped here in this flat, like a moth in a jar. She'd be a flavour in the atmosphere, detected and dismissed by the next tenants – until she evaporated like a dab of scent on a human throat.

June had organized things such that, when they returned from honeymoon, the house was ready to be lived in; there were clothes in the wardrobes, cutlery in the drawers, washing powder in the cupboard and Fairy Liquid next to the sink. There were flowers on the dining table, next to a *Welcome Home* card. Nathan examined the back of the card to see which of Hermes' rivals had produced it.

He set his luggage down next to the clean bed, never slept in, and said, 'This is so *weird*.'

Holly was still wearing holiday shorts.

'Well, from now on, this is it. So we'd better get used to it.'

He tested the bed with his hand.

'Shall we try it out?'

They tried it out. They tried out the other bedrooms, too: and the bathroom, and the living room. He fucked her on the windowsills and the stairs. Each time, it was quick. He would grasp her hair in his fist and she would arch her back and thrust herself towards him and he couldn't help it.

She didn't seem to mind. Afterwards, she would walk semi-naked and laughing, barefoot, brushing back her disarrayed hair with her palms, a pearl of semen glinting on her pubic hair.

Usually, Nathan was ready again in a few minutes. When that happened, he made sure it was okay; when her orgasm gathered he grinned to himself, and when he entered her, she screamed and dug her nails into his arse.

On her first day back at work, he looked at her in her sober grey suit and white shirt with wing collars, and he lifted the skirt to her hips and fucked her against the door; and when she came home that evening he undressed her before she said hello and fucked her on the sofa.

She said, 'It's only natural. Your body is trying to make me pregnant.'

'Reckon?'

'Reckon.'

'And how do you feel about that?'

'About what?'

'My body trying to get you pregnant.'

'Well, I don't want you to stop or anything.'

'But what if it worked?'

'What if what worked?'

'My body. Trying to get you pregnant.'

She sat up, propped on an elbow. 'How do *you* feel about it?'

'That depends.'

'On what?'

'On how *you* feel about it.'

She lay on her back with a forearm across her eyes, slapping at his upper arm.

'I feel pretty good about it.'

'What does "pretty good" mean?'

'I'm ready if you are.'

'Okay.'

'It's not too soon?'

'I don't see why.'

She sat up again.

'Have you been *thinking* about this?'

'Of course.'

'For how long?'

'Since forever. I don't know.'

She tickled the short hairs on the nape of his neck.

'You're sure you're sure?'

That night they stood together over the lavatory and, one by one, pressed her birth control pills from the blister pack and dropped them like confetti down the bowl. She pulled the flush and watched them bob and dance away.

She said, 'It's not too late.'

He led her by the hand to the bedroom and laid her down. When they were done, she placed the palm of his hand loosely on the soft swell of her belly, and they fell asleep like that.

Late that night, she turned on to her side and nuzzled him. He pulled the duvet over her. He lay awake. He thought of the dark rooms below, and the dark hallway, and the dark bathroom with its uncovered mirrors. He thought of the dark cupboard under the stairs, where a human form could curl, to reveal its smiling face when the door was opened. And he thought of the flickering scraps of life, his essence, struggling blind inside Holly.

Eventually, in the darkness, he slept.

*

When her period arrived, they pretended not to be disappointed. They'd only been trying for a couple of weeks. They were too polite around each other, but only for a day or two.

When it happened again, four weeks later, it was a little worse – but only a little. But it was a little worse again, the month after that, and the month after that. But it was still early days, and they were young, and it was still fun trying.

And they tried and they tried – but there was always blood at the end of the cycle. And with the blood came another spectral bereavement; the idea of a boy or a girl – no more than a scrap of possibility, but beloved for all that – had been wiped from the world.

Every year, as the anniversary of Elise's disappearance drew near, Holly became withdrawn. Slower to speak in the morning, she walked round the bedroom befuddled, as if her mind was elsewhere, before grabbing a towel or a clean pair of knickers or her watch.

One Sunday morning – near Christmas, 2004 – Nathan rose early and cooked Holly breakfast in bed, taking it up on a tray.

She sat up. Her hair was awry and the rucked bed linen was imprinted on her breasts and ribs. There was a diffuse red flush on her sternum. He passed her a T-shirt because she didn't like to eat naked.

She sat cross-legged with the tray balanced on her lap. She took a sip of orange juice, then coffee and said, 'So what's all this in aid of?'

'It's in aid of, I'm worried about you.'

She took the scrunchy band from her wrist and made a loose pony-tail. She pushed some scrambled egg on to an upturned fork.

'Worried about me how?'

'You know how.'

She popped the eggs into her mouth.

He watched her eat, saying: 'Look, it's not healthy.'

She gave him a silent warning.

He was longing for a cigarette. But he'd given up, long ago.

He said, 'You never really talk about her. Even now.'

'That's not fair. I talk about her all the time.'

'You *think* about her all the time. That's different.'

'What do you want me to say? You always look so uncomfortable whenever I mention her.'

He hadn't known that.

He said, 'That's not fair. How am I supposed to react? You don't give me any clues. Am I supposed to be comfortable about it? Because I'm not.'

'I really don't want to argue about this.'

'I don't want to argue about it either.'

'Then what were you saying?'

'Look, Jesus. You haven't got any *photographs* of her. Perhaps it would be better – I don't know, after all this time – perhaps it would be better if you just hung some photos or something.'

For a long time, she was very still. And then she said, 'Sometimes, I don't believe you.'

He looked at her with a swell of horror.

But she was paying him a compliment. She drained the coffee and leapt from bed and scuttled around the room, naked but for his T-shirt, the pale ghost of a suntan still visible around her arse. She was gathering clothes. She had a quick shower and soon they'd arrived at Graham and June's house in Sutton Down.

Nathan hadn't shaved. He wore old jeans, trainers and an over-coat. To his recall, he'd never allowed Holly's parents to see him dressed less than immaculately. Graham disapproved of slovenliness.

As ever, his parents-in-law were dressed as if to receive visitors, although June had yet to apply any make-up. She looked shockingly naked without it.

Graham said, 'There's nothing *wrong* is there?'

In answer, Nathan showed him the carrier bags containing fresh bread, eggs, bacon and fruit juice they'd just bought from the farmer's market. For the second time that morning, Nathan prepared breakfast. Holly made a round of coffee.

June said, 'To what do we owe this honour?'

Holly looked at Nathan.

'Go on. Tell them.'

'Tell them what?'

'What you told me this morning.'

Nathan looked down at his poaching eggs.

'Tell them what?' said Graham.

Holly folded her arms. 'Nathan had an idea. To mark the anniversary — we dig out all the old photos. The photos of Elise. And we rehang them. In our house and in yours. And I think he's right. I think it's the right idea.'

So they ate breakfast. Then Graham went and pottered in the greenhouse and Nathan sat in the conservatory reading the papers while Holly and her mother climbed into the attic and brought down several taped-up cardboard boxes. The framed photographs and albums had been parcelled up in bubble-wrap, secured with tape — how typical of June, he thought, to be so organized about something so unendurable.

He wondered what he'd been doing and where he'd been, the day these photographs had been boxed – and where he had been the day June decided to clear Elise's bedroom and put it to use as an office. She'd hooked up a network of computers in there, and printers and scanners and filing cabinets. She'd given Elise's bed and wardrobe and other furniture to one of her charities. Elise's personal effects were boxed in the attic. Her clothes would sit there, folded and vacuum-sealed, coming slowly in and out of fashion.

He couldn't imagine where he'd been, or who. That person was alien to him, more insubstantial than a ghost.

He wandered into the dining room, where June and Holly were laying out the photographs on the table. They held hands and laughed. They reminisced about certain photographs – Elise as a five-year-old, chubby on a Cornish beach; as a eight-year-old in a polo neck, wanting front teeth. A scowling schoolgirl in a blue A-line skirt she'd loathed.

Tenderly, June said, 'She hated that skirt. She bought another one and altered it, turned it into a miniskirt. Changed into it when she got to school. Came home every night and hand-washed it in the bathroom, using shampoo. Dried it over a radiator, disguised by her towel.'

Then Holly reminded June how all the teacups and coffee mugs in the house eventually found their way into Elise's room, such that June had staged a monthly raid, carrying downstairs armfuls of mouldy mugs and hairy biscuits.

By now, they had divided the photographs into two lots: Holly's had been loosely repacked in a box that stood in the centre of the table. Nathan glimpsed corners of Elise's smiling mouth, the edges of her hair, a laughing eye.

He went outside again. He sat on a bench in the garden, watching the gentle sway of the apple trees. He watched the bright clouds.

Back inside, Holly was getting her coat on.

Nathan carried the box of photographs to the car. He kissed June. They said goodbye, and drove home.

That evening, as Nathan watched television, Holly hung the photos. He listened to the sounds of measurement and concentration and short, precise flurries of hammer blows. Then an hour – a happy hour, he thought – arranging and rearranging them on the wall. By the time she'd finished, it was nearly eleven. Nathan called out for curry and they ate it, tired, in front of the late film.

They crept up to bed after midnight. In the darkness on the stairs, Nathan could feel Elise's repeated image smiling at him. He tried not to turn, in case in one of the photos her smile had become a wet leer.

But he was weak. He did turn on the stairs. And they were only smiles.

In their first year of marriage, Holly borrowed enough money to mortgage three run-down houses. Two of them she converted into flats, the third she gutted and extended, rendering its exterior starkly modernist. The five-bedroom was a big risk and she never repeated it. They spent many sleepless nights discussing it – but it sold, in the end, and she put the profits into more property.

She employed June as her sometime adviser and part-time PA. For a while they worked from home, but soon Holly rented some offices and expanded the business to incorporate third-party site management and architectural services. She employed four young architects, full-time.

Nathan remained at Hermes, where his early trajectory had been halted by Justin's profound tenacity.

He was offered other jobs, but Hermes always paid him to remain. It wasn't the money that kept him there, though. He stayed because he liked the configuration of his life. Monday to Friday, he worked. He set the alarm for 6.45 and rose at 7.15. Tuesday and Thursday evenings, he cooked. Fridays, they ate a takeaway, Chinese alternating with Indian. Saturday nights, Holly went out with friends – once a month, she slept round Jacki's house. Sundays they spent in Sutton Down. Holly and June were careful not to talk shop at the dinner table. Sunday evenings, Nathan and Graham went to the pub; Graham bought the first drink, lager and lime in summer and cask bitter in winter.

They took one week's holiday per year with Graham and June; alternating June's choice of destination with somewhere Graham could play golf. Nathan had once protested that he would sooner die than find himself on a golf course – but he didn't mind, not really, and Graham enjoyed it.

Every year, Nathan and Holly spent two weeks sizzling on a beach somewhere: Barbados or Bermuda. The deep-blue, gold-shot sarong knotted at her hip always aroused him. He liked to watch her walk into the sea; he loved the smell of salt and Ambre Solaire on her skin. To mark Holly's birthday, they'd go away for a long weekend. For their anniversary, they spent a weekend in London or Paris.

Once or twice a year, Nathan and Graham went away to fish. They'd erect tents by the river and lie in their sleeping bags, watching the stars. They rose early, while there was still mist on the water, and heated breakfast on a Primus stove.

He seldom thought about Elise. Except in the feverish immediacy of his dreams, he felt no link to the person he'd been the night she died. He still fell quiet when driving past the woods – the flickering in his peripheral vision – but it had become almost a learned response, a Pavlovian reaction to an ancient, forgotten stimulus. Like the genuflection of a lapsed Catholic.

By 2007, they'd saved enough to buy a larger house in a better area. But they knew they'd never leave this house while the painted nursery remained unoccupied. It would be bad luck.

The pattern of their sex life was ordinary – full of troughs and peaks. But Holly had long since given up elevating her hips on pillows after sex, and they'd long since given up holding hands and discussing names and local schools.

They took fertility tests. There was no pathology.

Nathan had no doubt the imperfection was his. He imagined Holly's gently luminous ovum withering at the touch of his infected sperm.

He'd first suggested the IVF programme a long time ago. Holly had rejected the idea: it would happen when it happened, she said, and it wasn't like they weren't busy. By now it was 2008 and they were considering it. Soon they were talking about names again, and schools. They stood in the doorway of the empty bedroom, looking to the future.

And then Bob came back, to tell Nathan they were digging up the woods to build a housing estate.

23

Bob looked at the photographs for a long time.

When he turned to Nathan, his voice had gone.

'What the fuck is *this*?'

'I told you not to come in.'

Using the wall for balance, Bob lowered himself. He sat on the stripped Victorian floorboards. He looked wrong, like an optical illusion, like a drawing where the perspective and the scale have been altered.

Fingertips brushed the hair on Nathan's nape.

In the living room, the TV flickered – and it seemed to Nathan that the lights dimmed, and flickered, then rose again.

Nathan said, 'My wife will be home.'

'I need to talk to you.'

'Then give me your number.'

From his pocket, Bob produced a diary. Once, he had constructed a makeshift Ouija board from an identical book. Now with a shaking hand, he scribbled a number in it, tore out the page, handed it to Nathan.

'You must call me.'

'I will. Now, you really need to be fucking off.'

They were lit yellow by the sweep of passing headlamps. It immobilized them. They heard the sounds of a parking car, nudging and edging into a small space.

Nathan said, 'Oh Jesus.'

'Is this your wife?'

Nathan followed the line of Bob's eyes and began to understand. Bob had assumed he was lying. Bob thought Nathan lived alone, surrounded by stolen images of a girl they'd buried in secret, face down, a decade before.

And now Bob was confused. What kind of woman allowed her husband to hang up so many photographs of a missing girl, a girl who never came home?

Nathan felt a flare of savage pity.

Then he heard the sounds of Holly's approach: the slamming of a car door, the small beep of remote central locking, the sound of jingling keys.

Holly always walked at night with her substantial key chain clamped in her fist. The urban self-defence classes she attended before taking classes in judo had taught her that keys were an excellent first weapon: ram them into an attacker's eyes, gouge his face with them.

Holly also carried mace in her handbag. In their bedroom was a stun gun that, at Holly's insistence, Nathan had nervously smuggled back from Paris on the Eurostar.

Holly was scared of strangers.

The key turned in the lock. By then, it had occurred to Nathan that he and Bob should have hurried to the kitchen and tried to do something normal –

– but they simply stood in the hallway, waiting until Holly opened the door. She was wearing a belted raincoat and indigo jeans. Her hair had gone to frizz in the damp air. Over her shoulder were a laptop bag, an overstuffed briefcase and a handbag. They made her walk leaning at an angle, like a vaudeville drunk.

She saw Bob and said, 'Oh, hello.'

'Hello,' said Bob, and extended his hand. 'I'm Bob.'

Nathan had to watch him, touching his wife.

'Holly.'

'Pleasure to meet you.'

She set down the bags by the telephone and closed the door.

'Bob's an old friend,' said Nathan. 'From university days.'

'Oh,' said Holly. 'Right.'

Bob said, 'He hasn't mentioned me, has he?'

Holly brushed a wet ringlet from her forehead, sheepish. 'Sorry. Not really. He doesn't talk much about the old days.'

'Well,' said Bob. 'They weren't much fun.'

Holly nodded. She glanced at Nathan and beamed a big, bright, private question.

'Anyway,' said Nathan. 'Bob popped round.'

'Right,' said Holly.

'But he's just off. So . . .'

Bob was trying without success to ignore the photos of Elise. Nathan clapped him fraternally on the shoulder, meaning *Fuck off*.

'Well,' said Bob. 'Nice to meet you.'

'And you.'

Nathan squeezed past Holly to open the front door. The rain gusted in.

'Anyway, mate. I'll give you a call.'

The hallway was narrow. Holly had to go up three stairs to let Bob squeeze pass. He stopped in the doorway and turned to her, saying: 'Girl trouble.'

'Right,' said Holly.

'Anyway,' said Bob, and to Nathan he mimed the action of picking up a telephone and dialling. Nathan nodded once, angrily – showing Bob his dog's teeth. Then he shut the door on him.

Holly sat on the stairs. She was still wearing her coat. A wet strand of hair was tickling her nose and her make-up had run a little. She said, 'Well. Who was *that*?'

'That was Bob.'

She was fiddling with something in her lap; a wet hair band. She squeezed it and stretched it and passed it through her fingers.

'Well, obviously it was *Bob*. Bob told me that. But who the hell is Bob?'

'Just a bloke.'

'He *smells*.'

Nathan hadn't noticed.

'Like vegetables. I don't know. Like rotten tomatoes or something.' She made a revolted face, then slipped the hair band over her wrist.

'How about a cup of tea?'

Finally, she stood and slipped off her coat, hanging it over the knob of the banister. She massaged the back of her neck.

'I think I'll have a proper drink.'

He followed her to the kitchen, where she opened a bottle of wine. Nathan badly wanted a drink. But he thought it would be dangerous to start drinking now.

Instead, he opened the muddle drawer in the kitchen and removed a cellophane-wrapped pack of emergency cigarettes he kept there, breaking the seal. Holly said nothing about it. She just opened the kitchen window to let the smell out. He stood in front of the open window and lit his cigarette, blowing a plume of smoke out of the window.

'So. Who is he?'

'Just a bloke.'

'Yeah, but what bloke?'

'I don't know. He's more of a friend of a friend really. He was a mate of Pete's.'

'Pete the pop star?'

'Well, I wouldn't say *pop star*, exactly. But yeah.'

'So, what's he doing here?'

'To tell the truth, I don't know. I mean, he just turned up. I don't even know how he got my number. I'm not in contact with anyone from back then.'

'And what?'

'I just wanted rid of him.'

'There's something wrong with him. Was he on drugs or something? He looked like he'd been crying.'

'I think he's had some problems. You know. Mentally. I think he might be on medication.'

'Jesus.'

He clutched the edge of the work surface and squeezed.

'Poor you,' she said, and laughed. She hugged him from behind, nestling her wet fragrant head in the crook of his neck. He could smell shampoo and the rain itself, the faint tang of pollution. She squeezed his arse and slapped it. 'So, what are you going to do?'

'I promised to go out for a drink with him. Is that all right?'

She nibbled his neck. 'Of course it's all right; I wish you'd go out more often, you know that. It just seems a shame that, when you do finally get a social life, it's with weird Bob.'

She knitted her hands across the bulge of his belly; he wasn't as skinny as he used to be. 'I'm sorry. Is that a really horrible thing to say?'

He patted the back of her hands – a signal to disengage. She stepped away and he turned to face her.

'Of course not. Do you think I want to go drinking with someone who smells like rotten tomatoes?'

She picked up her wine.

'Poor you.'

He turned to go upstairs, and Holly said, 'Who's the girl?'

'What girl?'

'He said he was having girl problems.'

'I don't know. He didn't even say.'

'Poor bloke.'

'Poor bloke? You've changed your tune.'

'I don't know. He must be lonely. Coming to you with his problems – when you hardly even know him.'

Nathan gave a non-committal grunt and made a gesture with his hands, exaggerated like a Hollywood Mafioso.

Then he walked past the photos of Elise in the hallway, and went upstairs and passed the photos of Elise on the upstairs landing. He let himself into the upstairs bathroom and turned on the light. He locked the door and rushed to the lavatory and was copiously but silently sick. He puked until he was passing green bile, and what looked like spots of blood.

24

In the morning, Nathan slipped out of the office and called the number Bob had given him. They arranged to meet.

Nathan had left a spare suit jacket hung on the back of his chair – this was to imply that he was still in the building, but away from his desk, perhaps in a meeting or on his way to the post room.

He walked to the main road and hailed a taxi. It took less than fifteen minutes to drive to Bob's house. He and Bob lived in the same city. They'd watched the same buses go by, had perhaps shopped in the same shops, seen the same films at the same cinemas. Perhaps at the same time.

The cab dropped him off at the corner. It was a street of Victorian mansion blocks long since gone to subdivision and seed. Nathan walked down an overgrown front garden to what had been a four-storey house. He stood on the worn stone step, reading the faded paper strips adjacent to the ranked doorbells. The ink in 'Morrow' had faded almost to illegibility.

He rang the bell and, waiting, lit a cigarette.

Eventually, the big, peeling door opened and Bob let him in. The hallway was dirty and dusty, grey-carpeted. An improvised mail-drop, a melamine bookshelf, was a landslide of bills and junk mail. A bicycle was propped against the two-tone walls, as were an empty plastic laundry basket and an old drop-leaf table. Nathan followed Bob along the hallway and down into the basement, where Bob lived in a single, under-lit room.

It was large and square and its walls were jam-packed with second-hand books. A home network of computers stood on a few junk-shop tables – three elderly laptops and four or five desktops, two of them brand-new Dells. Beside them stood a reel-to-reel tape recorder.

Musty sofas made three edges of a square. Nathan noticed a crusty towelling sock balled up in the corner of the kitchenette, by the fridge.

It smelled in there.

Bob shifted magazines and a frayed sweater from one of the sofas, bidding Nathan sit.

'Coffee?'

'No.'

'Right.'

While Nathan waited, Bob boiled the kettle, making himself a pint of black Nescafé. Then he lowered himself into a sofa opposite Nathan and said, 'So, how have you been?'

'How the fuck do you *think* I've been?'

'I don't know. Which is why I was asking.'

Nathan patted his pockets and produced a cigarette. He lit one. 'What's this all about?'

Bob sipped scalding coffee. 'Funny, isn't it?'

Nathan looked away, at the book-lined walls.

'The way things turn out,' said Bob. 'Did you hear about Detective Holloway?'

Nathan had. A few years back, Holloway had apparently absconded with some ransom money. Nathan and Holly had quizzed Jacki about it, but Jacki would say nothing. That was a while ago now, a few years. Holloway had been caught and, as far as Nathan knew, he was still in prison.

Nathan was looking at the reel-to-reel tape recorder.

Bob followed his line of sight. 'Don't worry. I'm not taping this or anything.'

'What is this stuff?'

'Research.'

Nathan looked away from it all. It gave him the creeps. He ran his hands through his hair and said, 'Oh, Jesus Christ, what am I doing here?'

'Who is Holly?' said Bob.

'My wife.'

'You know what I mean. I was thinking about it all night. I couldn't sleep. I couldn't put it all together. You know what that's like? Lying awake, worrying about something?'

'I've got a pretty good idea, Bob. Yeah.'

'She knows her, doesn't she?'

'Knows who?'

'Your wife knows Elise.'

Her name on his lips.

Nathan made a gesture with his fingers, like someone batting mosquitoes from his face, telling Bob not to bother him.

Bob jumped to his feet, apparently elated. 'I knew it! I knew it was something like that. Jesus. You're *sick*. It's unbelievable. Jesus. She even looks like her.'

Outside, a car went past.

Bob said, 'Is it, like, a *sex* thing? Do you get *off* on it?'

Nathan wanted to scream, but all the strength had gone from him. He said, 'Jesus, no.'

'Does she look like her? I mean, naked?'

He couldn't endure Bob even contemplating Holly's nudity.

He made as if to leave. The weight of Bob's eyes fell on his shoulders.

'Really,' said Bob, 'you have to stay.'

Nathan stopped. Eventually, he turned.

'Don't mention my wife again.'

'Fine. Whatever.'

'I mean, not ever.'

'Cool. You have to admit, though. It's pretty sick.'

They locked eyes. Nathan blinked first.

He looked at his shoes, then at a ball of soiled underwear lying dead on the kitchen linoleum.

'You wouldn't understand.'

Bob seemed about to speak. Instead, he slurped coffee and wandered to one of the tables, the one with the reel-to-reel tape recorder on it. Its plastic had yellowed with age and gone brittle. A crack ran across it like a fault line.

Bob pulled up an office chair, the kind Nathan used at work. It was threadbare and pilled and greasy.

Nathan said, 'So?'

'So. The forest where we buried her has been sold off to some property developer. They're going to build a new housing development – or extend a housing development they already built, a couple of years back. Depends how you look at it.'

Nathan reached out for the sofa, as if he were about to fall.

'In the course of doing this,' said Bob, 'they're almost certain to find her. It's not like the grave was very deep or anything.'

'I never understood why they didn't,' said Nathan. 'I was waiting for it. I expected it every day.'

'Who knows? They had their suspect. He didn't leave the party all night. So maybe they just didn't look in the right places. Maybe one of the sniffer dogs had a head cold. Jesus, I don't know.'

Nathan had a feeling like he was descending too quickly in a lift.

'If they find her,' said Bob. 'Which they will, they'll recover traces of semen from two different men. They'll assume, quite understandably, that she was raped and murdered. And they'll take a voluntary DNA sample from every man who attended Mark Derbyshire's party, and they'll identify us, and we'll go to prison for the rest of our lives.'

Nathan thought of Holly and he thought of Graham and he thought of June. He thought of the day they rehung the photographs.

He walked slowly round the sofa and sat in it. He put his head in his hands.

Bob said, 'We have to move her.'

'I can't do that.' The intervening ten years had not happened. 'Jesus fucking Christ. I can't believe this is happening.'

'It won't be difficult. There can't be much left. Not after all this time.'

'Then what's the *point*?'

'I mean, she won't be *heavy*. She won't weigh much.'

Nathan began to laugh. He clapped his hand over his mouth.

'Can we be sure they'd find her?'

'Your sperm is inside her. How much of a risk are you willing to take?'

'But won't it have – *rotted* by now?'

'They have forensic techniques that you wouldn't believe. All they need is a fragment of genetic material – just a tiny, a teeny tiny fucking scrap. They can amplify it. They, I don't know what they do, they spin it or something. It's called PCR. A polymerase chain reaction. Where there's a little DNA, suddenly there's a lot. And believe me, if there's anything left in her or on her, they'll find it. It's not like they don't know where to look . . . in her womb, her mouth, in her anus . . .'

'Fuck.'

'We drive down there, we park in the lane, we dig her up, we put her in the boot and we drive her to . . . I don't know where. I haven't thought it through yet. Somewhere they can't find her. We might have to pour acid on her or something. You know. On her, um, nether regions. Battery acid or something.'

'I can't do it.'

'Of course you can. You've done it once already. This time will be easier.'

'Not again.'

'You have to.'

'I'll take my chances.'

'How will Holly feel?'

A droplet of sweat ran the length of Nathan's spine. He was clammy, as on a thundery day.

'Because it would be a terrible thing to do to her,' said Bob. 'To let Elise be unearthed by a fucking bulldozer. And then learn it was you who put her there.'

'Do it by yourself.'

'I would if I could. But it needs two of us, to do it properly. Two pairs of hands. Two pairs of eyes.'

'I thought she'd be *light*.'

'I can't do it alone. Simple as that.'

Above them, a door slammed. Running footsteps descending the staircase.

Nathan said, 'Are you scared?'

'Wouldn't you be?'

'Yes. Yeah, I'd be scared.'

They sat in silence. Then Nathan stood. 'I'll be in touch.'

'Make sure you are.'

Nathan shuffled from the bed-sitting room, slamming the door behind him. He walked up the stairs and out the door and along the drive and into the daylight.

He sat on a wall from which the metal railings had been removed in 1941 – melted down for weaponry, their black nubs long since worn smooth. He took great lungfuls of air and watched the traffic go past.

Nathan walked in and dropped himself in the armchair. He sat with his coat on, looking at the television. It was *Coronation Street*.

Holly was on the sofa. She'd been on site most of the day, visiting a warehouse in Birmingham she was interested in converting. Then she worked for a couple of hours in the home office they'd installed in the second bedroom.

She'd taken a hot bath to unwind: if she didn't, she couldn't sleep, she'd be thinking about work all night. Sometimes that happened to Nathan, too. He'd wake at 2 a.m., fretting about some new line of cards that was failing. Now Holly smelled of bath oil. She wore tracksuit trousers and a T-shirt. Her hands and feet were soft and her legs were crossed beneath her. She was half-lying on the sofa, watching TV and doing a crossword.

She said, 'What's up?'

'Nothing.'

She put down the paper and muted the television.

'You look terrible.'

He touched his temple. 'I've got this really bad headache.'

She came over and sat in his lap. She was so clean. She laced her hands behind his head and said, 'This isn't like you. Have you caught a bug or something?'

'I don't know.'

She touched his burning forehead. 'God. You're really *sick*.'

She stood and led him upstairs and made him undress. She folded back the duvet and he lay, corrupt and sweating, in the clean bed. He left on his boxer shorts; he could smell his genitals. He cupped his throbbing testicles and slipped into a feverish sleep. The testicle ache spread to his lower back, like a bruise across his kidneys.

Elise's spectre lay a cool hand upon his forehead and he woke with a shout to see it was only Holly, his wife. She put a thermometer into the corner of his mouth. It was the instrument she'd once used to time her ovulation. She waited, then she removed it and held it to the hallway light.

'You're burning up.'

He reached out and held her hand by the fingertips.

She said, 'You sleep. I'll drive down to the chemist and get something for the fever.'

He sat up. Grabbed her wrist.

'Don't.'

'You need to get that fever down. I'll be back in twenty minutes.'

'Please don't go.'

She looked at him – backlit, the thermometer held high in one hand.

He said, 'Don't leave me alone in the house.'

Slowly, she lowered the thermometer.

'You're scared of the dark, aren't you?'

'Yes.'

She sat on the edge of the bed, holding his hand.

'You never talk about it.'

'Would you?'

'Did you think I'd laugh?'

'Yes.'

She laughed.

'You see,' he said.

She leaned in a little closer. 'What happened, to make you so scared?'

He turned away on his side.

'Nothing.'

He could feel her, looking at him.

She said, 'Shall I turn on the light?'

'Please. And leave the door open.'

She kissed his forehead and turned on the reading light. She left the bedroom door ajar. He heard her, descending the stairs; picking up the telephone and taking it through to the front room. She'd be calling her mother, seeking advice on how to treat a man who never fell ill, who wouldn't let her leave the house to get medicine.

He woke to a cool flannel on his forehead.

Holly pressed a mug into his hand; Lemsip Cold & Flu.

He said, 'Where did you get these?'

'Shhh,' said Holly.

He began to panic. 'Did you leave the *house*?'

Then he saw June, framed in the doorway. She'd driven to a twenty-four-hour chemist in the town centre. Nathan looked at her. Then he looked at Holly. She brushed back his sweating hair.

'Get better, now.'

Later, the sound of the front door closing: June going home. He imagined her at the wheel, a bubble of light in the darkness, hurtling past the earth where her daughter lay.

25

In the morning, Holly woke him with another Lemsip and a kiss goodbye.

He drank the Lemsip, then pulled on a tracksuit and thick socks and his dressing gown, and limped to the office.

Holly's workstation was a chrome and glass table: a Compaq desktop, replaced every couple of years; a filing cabinet, a cheap plastic desktidy, stacked in- and out-trays, a desk diary, a mobile phone charger. Nathan kept a smaller workstation in there – a corner desk, a laptop, not much else.

He logged on and skim-read his work emails. Later, he would answer the more important of them, because he wanted his bosses and colleagues to consider him a martyr and a workaholic. Then he logged on to the Internet and ran a search on the proposed Cabot Green estate.

There were dozens of hits – Cabot Green had been a local interest story for years now. According to the published minutes of the Sutton Down Action Group, Graham and June Fox had declined an invitation to act as group secretaries. (Probably they'd have thought it hypocritical to accept, given Holly's chosen career.)

Holly must know about this proposed development – all the local developers seemed know and enjoy gossiping about each other. She might even have mentioned it, over dinner or breakfast: Nathan had probably acknowledged her and immediately forgotten all about it, having little real interest in the matter – no more interest, say, than Holly had in the wholesale of greetings cards.

The final appeals had failed. Planning permission had been granted. Building work was due to commence.

Nathan navigated to the development company's website and found his way to a map of the proposed Cabot Green estate.

It took some time to make sense of the plans, but not as long as it might have – Holly often discussed similar proposals with him, and he'd learned how to read them.

Whoever now owned Mark Derbyshire's estate had sold off a good portion of it – including the woods that ran to the main road. On the map, Nathan was easily able to find and identify the lane. It was simply marked, given no name. He was able to trace the wiggling brook beside which they had laid her.

Superimposed on this map in dotted, coloured lines was the ghost of the housing estate to come. Around the brook, there was to be a modern playground with climbing frames and, across a small bridge, a picnic area. Nathan knew that such facilities were often designed into new estates' proposals – and were often dropped at the last minute, as a cost-saving exercise; such projects always ran above budget. But factoring in designated recreation sites helped get the project past the protesters. It helped foster the illusion that a new community was being designed from the ground up.

He could see written into the plans that Elise would be found. She would be disinterred by a mechanical digger, or by some boys who'd scrambled over the chain-link fence, drawn to the unexplored moonscape behind it, or she would be sniffed out by badgers or foxes or a domestic dog tempted by the thick, sweet smell of old carrion.

He cleared his Internet history, as if he'd been viewing pornography, then accessed his work emails. He answered several of them on corporate autopilot: they seemed to address problems that had arisen decades ago, and did not greatly interest him. Then he logged off and went back to bed. He couldn't sleep. He dragged the duvet downstairs and, wrapped in it, watched daytime television.

As a student and as a doley, he'd watched and thoroughly enjoyed daytime TV – but now the charm seemed to have gone from it. He watched tawdry, depressing quizzes, a sordid freak show disguised as a discussion programme, cookery programmes, yet more quizzes, and a comfortingly soporific programme about watercolours. He made beans on toast. He hadn't eaten beans on toast for a long time.

He called Bob at 5 p.m. – two hours before Holly was due back.

Bob said, 'How have you been? I've been worried.'

'I've been ill.'

'Stress, I expect.'

'Yes.'

'So. Anyway.'

'So anyway. Let's do it.'

'When?'

'Friday night.'

'What will you tell Holly?'

'That I'm going for a drink with you. And that I'm sleeping at your place.'

'Is that wise?'

'I never go out. The only nights I've ever spent away from my wife, I've been at a sales conference. And there isn't a sales conference for five fucking months, and it's in fucking Dublin. Okay?'

'Okay. Steady on. Whatever.'

'I'm sorry. I'm on edge, here.'

Bob said, 'I'll be in touch', and hung up.

Nathan wrapped the duvet tighter round himself and turned up the volume on the muted television. He watched a shrieking advert for loan consolidation, then a quieter ad for orthopaedic beds, a third for stairlifts, and a fourth for a flu remedy which took the form of a macho, corporate mini-drama.

So this is who was watching with him. The unemployed, the elderly and the sick. A silent nexus of them, in lonely communion.

He turned it off.

26

On Friday night, Holly kissed his cheek and told him to have a good time.

In the hallway, he crushed her to him and she pulled back, laughing: 'You're only going for one night.'

She brushed down his lapel – he was wearing a good suit and carrying an Adidas sports bag – then turned him round, swatted his arse and shoved him through the front door. A taxi was waiting at the kerb.

He took it into town and met Bob, who was waiting for him at the wheel of an old Audi 100. Its rear bumper was gaffer-taped and his tax disc was out of date.

Nathan got in, pointing to the tax disc.

'That's a good idea. Get us arrested.'

'It's a detail. What's in the bag?'

'Clean underwear. Nurofen Plus for the hangover. Lucozade. That sort of thing.'

'It's like she's sending you off to *camp*.'

Nathan belted himself in, saying: 'That's the last time you mention her this evening.'

'Fine,' said Bob, and pulled away.

They drove.

Nathan asked him, 'Have you got everything?'

'Pretty much. Do you want to stop somewhere? Pick up some cheap clothes?'

Bob waited behind the wheel in an NCP car park while Nathan went to Millets in the mall. He bought a dark-green fleece and a black cagoule, some hiking shoes, a pair of khaki trousers. Also a balaclava.

He paid cash.

Back at the NCP, he dumped the carrier bags on the back seat of Bob's car, next to his overnight bag.

Driving, Bob said, 'How are you coping?'

'I feel sick. You?'

'I'm all right. A bit hyper. Like I had one coffee too many.'

To calm down, and to kill some time until it was late enough, they stopped at a pub.

Bob moped over a pint of Guinness. Nathan drank several tepid gin and tonics. They sat in a booth, unwilling and unable to talk – the jukebox was too loud. Before they left, Nathan went for a long piss.

They turned off the motorway and on to the B-roads. The night was overcast, with multiple layers of quick-moving clouds, backlit by the moon.

They left the yellow lights of the city behind them. Nathan turned to see it, sitting in the valley like a UFO. Bob took the familiar route to the forest and located the lane with almost no difficulty.

He slowed and, with a heave on the wheel, he turned the Audi into the slot of darkness. They followed the beam of its headlights. The trees shifted in the edge of their vision.

They came to the right place.

They knew it was the right place.

Bob stopped the car. They heard its engine ticking. The wind through the trees. Nathan remembered the last time he'd sat here. He remembered Elise. Laughing, naked. The way her fingers tightened then relaxed on his arms as he entered her. He thought of the semen he'd pumped into her.

The sound of them breathing.

Bob said, 'I used to come here sometimes. In the early days. Just drive past. Y'know.'

Nathan didn't want to listen. He freed his seat belt and scrambled on to the back seat. He took the new clothes from the carrier bag and began to rip the tags from them. Then he began to undress.

'Just like old times,' said Bob.

Nathan was pulling off his smart trousers.

'You,' said Bob. 'Taking off your trousers in the back of my car.'

Nathan had folded the clean trousers next to him and removed his shirt. He was pulling on a Millets T-shirt. His hair stuck up.

'Make sure you get all the tags off those clothes,' said Bob. 'You don't want to leave any behind.'

Nathan brushed his hair flat.

Bob said, 'Look, I'm sorry. I just thought it was pretty freaky, that's all. You undressing in the back of my car. Here, of all places. You have to admit.'

Nathan said, 'If it gets any more freaky I'll go fucking mad. Do you know what I mean, Bob? They'll find me in the town fountain, hitting myself with bricks and eating dog shit. So give me a break, all right.'

Bob smoked a cigarette while Nathan finished dressing. The clothes smelled new; they were still creased with their shop folds. The boots had been expensive – he didn't want to wear something that might give him blisters.

He and Bob looked straight ahead, through the black windscreen.
'Shit,' said Nathan.

His voice, so loud in the confined space of the car, seemed to galvanize Bob, who slapped his leg and opened the door. He walked round to the boot. Nathan joined him. In the boot were two shovels and a big roll of clear plastic. There were two rolls of duct tape and two pairs of gardening gloves.

They listened to the wind. The clouds moved fast overhead, lit silver by the moon.

'We are going to do this,' said Bob.

He reached in and grabbed two shovels in his fist. He passed them to Nathan. Bob lifted out the bulky roll of plastic. He rested his chin on top of it and said, 'Right.'

Nathan looked at the trees: the oaks, the silvery ash, the swaying ferns and the soft moss. The smell of it.

'Are you sure this is it?'

'Pretty sure.'

So was Nathan. He followed Bob into the trees. After a single step, the moonlight winked out and the darkness was complete. He could hear Bob's exerted breathing, the rustle of clothing. But he could see nothing. The canopy of branches formed a rustling, shifting membrane above his head.

Bob's harsh whisper:

'Are you there?'

'Yeah. I can't see a fucking thing.'

'Press on a few feet. I'll turn on the torch as soon as it's safe.'

'But I can't fucking see.'

'Then be careful.'

Nathan moved with great caution. But still, he caught his foot in the twisted root of a tree. For a terrible moment, he believed that a human hand had reached out and grabbed his ankle.

He'd fallen before he could scream.

A cold point of light popped on and passed across him. Bob's torch. Nathan stood, brushing himself down, and picked up the shovels. Bob's face was blanched by the torchlight.

He handed Nathan a torch. Nathan tucked the shovels under his arm and followed its wavering beam deeper into the forest.

Eventually, they found the brook. Its waters were black round white boulders. They stuck close together, did not speak, and began to dig around. In less than half an hour, they had found the place. They had buried Elise near the fork of a massive old tree, adjacent to the brook. The bank had crumbled away since, exposing the tree's root base.

Further up the bank, where it began to level off, they lay out the plastic sheeting, weighing down the corners with branches and rocks. Weighed down, it inflated and deflated with the wind, like something breathing.

Bob laid his torch on the ground. Then he thrust the blade of his shovel into the earth. It made a slicing sound. He looked at Nathan, then turned off the torch. To Nathan's eye, he simply disappeared. Nathan whirled the beam of his torch until it crossed Bob's form, made him briefly luminous like the moon. Bob paused, spade in hand and whispered, 'Turn off the fucking torch and give me a hand.'

It was hot work, far hotter than burying her. Nathan removed his fleece and cagoule and worked in his T-shirt. His trousers and boots were muddy to the knees and clagged with clots of mud and soil.

They wished they'd remembered to bring the water. It was in the boot. It was thirsty work.

They dug around for an hour or more. Then Bob hissed for him to stop.

They kneeled, brushing at the soil with their clumsy gloves. Bob had overturned a white knob of something.

Nathan stood. He walked to the water's edge and breathed rapidly through his nostrils. Leaning on the shovel, he looked at the racing sky. Then he looked at the water.

He walked back to Bob.

'What is it?'

'I don't know. An elbow?'

'Or an ankle.'

'Whatever.'

In the black soil, it looked like the head of a mushroom.

They got down on their knees and began to dig and sift the soil with their gloved hands. The cold seeped through until their fingers ached.

Bob told Nathan to stop. Under his hand was a long bone. It looked cracked and old, even in the darkness.

Nathan sat.

'There's nothing left.'

He was on the edge of the excavation. The soil was cold and it wet his arse. He wanted a cigarette. He said, 'What do we do?'

Bob leaned on his shovel. Dirt like camouflage on his face.

'Find as much as we can. The skull. The hips. The important bits.'

'It's a fucking *skeleton*, Bob. She's gone.'

Bob was breathless. He looked at Nathan, and then began digging.

Over the next forty-five minutes, they found a number of vertebrae; they were scattered through the soil like the beads of a snapped necklace. They found a few dozen smaller bone fragments. They threw them all on the plastic sheeting. They found two more long bones. They chucked them on the sheeting, too. They lay like firewood.

Then Bob stooped, examining the ground.

He'd found Elise's skull. It lay close to the river's edge.

It was no longer face down.

Close by, Nathan spotted the edge of her lower mandible, protruding from the soil. He lifted it clear and placed it on the plastic. Then he joined Bob, digging under the skull with his fingers, prising it from the soil.

They placed the skull on the plastic. Nathan turned it to face away from them, into the trees.

An hour later, they found the carrier bag. It was black and oily and had been compressed by the weight of the soil, but it was intact. Inside were the damp remains of Elise's clothing. Nathan felt it: congealed fabric gone black and rotten. Even the rubber remains of the Adidas had perished. But they threw the bag on the plastic sheeting too.

Then they stopped to examine it all. It didn't look like much. A broken skull, a few cracked bones. A bag of rags. Nathan looked down at the churned soil.

'We'll never find it all.'

'It doesn't matter. If a builder unearths what he thinks is a human skeleton, he's obliged to call the police. But if he finds a few scraps of bone by a river in the woods, what's he going to think? He's going to think it's an animal. I mean . . .' He stooped to lift a chipped fragment from the plastic. He cleaned the caked earth from it and said, 'What's this?'

'I don't know.'

'I don't know either. It might not even be part of her. And we're the ones who put her here.'

Nathan counted the long bones.

'Bits are missing. A leg, or something.'

Bob considered the plastic sheeting.

'It was probably dragged off and eaten in the early days. By a badger.'

'A *badger*?'

'How the fuck should I know?'

'A fox. A dog maybe.'

They examined the grave.

Bob said, 'What time is it?'

'Gone three.'

'Right. So we don't have much time.'

They rolled the bones into a plastic bundle and sealed it with duct tape. They left the bundle in the woods and began to fill in the hole. They threw rocks and rotted leaves and twigs and branches at the area where they'd been digging. It hurt to breathe. Nathan's hands were numb.

When they were done, Bob evaluated the scene. He probed at the ground with the beam of his torch.

He said, 'Now, have you got everything? Keys, wallet? Glasses? Everything you bought. You haven't left anything? Your mobile phone?'

'No.'

'You're sure?'

'Pretty sure.'

'Two torches,' recited Bob. He counted off on his gloved fingers. 'Two shovels. Carpet knife. Tape.' He looked round himself. 'I think that's it.'

He patted his pockets.

'Car keys.'

Nathan waited until Bob found the keys. They walked into the trees. They'd come to the end of their endurance, and their tempers. Nathan took the shovels. Bob lifted the plastic-wrapped remains.

They were light, but bulky, and Bob's arms were tired. He couldn't carry it alone. He couldn't drag it; it might rip open on a tree root. Nathan would have to help. But Nathan couldn't do that and also take the shovels.

'One of us will have to come back for them,' whispered Bob. 'We'll draw lots.'

'Fuck that. Let's throw her in the river.'

'What?'

'For Christ's sake. We wore gloves. We haven't bled or spat or whatever the fuck else. The river will wash away any trace elements. And it'll scatter the bits: it'll wash them all the way downstream. To the sea maybe, to the ocean. It's the safest thing to do.'

'Are you *mad*?'

'No. What's mad, is to dig her up, then take her home in the boot of your car. Why not just get rid of her now?'

'It's leaving too much to chance.'

'Not so much as driving out of this lane at 4 a.m. with a fucking *skeleton* in the boot.'

'If we abandon the evidence, just throw it in the river, then we have to spend the rest of our lives worrying that someone, somehow, is going to find it – and identify it. And we'll have to go to bed at night hoping we haven't left some clue, some trace of ourselves, that can be traced back to us. Christ, I don't know – maybe one of your *hairs* is trapped between her teeth or something, maybe it lodged there when you lifted the skull from the ground.'

'The river would wash it clean.'

'Maybe it would. Maybe not. Do you fancy taking that risk?'

'The hair would rot.'

'Maybe the cold water would preserve it.'

'Fuck,' said Nathan, knowing Bob was right.

They glared at each other and at the plastic-wrapped remains.

They taped the spades to the parcel and carried it between them like a stretcher. It took a long time to retrace their steps. They left behind several hundred muddy footprints. They used no torches and it was very dark. Because their arms were weary, the remains of Elise eventually grew very heavy.

Back at the car, they removed their shoes and shoved them into a black bin liner. They removed their clothes and shoved these into another bin liner. Inside the boot were six large bottles of Evian. They used these first to slake their thirst, then to rinse the worst of the mud from their hands and face and hair. The water was cold. They spluttered and swore. Bob had not thought to bring a towel.

Bob put Elise in the boot while Nathan put his suit back on. He was cold and wet and muddy, and the clean fabric abraded his skin. His fingers shivered as he laced his shoes. Bob closed the boot. He supported his weight with one hand on the roof while he dressed in a pair of jumbo cords and a cable-knit sweater gone in the elbows. It smelled of motor oil.

They sat in the Audi, shivering.

'Right,' said Bob.

He engaged the engine and pulled the car through a U-turn. Nathan turned in his seat to see how the red brake lights illuminated the half-moon of tyre tracks they left on the road behind them. Bob told him not to worry. The tyre tracks and the footprints would be long gone before the builders got here, let alone the police: erased by the wind and the rain and the passage of other cars with muddy wheels, cars that brought young lovers down this dark lane. And when the footprints and the tyre prints were gone, they would be gone forever. Any fresh traces they'd left behind would be hopelessly compromised.

The Audi stopped where the lane joined the road.

Bob waited until he was sure no cars were coming – no car whose driver or passenger might take note of the old Audi slipping out of such a sinister track, so late at night. But it was late and there was no traffic. The road stretched empty in both directions.

They barely saw another vehicle until they pulled on to the motorway, and even then the traffic was intermittent and forlorn. Bob drove at a measured pace in the inside lane. They passed two flashing police cars breathalysing somebody at the roadside. They grew tense. But that was it.

It was after 5 a.m. when they arrived at Bob's house. People on early shifts were leaving for work. Clubbers were still getting home. It was dark but the night had gone. It was a new day.

27

Bob had rented a lock-up garage just round the corner from his house. The Audi idled in front of the doors while Nathan fiddled with numb hands at the padlock.

The garage was dark and smelled of mildew and oil, exactly like Bob's sweater. Nathan stepped inside its damp mouth, fumbling for the light switch. He found it on the breeze-block wall and now the garage was filled with wan radiance and dark corners. Nathan stepped aside to allow the car to enter.

It crept in, brushing its snout against the far wall. Nathan pulled the garage door closed, engaging the four heavy-duty slide bolts Bob had fixed there.

Inside the garage was a workbench. Its corners and holes were linked with ancient cobwebs. There were some oil canisters, a hat rack against one corner, and there was a chest freezer with rusted hinges. Nathan looked at it. He could hear the low humming of its motor.

Bob got out of the car. He dug his knuckles into the small of his back and lit a cigarette.

'What a night.'

Nathan lit a cigarette too.

'What now?'

'I'll keep it in the freezer until I've researched the best way to get rid of it.'

'Just *burn* it.'

'And where do you suggest I burn it? Where do I procure a heat source powerful enough to break down human bone? Would you like me to take it home and do it in the oven?'

'All right. The clothes. Let's just douse them in petrol and burn them on the floor. We can do that right now. Right here and now.'

'And what if they leave trace elements?'

'They won't, Bob. There's nothing *left*.'

'And you know that, do you? You can be certain?'

'Pretty certain, yeah.'

'I wish I could be.'

Nathan was exhausted. The walls seemed far away.

'It's all going in the freezer,' repeated Bob, patiently. 'Until I've found the best way to dispose of it.'

Nathan threw down his cigarette and drew near to Bob.

'We just took a stupid risk, digging this stuff up. Now you want to keep it in your garage, for Christ's sake? What's the matter with you?'

'Are you going to tell anybody it's there?'

'Of course not. But Jesus, you can't just leave it there. We should be dissolving it in acid or something.'

'Good idea. Do you know where to get it?'

'I'll Google it.'

'Excellent idea. And do you know how to handle it safely?'

'I'll Google that, too. I'll go to an Internet cafe, right now, and I'll order a coffee and I'll . . .'

He trailed off. Then he kicked the car, almost hard enough to break his toe. Then he leaned on the bonnet and said, 'Jesus fucking Christ. What a mess. What a mess.'

Bob said, 'Look, okay. It's been a long night. But we did it. So let's not fuck up now, by doing something rash when we're both so tired. The truth is, that's how people get caught. They do something stupid when they're feeling exactly the way we're feeling right now. Like going to an Internet cafe and looking up how to dispose of a body and being caught on CCTV.' He held up a hand – pre-empting Nathan's interruption – and said, 'Look, I'm sure you're right. I'm sure we can just douse the clothes and burn them. Fine. But what if, I don't know – you've seen the way stuff floats around when you light a fire. The embers, whatever. What if, by burning the clothes, you're leaving little fragments all over the garage? The kind of thing you can't see, but that Scene of Crime Officers can detect in two minutes flat? Traces of human fat, or whatever.'

'It sounds pretty unlikely to me.'

'And to me. But I'm not *sure*. Okay? I'm not sure. I just want to research this stuff. Believe me, it's the best way.'

'Keeping her in a *freezer*?'

'It's as good as anywhere else. It's better than where she was.'

He watched Nathan's eyes flit to the boot, and said, 'Look, we got away with it. We're not even suspects. But we'd *become* suspects if they found her, out there in the woods. But they're not looking, Nathan, they're not even looking. We just have to make sure that, if they *do* come looking, they find nothing. Absolutely nothing. And I want to find out the best way to do that.'

There was a standing pipe in one corner. Nathan flicked away the cigarette and walked over to it. He ran the tap. He took off his shirt. The water was unbearably cold. He forced his head under. His scalp constricted. He straightened, spluttering. Goosebumps ran the length of his torso. His sparse body hair stood erect, his hair in wet-cat spikes.

He was shivering when he said, 'You're right. I can't think straight. I don't know what to do for the best.'

Bob nodded, with gravity.

Then he opened the boot and hoisted the plastic-wrapped remains in his arms and carried them to the freezer. Still half naked and shivering, Nathan opened the lid. He removed the baskets of frozen vegetables. They put Elise in the bottom and hung the racks of frozen vegetables above her.

Then Bob closed the lid and secured it with a padlock.

Nathan watched him do it. 'Now *that's* suspicious.'

'What is?'

'Padlocking a freezer. Who padlocks a freezer?'

'What if some kids decide to burgle the place?'

Nathan buried freezing hands in the pockets of his trousers. He hurried to the bonnet of the car, where his clothes lay, and pulled the T-shirt and shirt over his head.

'I'm going home.'

'Do you want a lift?'

'I'll take the bus or something.'

'Are you sure? You look like shit.'

'I'll be fine. I need to get my head together.'

'What will you say to Holly?'

'She'll be gone when I get home.'

'Better make sure she is.'

'She will be.'

'Because you look *fucked*, mate.'

'That's pretty funny.'

'Can you do me one favour?'

'What?'

'Take our clothes and dump them somewhere?'

Nathan sagged. He reached into the boot and removed the bag of muddy clothing. It smelled of soil. He tied a knot in it.

'Just dump it outside one of the shops on Endymion Road,' said Bob. 'There's always rubbish piled out there.'

Nathan tested the bag's weight. It seemed heavy. His arms were so tired.

He said, 'What are you going to do?'

'Sleep. Then get rid of the car. The spades. The rest of it.'

'Okay.'

There was nothing else to say. So, clasping the bag of evidence in his fist, Nathan unbolted the garage door and stepped into the fragile morning.

Behind him, Bob slid the bolts shut, one by one. Locking himself inside with the bones.

28

Nathan carried the binbag along the tree-lined street of Victorian bedsitters.

At the corner, it joined a main road. A yellow skip stood outside the gutted shell of a house in the early stages of renovation. The skip was half full of plasterboard and broken bricks and rusty wire frames. It was still early. Nathan leaned in, lifted a piece of plasterboard and wedged the binbag in the bottom corner of the skip. Then he dusted his hands and turned on to the main road.

At the bus stop, he paused to open his Adidas sports bag. He removed the pack of Nurofen Plus and dry-swallowed a handful.

There was a greasy spoon across the road. Nathan half-jogged over to it. His legs were stiff, on the edge of cramp. Inside, there was the sound of frying and hot water jets and local radio. He ordered a full breakfast and a mug of tea and sat down with a copy of yesterday's *Sun*. When the breakfast arrived, he looked at it without conviction. But hunger found him. He ate the breakfast and drained the tea and hoisted his bag on to his shoulder. He left the cafe and caught the bus home.

It was full daylight when he opened the door. The house was quiet. He could smell Holly's perfume in the hallway. A floorboard creaked, the house warming to the new day. He set down his bag by the telephone and stared at the photos on the wall. He could not connect that laughing girl to the cracked remains in Bob's freezer. He reached out, to straighten a frame. But he couldn't touch her. He thought of those rattling teeth, loose in the skull. And those clean limbs, gnawed at by foxes and badgers and local dogs drawn to the scent of rot.

He couldn't go upstairs.

He put the kettle on, and the television. While he waited for the kettle to boil, he sat in the armchair and fell asleep.

In the dream, he awoke. Elise was in the room with him. She didn't say anything. She was on the sofa, legs crossed. She looked at him. He felt a swell of love for her, as he might for a lost child.

He said, 'I'm so sorry.'

Elise said, 'I'm cold,' and then she began to scream.

Nathan woke in the act of wetting himself. The warm–cold stain spread across his crotch and thigh.

He moved to the centre of the room and stood there with his back to the bay window, until his queasily thrashing heart had slowed. He stood there so long that twice he nodded off, his head dropping to his chest. He saw Elise tearing at her hair, hanks of it in her fists.

He jerked awake and sat on the windowsill. The television was meaningless and brash.

He stayed there until 1 p.m. He walked to the kitchen. With every footstep he glanced over his shoulder. Each creak of the house made his heart lurch.

He opened the fridge. Looked at the eggs and the cold meats and the milk and the remains of a chicken, the half-drunk bottle of wine. He closed the fridge door. Got himself a glass of water. He was shivering. He went to the thermostat and turned up the heating.

He was asleep, face down on the dining table, when Holly got home.

Her smile fell.

'My God, are you all right?'

Opening one eye, he said, 'Heavy night.'

He wanted her to lower him into a hot bath, to let the heat seep into his frozen bones that felt like rods of cold steel inside him: he wanted her to wash his hair with her fragrant shampoo, and he wanted her to wrap him in a warm towel, and then he wanted to undress her, her warmth and her softness, and he wanted to smell her and he wanted to make love to her; he wanted to make her pregnant, he wanted to make a little comma of life, something to double and increase in the secret heat, the pink half-light inside her.

'What happened? Where did you go?'

He waved a hand. His fingernails were dirty.

'We went to the pub. And then back to Bob's. It all got a bit out of control. He had some drugs. Some cocaine. We were up all night.'

'It looks like it.'

She went to the kitchen: brisk and businesslike.

'Have you eaten?'

'Yes.'

'Eaten what?'

'I went to a cafe.'

'Are you hungry now?'

'No.'

'Right.'

She slammed the fridge door.

'Holly, I'm sorry.'

'There's no need.'

'I've got this problem.'

She hesitated.

'With cocaine. I'm not an *addict* or anything. But I've got a problem with it.'

'What sort of problem?'

'Saying no. Knowing when to stop. How to stop.'

'You never even mentioned drugs to me.'

'Because I stay away from them. I just – y'know. I was drunk. And my judgement was off. Believe me, I'm paying for it now.'

She looked at him with something like pity. A knot of hope rose in him. Pity was good. He could start at pity and work up.

She said, 'I tried it a couple of times. Cocaine. I didn't like it much. It made my heart all biddy boom.'

He said, 'You're a dark horse.'

'Well. There's a lot about me you don't know.'

'I don't doubt it.'

'Good.'

He lay cold in the dark with his wife asleep beside him. When he cuddled up to her she made a sleepy noise and rolled away.

At some point, he must have slept because he woke in the dark. Holly was raising herself above him. Her hair tickled his face. Her nipples brushed his chest. She was shaking his shoulder.

'Are you all right?'

'Why?'

'You were talking in your sleep.'

A fluorescence of terror.

'What did I say?'

'I don't know. You were mumbling.'

'I'm sorry.'

'I'm worried, that's all.'

'I'm fine.'

'Is it the drugs?'

'Probably.'

'Don't touch them again.'

'No chance.'

'Your feet are *freezing*.'

'I know. It's cold in here.'

'It's *boiling*. It's like somebody turned up the thermostat.'

He'd forgotten about that.

'Anyway,' she said. 'Get some sleep.'

'I'm sorry.'

'Don't be silly.' She turned over. She reached behind her and cupped his flaccid cock and balls in her hand. She gave them a friendly, gentle squeeze, and fell back to sleep.

She phoned her parents and told them Nathan was too fragile for Sunday lunch. So they stayed home and Nathan had a long, very hot bath. With each tick of the clock, it got further behind him. Time – a few more days, weeks, years – would push it inside him like a prolapse.

On Sunday night, as he showered and shaved and cleaned his teeth and laid out tomorrow's work clothes on the bed, he felt something like confidence, almost pleasure. It had been bad. It was still bad. But eventually it would go away.

Sometimes he believed this for minutes at a time. Then he remembered what lay bundled up in the freezer, in Bob's garage, and the chill crept back into him.

Monday morning, he went to work.

Everything was the same: there was reception and there were Fiona and Maude, the receptionists. Here were the pot plants on either side of the lift doors, and here was the same lateral scratch across the door, like a key-vandalized car. And here was the first floor. Take the first turning on the left for the sales department. And here was the same open-plan office with the same furniture and the same computers, smudged with inky fingerprints. Here were the same novelty gonks and teddy bears and amusing mugs and family photographs, and here were the same staff, and here was the same glass-fronted office with the same laptop computer, and here were the same problems, the same cock-ups and blunders and lost orders and pissed-off reps, the same staff complaints and affairs and annual appraisals, the same marketing meetings and board meetings and finance meetings, and here was the same Justin, the same mendacious, pitiful Justin with his too-short trousers and his six-pint lunches and his little breath mints, and this was the calm place the dread had dumped him – this was the place that did not change, and as long as he was here, he was safe.

Two weeks later, Bob called.

29

'Hello,' said Bob.

'Hold on,' said Nathan, cupping the mouthpiece. He leaned over and, with the tips of his fingers, closed the office door.

'How are you? How's the research coming?'

'Not good.'

'You or the research?'

'Both. We've hit a snag.'

'What snag?'

'I can't talk. Can you get over here?'

'As soon as I can.'

He put the phone in its cradle and consulted his diary. He had a meeting at 2.30. He told Angela he was stepping out for an early lunch – it was 11.30 – and he grabbed his coat and made straight for the door. Outside, the taxis weren't biting. He stood for a long time on the corner, hailing cabs that were already occupied. His tie flapped at his shoulder like a flag.

Eventually, a taxi stopped for him. But they hit every red light on the way. It took forty-five minutes.

Bob came to the door scrub-bearded and hollow eyed. Over his jeans and T-shirt, he wore a tatty, dirty pink chenille bathrobe; it looked like a woman's. He smelled bad, like milk left too long on a July windowsill.

Nathan followed him downstairs. The bed-sitting room was yet more shambolic. Improvised ashtrays had been placed on the tables, the bookshelves, the kitchenette, the windowsill, the arms of all three sofas, alongside the computers, the reel-to-reel tape machine. All of them were overflowing.

Nathan said, 'What's wrong?'

Bob lit a cigarette. His hand was shaking.

'I want you to sit down and listen to something.'

Nathan hitched his trousers and sat.

Bob walked to the reel-to-reel. He manually rewound it several inches, saying: 'Now, this is going to be loud. Okay? I'll explain why in a minute.'

'What is it?'

'Just listen.'

Bob pressed *Play*.

He'd hooked the reel-to-reel through to a pair of floor-mounted loudspeakers. From them emanated a painful blast of white noise, like the static on an untuned television turned up to maximum volume. Nathan looked at him in baffled discomfort.

Bob pressed *Stop*.

The silence was sudden and total.

Nathan shifted in his seat. 'What am I supposed to be listening to?'

'You might have to listen a few times. It does that.'

'Listen a few times to what?'

Again, Bob was manually rewinding the machine, saying: 'Try to listen through the background noise.'

Bob pressed *Play* again.

The same abrasive static.

Then, mumbled and indistinct, something like a voice. It was murmured, and very quick. When it was gone, Nathan doubted that he'd even heard it.

Bob stopped the tape.

'You heard it.'

'Heard *what*?'

Bob played the tape again.

On a third listen, there was something behind the white noise, like someone murmuring through a hotel wall.

'Okay,' said Nathan, in the ringing silence that followed. 'What is it? Someone speaking?'

'I don't know about someone *speaking*. But it's a voice.'

Nathan's palms were wet.

'Whose voice?'

'Elise's.'

Nathan laughed. His mouth was numb.

'And what do you think she's saying?'

Bob swallowed.

'I believe she's saying "I'm alive".'

There was a long silence between them.

Nathan said, 'You're mad.'

'It's called EVP,' said Bob. 'Electronic voice phenomena. I've been researching it for years. You run a tape in an empty room. You make sure it's isolated from stray radio broadcasts, yada yada yada, you ask it a question. You go away. You come back, you've got voices on the tape.'

'Whose voice?'

'The dead.'

'Who else?' said Nathan, and began to giggle. He said, 'Jesus Christ, Bob.'

Bob waited until the laughter had passed.

'Play it again,' said Nathan.

Bob played it again.

This time, Nathan heard a clear pattern beneath the shifting, oceanic hiss.

It was the sound of a human voice. It was a woman.

She was saying, 'I'm alive.'

Or perhaps it was 'line five'.

Nathan shouted over the noise, 'It's off the radio or something. It's one of your neighbours. It's somebody walking past the house.'

Bob pressed *Stop*.

'I have eliminated those possibilities.'

'How?'

'Trust me. I know what I'm doing. I've been doing this for twenty years now.'

'And what? This is the first voice you've heard?'

Bob reached under the table and drew out an old blue suitcase, worn white at the corners. He opened it. It was filled with reel-to-reel tapes.

'There are voices on each one of these, sometimes dozens of them. I've also got several hours archived on the hard drives of these computers. They talk all kinds of shit – just like the Ouija board. That's what makes it so fascinating. They sound confused, disconnected. Maybe not even conscious. So no, Nathan, this is not my first voice. But it is the first voice I ever *recognized*.'

Nathan felt something rise inside him. He said, 'You *can't* have recognized it. You only knew her for one night, and that was years ago. Ten years! And you'd been drinking. And taking cocaine.'

'Listen again.'

Nathan didn't want to hear it. But he didn't want to admit that. So he sat through it, once more.

I'm alive

'There's more,' said Bob. 'Wait.'

He fast-forwarded the same tape. Nathan had learned how to filter the static by now, or perhaps to impose order on it. This time, quite distinctly, but as if at a great distance, he heard a woman's voice shouting:

Bob! I'm here!

Nathan stood up.

'Fucking turn it off.'

Bob hit the *Stop* button.

'There's more.'

'I'm not joking. Fucking turn it off.'

'Don't you want to hear what she says?'

'She's not saying anything. It's, I don't know what it is. But one thing I know it's not, it's not Elise. All right. Jesus. Get a fucking *grip*.'

Quietly, Bob said, 'I think you should calm down.'

Nathan's legs were shaking. 'If you put your finger back on that fucking button, I swear to God I'll break it. I fucking promise you, Bob. Don't touch that thing again.'

Bob sighed. He slumped in the office chair.

'Usually there's more than one voice. Sometimes there's three or four. Sometimes half a dozen. Sometimes, there's twenty of them. Twenty distinct voices. They're temperamental and sarcastic. Sometimes they manifest at different speeds. Sometimes they talk gibberish. But on this tape, *this entire tape*, there is only one voice.'

'Shut up,' said Nathan.

'What are we going to do?'

'I'm not joking. Shut the fuck up.'

Bob pressed *Play*. Nathan heard it plainly. A young woman, clear and crisp behind the hiss, like someone shouting from the edge of the sea.

Bob! I'm here!

Nathan waited until he had some control over his voice and said, 'Bob, if you don't get a grip on yourself, this is all going to fall apart. All right?'

'Don't kid yourself.'

'Kid myself what?'

'That it's not her.'

'Fuck you.'

Nathan was running before he reached the bedsit door. He sprinted up the stairs and ran on to the street. And he was panting and wheezing and had a stitch in his side when finally, a long way away, a taxi finally stopped to pick him up, and take him back to work.

He sat through the meeting without making a contribution. When the meeting was over, Justin automatically invited Nathan to an afternoon meeting in the Cricketer's Arms.

Nathan said yes.

They sat in the pub. It was almost empty. A scrawny, prematurely wizened barman with baby-soft hair served them drinks at the table, Justin being a precious slow-time regular. Nathan ordered a double whisky with his lager. When the drinks arrived, he downed the whisky and ordered a second.

Justin laid a hand on his shoulder.

'What's wrong?'

Nathan sipped lager. 'What's the worst thing you've ever done?'

Justin pretended to think. 'I was best man once, for an old school friend. I shagged the bride the night before the wedding.'

'That's pretty bad,' said Nathan, not believing him.

'And I shagged her on the morning of it. She was wearing her bridal underwear, and her dress was all laid out on the bed. The full wedding cake. One of the white ones.'

'Did you get caught?'

'No. You don't want to worry about that. I had the bride's mother the same day, just after the speeches. I didn't really fancy her. It was for the thrill, you know?'

Nathan took a long draught of his beer.

'So, it's possible to do something you regret, and get away with it.'

'If you do it with enough style, nobody will ever know.'

Nathan stared at him with sadness where the incredulity should be. He happened to know that Justin had been impotent for many years. He knew because Justin's wife had used his impotence as a pretext to attempt the seduction of several members of staff – and once, Nathan himself. Two or three of them had obliged her in the back of company Mondeos or in wine-bar toilets. Nathan hadn't.

Justin never got away with anything. He just thought he did. And yet, here he was. Still here, long after he should be gone.

'So,' said Nathan. 'What's your secret?'

'Never sleep with anybody who has less to lose than you do.'

Nathan pondered the wisdom of this, then drained his pint and raised his hand to order another.

Justin said, 'So who is she?'

'Who's who?'

'Your guilty secret.'

'Nobody.'

'You can tell me. You know how good I am at keeping secrets.'

Nathan knew exactly that.

'It's nothing like that.'

'It's always something like that. You wouldn't be human otherwise.'

They stayed in the pub for hours. Justin seemed to think of it as a special occasion and, after the fourth pint, he ordered a bottle of champagne.

He spent a long time talking about office politics. And he kept asking who *she* was. Nathan maintained that *she* was nobody.

When Nathan got home, he was drunk. Holly was watching television in bed. She watched from the corner of her eye as he fell over, trying to get out of his trousers. When he leaned over the bed to kiss her, she turned her face away. She got up to visit the bathroom, and when she came back she was wearing a nightdress.

He woke, as he always did when he'd been drinking, in the early hours of the morning, badly needing to piss. But he lay curled on his side, the duvet clutched over his head, trying to sleep.

In the morning, he said, 'I'm sorry.'

She said 'Fine, whatever,' and stomped downstairs. Halfway down, she paused, saying: 'You could've called.'

'I know. I'm sorry.'

'I don't care what you do. I just want to know that you're okay. I just want to hear your voice.'

Nathan sat on the bed. Yesterday's clothes, reeking of smoke and beer, lay in a pile beside it. He wanted to burn them.

30

In Nathan's pigeonhole that morning was a tatty buff envelope. Because PRIVATE AND CONFIDENTIAL had been scrawled across it in red ink, Angela hadn't opened it for him – she'd placed it on top of his other post, internal and external. Sometimes, people were offended by one of Hermes' cartoonish and lewd greetings cards. The complaints often came in envelopes like this.

He opened the envelope and unfolded the letter inside.

Dear N

Naturally I understand your reaction.

Here are some transcripts of further conversations. At all times, only a single voice (1) appears on the tape. I should reiterate how unusual that is.

Tape 1, Monday, 12 am
Duration: 17 minutes

Bob, I'm here

you bastard (Jew bastard?)

cold here

Tape 1, Monday, 3.40 pm
Duration: 9 minutes

didn't get there

Bob!

Tape 1, Tuesday, 7 pm
Duration: 3 minutes

my eyes

my teeth

Tape 1, Tuesday 11.30 pm
Duration: 1 minute

oh god

horrible

The office door opened. Nathan jumped.

It was Justin. He leaned, cross-armed, in the doorway – working at being rakish and hungover. 'Christ. You look awful.'

Nathan crushed Bob's letter in his fist. 'Cheers.'

'Can't take the pace?' He walked in, closing the door behind him. His perfumy bulk took up much of Nathan's little office and the smell – stale booze and tiny breath mints and too much Issey Miyake – was intimate and revolting, like busy airport toilets. Nathan breathed through his mouth.

Justin said: 'Just like old times.'

'Yep.'

'Before she tied you down.'

'She didn't tie me down.'

'Anyway. We should do it again.'

'Yeah.'

Justin said, 'Cool,' and left the office without bothering to close the door. Nathan leaned over to close it, then called Bob from his desk phone.

'Bob. It's me —'

'Did you get it?'

'Yes, I got it. What the fuck did you think you were *doing*?'

'Did you read it?'

'No,' said Nathan, and glanced through the office window. The new graduate trainee stood, infinitely bored, at the photocopier. Every few seconds, he was scanned by a bar of light.

Then Nathan said, 'Listen, Bob. We've been through a lot of stress, all right? I mean, really a great deal of stress. And stress does funny things. It's dangerous. What you need, you need to get away for a while. Get away for a few days. Book yourself a holiday.'

'Don't patronize me. You're the one who's denying the evidence.'

'Evidence of what? A voice you think you can hear on a blank tape? Jesus Christ, have you got the slightest idea how *mad* that sounds? I mean, even the faintest inkling?'

In the silence that followed, Nathan could hear Bob, breathing through his nostrils, until he said: 'I know about this stuff.'

Nathan wanted to light a cigarette. Instead, he pressed on his temples with his thumb and second finger and spoke very carefully. 'Okay. We're not going to agree about this. We're just not. So answer me one question. What bearing does this have on the rest of – the project?'

'Are you referring to the recovered materials?'

'Yes, I am referring to the recovered materials.'

'Well, obviously it changes everything. We can't just destroy them.'

Nathan stood up so abruptly the telephone lifted from the desk and hung there, spinning on its cord.

'And why not?'

'Because we need to give her a proper burial.'

'And how do you propose to do that?'

'I don't know.'

'Bob, this is totally unacceptable, this is completely unacceptable.'

'It's completely non-negotiable.'

'There's no way I'm doing this.'

'There must be a way. Even if it means we go to prison.'

'I'm afraid I don't see how that would improve the situation.'

'She's *haunting* us. Do you know what that means?'

'What are you talking about?'

'She's lonely. And she's angry. She's really, really angry.'

Incredibly, Bob began to snivel.

Nathan took this in. And said: 'We'll talk about this later. Don't do anything hasty. Please. Promise me that.'

'Fine.'

'Hasty about what?' said Angela, who was standing in the door-way, about to offer him a cup of tea.

Nathan screamed.

31

He and Bob met in the park. They sat on a bench, watching children play. The wind flapped at the tail of Nathan's coat. He was smoking a cigarette.

Nathan said, 'Bob, what you have — what we both have — is a burden of guilt. All right? You've got to face that. You've got to face it head-on, and you've got to deal with it. You've got to get through it.'

'I don't feel guilty. Why should I?'

'Because we both fucked a nineteen-year-old girl who died. And we buried her in secret. We buried her naked and face down in the fucking *woods* with our come still dripping down her legs, and nobody ever found her.'

Bob shrugged again.

'Guilt isn't the problem.'

Nathan stood. 'This is going nowhere.'

'We have to bury her. No choice.'

'I have to get back to work. So let me think about this. Don't make any rash decisions. We'll work this out. Okay?'

'Fine.' Bob stood too, massive hands buried deep in the pockets of his blue-grey overcoat.

'Okay,' said Nathan.

They walked away in different directions.

Even before reaching the park gates, Nathan had called Justin's mobile. They agreed to meet in the Cricketer's in half an hour. By the time Nathan arrived, Justin was on his second pint. He stood, shaking Nathan's hand. He and Justin were always shaking hands; they shook hands half a dozen times a day. It was a ritual they had fallen into, long ago.

There were drinks waiting for him: a double whisky and a pint of lager. Nathan had downed the whisky before unbuttoning his coat.

Justin asked, 'To what do I owe the privilege this time?'

Nathan removed his coat and laid it over the empty stool. His phone rang. He turned it off. He sipped lager.

Justin said, 'I wish you'd tell me what was wrong.'

'Nothing's wrong. Except that, of all the possible best friends in the world, I end up with you.'

'It's not so bad.'

'Nah,' said Nathan. 'It's not so bad.'

He was late home. Holly was waiting. She was pretending to watch television. 'Where have you been?'

'With Justin. Having a beer.'

'Then why did Justin's secretary call to ask where you were?

Apparently there was some kind of presentation. Someone called Steve Jackson had to do it for you. There's been a bit of a fuss around the office.'

Nathan slumped in the chair.

'Fuck. I forgot.'

'Where were you?'

'With Justin.'

'Well. That's what I said to Miriam: "He's probably with Justin." But she told me Justin was in a meeting.'

'It's her *job* to say that. She says it a hundred and fifty times a day. It's never true.'

'I've got no reason to disbelieve her.'

'You have every reason to disbelieve her. She's Justin's PA. Her job is to lie.'

'Apparently you had your phone turned off.'

'That's true enough.'

'That's not like you.'

'No.'

'Are you seeing someone?'

'Excuse me?'

'Are you having an affair?'

He wanted to stand in indignation, but he was far, far too tired.

'You should know better than to ask that.'

'What am I supposed to think? You're like a different person.'

'I'm sorry.'

'If you're not seeing someone, then what is it?'

'I can't explain.'

'Is it Bob?'

'No. Why?'

'Because you haven't been yourself from the minute he came round that night. Right from the minute.'

What could he say? She was right.

She said, 'I'm going to bed.'

'Me, too.'

'Whatever.'

He followed at her heel. Trying to minimize at least the physical distance between them.

32

In the morning, having gone to some effort to look and act less hungover than he felt, he told Holly, 'I'm going to see Brian.'

Brian was their family doctor; he was one of Graham's domino-playing cronies.

She said, 'Good.'

Nathan knew Brian socially – they'd spoken at various fetes and barbecues and New Year's Eve parties. It was to Brian that Nathan and Holly had gone, when first trying to conceive. So he was able to book an appointment for that afternoon.

Brian was petite and aquiline and dapper – sixty-three and unmarried.

Nathan liked Brian – they often gravitated to one another at parties. Nathan thought they recognized a secret in each other – although Nathan supposed his secret was not what Brian imagined.

Now Nathan described to Brian his anxiety, his inability to sleep.

'But I don't want anti-depressants. They don't work. I'll get through it without them. All I need is sleep. Just a few good nights' sleep, and it'll be okay.'

Brian wrote Nathan a prescription for three months' supply of temazepam, telling him: 'Everyone has their ups and downs. You've probably been working too hard. I've seen it all before, more times than I can count. You need to slow down, take some time out. Graham and June are always telling me how hard you're working.'

'You're probably right.'

'Come back and see me, if you need to.'

'I will. I will. But I'm sure I'll be fine.'

He stood outside Oakley's the Chemist while the pharmacist prepared his prescription. Wandering up and down the pavement like a polar bear in a zoo enclosure, he called Bob. Who said, 'How are you?'

'Tired. We need to talk again. Can we meet tonight? In the Plough?'

'I can be there at eight?'

'I'll see you then.'

Nathan pocketed the phone, went in to Oakley's to collect his prescription, then drove back to work. On the way, he stopped off at Travis Perkins, building suppliers, where he bought a pair of heavy-duty bolt cutters.

The man behind the counter looked at Nathan in his suit and his good tie and his haircut, buying bolt cutters. Nathan smiled tightly and walked out, dangling the bolt cutters in his fist by one long handle.

He called Holly from the office.

She said, 'How are you?'

'Tired.'

'How did it go with Brian?'

'Good. He says I've been working too hard.'

'Well, we know that's true.'

'He offered me something. To help me sleep.'

'What?'

'Temazepam. But I've kept the prescription. I don't think I need it.'

'That's good. It's good to hear you say that.'

'I'm going to be fine.'

'I know.'

'And so are we.'

'I know.'

He took a breath and said, 'I'll be late tonight.'

A moment of silence on the line. 'Where will you be?'

'Look. You're right. Part of it is this bloke, Bob. He's been on my back. He's unhappy, he's got no friends. He's really needy. You know what I mean.'

She said nothing, which meant she did.

'Well, it's too much,' said Nathan. 'I feel sorry for him and every-thing, but I'm sick of it. I hardly even *know* him. So tonight, I'm going to tell him: I've got my own problems, leave me alone.'

Now he could hear her smiling as she said, 'Okay.'

'I'll see you later,' he said. 'Don't wait up.'

At 7.45, he called Bob.

'Hello?' said Bob.

'Where are you?'

'Why?'

'Noise in the background.'

'I'm in the pub.'

'Okay. Good. Look, I've got an issue at work. I'm stuck in the office. I'll be fifteen, twenty minutes late. Is that a problem?'

'No problem.'

'Then I'll see you about quarter past.'

He terminated the call and turned off the phone, placing it in the glove compartment.

He wasn't really at work. He was parked outside Bob's lock-up garage.

He waited until the street was empty, then got out of the car – his coat slung over his forearm – and went to the boot. He took out the bolt cutters and slipped them under the coat, then slammed the boot closed. He walked to the garage door. He looked left and right, then applied the cold beak of the bolt cutters to the padlock chain. He gripped the long handles in his fists and leaned into them with all his weight.

It was harder than he expected, much harder than they made it look on television. He was sweating when the chain finally gave, and there was a band of pain across his chest and under his armpit and across his guts.

He edged into the garage and turned on the lights. He closed the door behind him and slid the bolts closed. The Audi wasn't there: Bob had sold it. He'd yet to buy another car and the garage was weirdly empty, except for the old Workmate and the utilitarian shelving and the rusty, humming freezer. It smelled of damp concrete and spilled oil and old exhaust.

He examined the freezer. At the rear, it was connected to the breeze-block wall by thick, dusty cobwebs. Nathan took a moment, then employed the bolt cutters to the small padlock on the freezer lid: they took it apart with comparative ease.

Nathan lifted the freezer lid. Its cold exhalation chilled the sweat on his face and the front of his shirt. He lifted aside the baskets of frozen peas and sweetcorn, setting them carefully on the floor.

He wondered if there was time to burn Elise's clothing before his meeting with Bob. The bones he could pulverize, then soak in quicklime: it was the semen-steeped clothing, those fungal rags, that presented the biggest threat.

Nathan leaned deep into the freezer.

But the taped-up plastic parcel was not there.

The bones and the clothes had gone. Bob had moved them.

33

He left the garage door hanging open like a broken limb; perhaps Bob would suspect local kids of breaking in. He threw the bolt cutters into the thick bushes and walked back to the car. He started the engine then spun the wheels up to 60 miles an hour, screeching to a halt at the lights. He tapped the steering wheel, waiting for people to cross the road.

Pulling away, he drove less aggressively. He didn't want to get arrested. He drove around the corner to Bob's flat and parked outside, across the road. Then he walked to the pub.

Outside, he paused to straighten his tie. Then he walked into its familiar fug, convincingly flustered and breathless.

Bob was hunched over a table, reading *The Times*.

Nathan sat down, saying, 'Blimey.'

He loosened his tie.

'Fuck have you been?'

'I've got a *life*, Bob. I've got a mortgage to pay.'

Bob nodded at a pint of lager sitting on the table opposite him. 'I got them in.'

Nathan watched bubbles unlatch themselves from the base of the lager glass, leaping for the unknown surface. He took a sip. He wanted to smash the pint glass on the edge of the table and grind the remains into Bob's face.

He said, 'Look. We can't talk here. Let's go back to your place.'

'I thought my place scared you.'

'Not at all.'

Bob grinned, knowing the lie.

'Shall we finish these?'

'Fine,' said Nathan, and downed his pint in seven or eight gulps.

Bob watched him, then raised his glass.

'One more. Same again. Your round.'

So Nathan got them in.

After the pub, they stopped off at an off-licence. Nathan bought a bottle of whisky, eight cans of Guinness, cigarettes. Then he and Bob trudged home.

They paused in the stone doorway of the Victorian mansion block, overgrown with weeds and wet, black trees. Bob dangled his house keys from an index finger: made them dance.

'Are you sure?'

'About what?'

'Going inside.'

Nathan tutted and followed Bob into the mouldy, darkened hall-way. The light was on a timer; halfway down to Bob's flat, it turned off. Nathan and Bob stood while their eyes adapted to the sudden dark. Sounds of their breathing, the clinking of the whisky bottle in the carrier bags.

Bob went down. He found his keys and opened the door. Pale

light sneaked into the stairwell. Nathan went down, into the bedsit.

He walked straight to the kitchenette and broke the seal on the bottle of Macallans.

Bob told him, 'Use water. I finished the ice.'

So Nathan poured whisky into two cloudy tumblers. Topped them up with a dash of water from the tap.

They sat down.

Bob nursed his glass. 'Can you feel her?'

Nathan said, 'No.' Swirling the whisky, he said: 'For years after it happened, I thought she was there. But she wasn't, Bob.'

Bob drained his drink and stumbled to the kitchenette to pour himself another, no water. He wandered back to his seat, clutching the bottle. He looked blue-jowled and exhausted.

Nathan glanced at the reel-to-reel tape recorder and said, 'You're going through exactly what I went through. You're just going through it a bit *later*, that's all. You were able to cope with . . .'

His voice fell. He was too aware of the way it echoed from the low ceiling.

'. . . you were able to cope with it first time round. I don't know the proper word for it, the doctor's word for it. But you *buried* it. Do you know what I mean? You buried it. And now it's all bubbling to the surface.'

'To haunt me.'

'Yeah.'

'So, it's all in my mind?'

'It's all in your mind.'

Nathan watched Bob struggling to light a cigarette, then went to examine the books, as if it were a CD collection. *Breakthrough! Life After Death: the Truth. Whispers From Beyond. Grave Secrets.*

'I thought you'd've given this stuff up years ago.'

Bob grinned secretly into his glass.

'No.'

Someone whispered into Nathan's ear.

He stepped away from the bookshelves, away from the reel-to-reel recording machine.

'What does that mean – *no*?'

Bob's smile widened into a grin, and the grin widened into a leer.

'Come on.'

Nathan had a feeling in his stomach.

'What?'

'The dark woods,' said Bob. 'The running water. Lovers' lane.'

'Bob, I'm not sure what you're telling me here.'

'The thing about ghosts; you go looking for one, you're already contaminating the data – by looking here and not there, choosing this site over that one. You're not being objective.'

'Ghosts aren't real, Bob. They don't exist.'

'One of your most common forms of haunting, it's actually the roadside ghost. In England, anyway. Usually it's the shade of a young woman. She died violently, after sex. She's been buried on unhallowed ground. Usually between a road and a river.'

The strength drained from Nathan's legs.

Bob was saying: 'For years, I thought I'd cocked it up. I used to scan the papers, to see if something had been reported by the roadway. Phantom hitch-hiker. Anything like that. I used to drive down the lane – twice a week, in the early days. But there was nothing.'

'I don't think I understand what you're saying.'

'I thought she'd haunt the woods.'

'Who?'

'But it was us. She stayed with us.'

'Bob, what did you *do*?'

They stayed like that for a while. Until Bob said: 'I was trying to make a ghost.'

Nathan dropped his glass.

It rolled on the carpet. Its base described an arc. Nathan and Bob fixed their eyes on it and watched until it had stopped.

34

Nathan wanted to laugh.

Then he wanted to cry.

He ran his hands through his hair. His hair stuck up.

He said: 'You know you're mad. You do know that? There's something wrong with you. In here . . .' He tapped his head. 'You're all wrong. Jesus. You're fucked in the head.'

For a passing moment, Nathan felt eight years old and helpless. He said: 'What have you done to me?'

He went to the kitchenette and slid open the cutlery drawer. He itemized the contents: forks, spoons. Knives.

Bob turned slow eyes upon him.

Nathan closed the cutlery drawer and poured off a dirty glass of clean water. While draining it, he turned briefly to follow Bob's eyeline. In the far corner, near the rotting velveteen drapes, stood a heavy-duty combination safe. It was green, and flecked with dull metallic chips.

Nathan tugged at his lower lip and muttered, 'Sweet Jesus Christ.'

And he stood there, blinking rapidly. He did not want to cry.

He looked up at the ceiling. He could hear furtive movement up there: scratching. The neighbours, perhaps, or rats.

'You said she had a *fit*.'

Bob shrugged, red-eyed.

'Sorry.'

'How did you . . .?'

Bob held up his hands. Flexed them.

Nathan was still looking at the ceiling. The machinery in his head was running out of control.

The weak overhead bulb flickered three times. The darkness stuttered around them.

Nathan said: 'I didn't know.'

He wasn't talking to Bob; but Bob was watching.

Bob said, 'She's haunting us.'

'No she's not.'

'She should be at the roadside, close to where she's buried. That's what road ghosts do. But I woke up, and there she was. In my room. Next to my bed. Just standing there and hating me. She's here now. Can you feel her?'

'No.'

'Liar.'

'You're delusional. It's not real.'

'You've seen her.'

'No.'

'Yes.'

'No. It's not real.'

Bob said, 'Second drawer down. Near the bottom.'

Nathan took a moment to work out what Bob was saying. Then

he opened the middle kitchen drawer and rooted around. Beneath carrier bags, broken corkscrews, dead biros and stray 9-volt batteries, he found a note that had been printed and laminated on A4 paper: *These are the remains of Elise Fox, who died an unnatural death. We commend her into your care and wish her peace.*

Bob let him scan it two or three times, then said, 'I did it in an Internet cafe. You might want to think about washing your fingerprints off it, though. Use Fairy Liquid and a sponge.'

'And what do you want to do with it?'

'We drive her to a church.'

'We can't just dump her.'

'That's my point. We're not. A church is hallowed ground. If we're careful, nobody ever knows. Not Holly. Not anybody. And soon after that, it's done and dusted. Elise is gone. Out of your life. Me, too.'

'It's not real, Bob. It's not real.'

'Tonight.'

'Not tonight.'

'Yes tonight. I'm ready.'

'We've been drinking.'

'Exactly.'

'So let's not do something careless.'

'I have to make her leave. I have to do that.'

'It's not real.'

'She's here.'

'Nothing's here. She's dead.'

'Both of us did this. Both of us put it right. That's the way it works. Both of us put it right – or it just goes on and on.'

He scrubbed at his face with dry hands.

Then he said: 'Having her with you. Every minute of every day. It's horrible.'

Nathan began to shiver. He wasn't cold.

He said, 'Tomorrow.'

'Tomorrow.'

'Tomorrow.'

Nathan walked to the door. He could feel the foul bedsit behind him; its filth and its corruption. He opened the door and hesitated there – looking up at the long, dark stairwell.

Then he reached out and hit the timer switch and raced the light all the way upstairs and out, into the cold unsoiled night.

35

Nathan was on his knees before the lavatory, shaking like a sick dog.

Holly walked in. She was topless in silky pyjama trousers. On them was a design: swallows and brambles and delicate spring flowers. Her hair was a mess. It was 6 a.m.

She sat on the edge of the bath, gripping the sides. Waiting for Nathan to pull the flush, then turn and sit on the tiled floor, his back to the cold porcelain lavatory.

He said, 'Did I wake you?'

'Is it the drinking?'

'No.'

'Are you ill?'

'No.'

She softened. 'Then what is it?'

'I don't know. Stress.'

She reached out a bare foot and gave him a friendly nudge. He took the foot in his hand. He would have kissed its soft and tender sole, had his mouth not been so rancid.

She said, 'Don't, my nails need doing.'

'Your nails are fine.'

She crossed her legs, still sitting on the edge of the bath, and lifted one foot so it was inches from her face. Quickly and efficiently, she inspected her nail varnish, toe by toe, then let go of her foot.

She said, 'You're a mess, aren't you? And nobody knows. Nobody knows what kind of mess you are, not even me.'

'That's not true.'

'Look at you.'

'I'm fine.'

'Right.'

'Really.'

'Are you going to tell me?'

'Tell you what?'

'What it is.'

'Yes.'

'Today? Now?'

'I can't.'

'I'm your wife.'

'I know.'

'I'm your friend.'

'I know.'

'You don't think you sleep. But you do. You make noises.'

'I'm sorry. I don't mean to.'

'Don't be sorry. What is it? What are you dreaming about?'

'I'll tell you.'

'When?'

'When I've sorted it.'

'When will that be?'

'Soon. Today.'

She considered it. 'Or we could take a day off,' she said. 'Catch a film. Go to London. Go to the zoo, maybe. Take a day trip. Go to the beach.'

He began to cry, because she was scared.

He sobbed into his knees. He said, 'I'm so sorry, I'm so sorry.'

She climbed down from the edge of the bath and hugged him. Her breasts squashed against him. Her sleep-breath was sweet to him, the musk of her that was like no one else. His tears made wet the soft skin of her shoulder, the fine strong clavicle.

She rocked him, saying, 'Don't be sorry. Don't be sorry. Don't be sorry.'

Nathan took the morning off. He and Bob met in the village of Woolhope Ashbury. They walked through the little high street. The people around them were elderly, slow, retired.

At the edge of the village stood a Norman church: grey stone, simple geometries. Nathan and Bob wandered the graveyard. The stones leaned at crazy angles, green with lichen and rubbed smooth. All the names had gone from them. They wandered around like amateur local historians.

Nathan muttered, 'Do we even know she was Christian?'

'Doesn't matter.'

'It seems to matter to you.'

'Not at all. Look at that.'

He was pointing to a yew tree that stood in one corner of the churchyard. It was an old and hideous thing. Four people, linking arms, could not have encompassed its girth.

'That tree's a thousand years old. And there would've been another tree, a thousand years old, on the same ground, before it. This church was built on ground sacred to the Druids. It's not the church which is sacred. It's the earth itself. You can feel it. It's like electricity.'

Nathan didn't feel anything, except thirsty.

Bob said, 'It's the ground that sanctifies the building. Not the other way round.'

'Fine. So we come here. In your car, not mine.'

'Why mine?'

'Company car. I can't get rid of it.'

'Fair enough. We'll bring mine.'

'So we leave Elise. Leave the note—'

Bob pointed to the nailed and banded double doors, restored in the nineteenth century and now polished with time.

'Right there.'

'And then it's done?'

'I hope so.'

On the way to work, Nathan called Jacki Hadley.

'Nathan? What is it? Is it Holly?'

'No. No, it's not Holly.'

'Is she okay?'

'She's fine. She doesn't even know I'm calling.'

'Okay.'

'Can we talk?'

He met her in a coppers' pub not far from the station. A few thick-set men sat at the bar. A fruit machine flashed in the far corner. Nathan got the drinks – two Cokes with ice and a limp slice of lemon.

'So,' Jacki said. 'What's going on?'

'What's going on. I told you a lie.'

'What sort of lie?'

'When you questioned me.'

'About what?'

'Elise.'

Before his eyes, she became a police officer.

She waited.

Eventually, Nathan said, 'Bob Morrow and I – Bob Morrow's the man I was with—'

'That night. I remember.'

'Well. The statement I made. It wasn't completely true.'

'In what way?'

'Well . . .'

'Go on. It's all right.'

'Well, I said I'd stormed out of the party—'

'Because you'd seen your girlfriend dirty dancing with Mark Derbyshire and got jealous. Your girlfriend being Sarah Reed.'

'*Sara*. You remember this stuff?'

'I remember this stuff.'

'Anyway. So that's true enough: I saw Sara flirting with Mark, and I stormed off. I mean, I hated the bloke. Really hated him.'

'And . . .?'

'I told the police that Bob was driving home when he saw me by the side of the road. I was trying to walk into Sutton Down to find a minicab.'

He made a scoffing noise at that, because in truth Sutton Down was the last place in the world to find such a thing.

Jacki said, 'So Bob pulls over, picks you up. You have a chat, love and life. He drives you back to the party. You have an argument with Sarah—'

'Sara.'

'You try to hit Mark Derbyshire. You fall on your arse. Bob picks you up and drives you all the way home. So that's not true?'

'Well, it's kind of true.'

'How true?'

'It's essentially true. Bob did see me by the side of the road. He did pull over. We did a few lines, had a chat.'

'Love and life.'

'Love and life.'

'But . . .?'

'But when he saw me, he wasn't headed away from the party. He was heading back towards it.'

She took this in.

'Where did he say he'd been?'

'Into town. To score.'

'To buy drugs?'

'Cocaine.'

'And had he?'

'He had loads of it. Five, six grammes. The most coke I'd ever seen. And now he was headed back to the party. He was pretty wired. Like, gibbering. Off his trolley.'

'And why didn't you mention this before?'

'He asked me not to. Kind of begged me.'

At the far end of the bar, the group of coppers suddenly laughed at something. Jacki glanced their way – as if she'd heard what they were saying and didn't like it. Then she turned back to face Nathan.

'And from the infinite kindness of your heart, you said okay.'

'Look, when Elise – when this thing happened, Bob called me.'

'When is this?'

'On the Sunday, the Monday maybe.'

'Go on.'

'We talked about being interviewed – we thought everyone at the party would be. So we knew the drug thing would maybe come out. But Bob's got a conviction, apparently. Intent to supply. Selling a bit of weed when he was a kid, funding his degree.'

'So you agreed to say the cocaine was yours.'

'I didn't want to see the poor bastard go down. And – well, Mark Derbyshire was all over the newspapers. I thought you had your man. We all thought you had your man. It didn't occur to me. Not in a million years.'

'And why are you telling me this now?'

'It's probably nothing.'

'If you thought that, you wouldn't be here.'

'Okay.'

He tried not to blurt it out – he wanted Jacki to think him reluctant. He said, 'After that night, I didn't really see Bob Morrow again. I didn't want to, to be honest. He kind of gave me the creeps.'

'In what way?'

'I don't know. I couldn't put my finger on it. He was just – *not right*, y'know. Just not right. And anyway, after the party – after Elise and the rest of it – I lost my job.'

'Because of the Mark Derbyshire thing.'

'Yeah. Plus, Sara and I split up. I had nowhere to live. I just wanted to forget about the whole thing. The entire night was a disaster. You know what I'm saying?'

She said she knew.

'So then, a few weeks back, Bob Morrow turns up at my door. I don't even know how he got my address.'

'What did he want?'

'Well, this is it. He said he didn't want anything. He said it would be nice to catch up, go for a drink.'

'And you hardly know him?'

'I don't know him at all. We were just at this party together. But now he says he's split up with some girlfriend, he's a free man. You know how it is. So I'm thinking, fuck, what do I do? I want rid of him. If anything, he's worse now than he was then. He smells a bit. I'm not sure if he's working. He says he's a research assistant at the university, but he never seems to be there.'

'So?'

'So, anyway. We go for a drink. And after a couple of pints – where have we been, what've we been doing – he starts to ask about the worst thing I'd ever done.'

He paused, to take a long sip of Coke. He wanted a proper drink, but he also wanted to impress Jacki with his considered sobriety.

'I said – oh, I don't even know what I said. Stealing from my friend's stash of porn mags when I was a kid. *Club* Celebrity Edition, 1979. It had Victoria Principal in it.'

Jacki smiled and nodded. But the smile did not belong to Jacki. It belonged to the police officer who was interviewing him.

Nathan said, 'Anyway. So then, Bob starts talking about Elise.'

'Elise Fox?'

'Yes, Elise Fox. What other Elise is there?'

'Keep it down. What did he say?'

'Do I ever think about her? Do I ever dream about her?'

'And what did you say?'

'I said, who wouldn't? I never even met her, but she changed my entire life.'

'Did you tell him about Holly?'

'God, no.'

'Why not?'

'He was giving me the *creeps*. I kept trying to change the subject. But he kept getting back on to it. Asking if I believe in ghosts.'

'In *ghosts*?'

'In ghosts.'

'And have you seen him since?'

'A couple of times.'

'And?'

'More of the same. He's, like, really depressed. Drinking heavily. Absolutely fixated on Elise. I kind of convinced myself he was just a weirdo. Maybe things had gone wrong for him too — after the party. And he'd been stuck there ever since. Does that sound stupid?'

'Not at all. Do you still think that?'

'No.'

'Why not?'

'Look, I don't know about this sort of thing. But I started thinking about it. Bob coming back — from wherever he'd been. It seemed so unimportant back then. But now. Jesus. I don't know. Do you think — y'know?'

She didn't answer.

He said, 'I feel embarrassed, talking about this.'

Outside, a bus went past.

Jacki said, 'Are you sure you know what you're doing here?'

'Absolutely not, no.'

'You're setting wheels in motion. They grind slow at first, but once they're going, there's no way of stopping them. If — *if* — it should ever happen that Bob Morrow was charged with something, then the lies in your statement will be important. That means Holly will find out you were at Mark Derbyshire's party. Can you deal with that?'

'What else can I do?'

'I told you this would come back to haunt you. I told you that years ago.'

'What can I say? You were right.'

She took his hand and squeezed it, once, then let go.

'You got plans to see him again?'

'Tonight.'

'Then see him.'

'I don't know if I can.'

'You have to.'

'Do I have to wear a *wire* or something?'

She laughed at that, with more pity than scorn. 'I'm just – I don't know. I need to think about this. I need to check Bob Morrow's form and go over his statement. Probably there's nothing in all this. Almost certainly there's nothing in it. But if there is – big *if* – then I don't want him freaked out because you haven't shown up. So see him tonight. Make your excuses, leave early. But see him. We'll talk tomorrow.'

'I don't know if I can be in the same room as him.'

'You have to be. For Holly. In case there's something to this.'

Before leaving the pub, she shook his hand.

At the wheel of his car, he had an anxiety attack. He thought he was dying. He grabbed the steering wheel. He pulled over, on to a double-yellow line, and listened to the radio until it had passed.

At work, he splashed cold water on his face then went to attend his scheduled meeting. Secret talks were being held about changing distributors.

Secret talks were held about changing distributor once a year. Most of the personnel involved, including Nathan, pretended not to notice this.

After the meeting, Justin shook Nathan's hand and told him how well he'd done. Nathan said they should go for a drink, sometime soon.

In the late afternoon, there was a marketing meeting pre-meeting. He got through it, and later in the afternoon he dealt with a couple of difficult customer calls. At 6.15, he checked he had everything. He said goodbye to everyone in the office – he didn't know why, they only did that at Christmas. Then he went to get his car.

36

He parked outside Bob's house. He sat at the wheel, wondering if he could go through with it. On the radio, they were playing songs from the 1980s – Rick Astley, Mel & Kim. It was stuff he'd despised at the time, but now it filled him with acute and painful nostalgia. He wondered how he'd come to be here, in this car, tonight. He listened to the beginning of the 7 p.m. news bulletin. He looked at his wristwatch.

At best, his timings were approximate. At worst, they were arbitrary. Justin would have called what Nathan was doing 'winging it'.

Bob answered the door. He'd shaved, but his hair was a tangled mess, greasy at the scalp.

Clutching his briefcase, Nathan allowed himself to be led inside. He trudged down the hallway in Bob's heavy, flat-footed wake, saying, 'Have you even left the house recently?'

'To get milk. Why?'

'You need some fresh air, mate.'

Bob snorted like a bull, and they went downstairs.

The bedsit was different. All the clutter had been pushed to the edges. So had most of the furniture. The carpet had been ripped up and dumped, half-rolled and folded, in the kitchenette. Bob had taken up the grey underlay. Patches of it still adhered to the concrete floor. On the concrete, Bob had drawn a large chalk circle. Outside the circle he'd etched a series of glyphs. They were elaborate, possibly zodiacal. Into the circle he'd moved a sofa and the television.

Nathan said, 'What the fuck is this?'

'It's protective.'

'Do I have to do anything, before I can step into it?'

Bob contemplated Nathan as if he were an idiot.

'No.'

'Okay.'

Nathan opened his briefcase, taking out a bottle of Laphroaig. 'Drink?'

'We need a clear head.'

He showed the bottle to Bob.

'This is fifteen years old.'

Bob considered it.

Nathan said, 'I can't do this without a drink, Bob. So please yourself.'

He walked to the counter. Earlier that day, he'd dissolved thirty caplets of temazepam in the whisky. Then he'd gone to a great deal of effort to hand-solder the bottle's metal seal, working on his knees in the front seat of his car. He now saw the job was not a good one: small globs of solder were visible at the joins. But he wanted Bob to hear the faint crack as the seal broke, so he turned to face him as he opened it, like people do when opening champagne.

'Ice?'

'There's no ice.'

Nathan poured Bob a tumbler, topping it up with a dribble from the tap. Then he poured himself a tiny measure. He filled the glass to the brim with water.

He stepped into the circle and passed Bob the glass.

'Cheers.'

Bob downed half the drink. He was surly and red-eyed. Nathan took the tiniest sip possible. He held it in his mouth. When Bob looked away, he spat it back.

'This tastes weird.'

'It's the peat. It's a very peaty whisky.'

Bob swirled the dregs in the bottom of the tumbler.

'It's got an aftertaste.'

'It's fifteen years old.'

'Whatever.'

Once again, Nathan spat back into his whisky as Bob drained his drink and set down the glass.

'Right. Let's get this over with.'

He walked over to the filthy bed. Stooped down and rooted around underneath. From underneath, he dragged an old Samsonite suitcase.

'You're going to put her in a suitcase?'

'What do you suggest?'

Nathan couldn't think of anything. A suitcase was the least suspicious thing in the world.

He shifted his weight a little and fished in his pocket, making sure the latex gloves were there, balled up. He took out his pack of cigarettes. It was empty.

'I'm out of cigarettes.'

'Smoke mine.'

'I'll be back in five minutes.'

'We need to do this.'

'I can't do it without cigarettes.'

'Fine. Whatever. Hurry the fuck up.'

'Five minutes.'

'*Okay*. Whatever.'

'Lend me your keys?'

'Leave the door on the latch.'

Nathan clenched his teeth. Then he made his fists relax.

'Fair enough. See you in a minute.'

He walked upstairs. He left the front door on the latch. At the gate, he lost control. He began to shake.

He sat on the low wall until it had passed.

He walked to the corner shop. He fought the urge to hurry, even to run. It made his legs hurt.

He wondered how he'd ever get hold of the keys.

At the corner shop, he bought two packs of Marlboro Lights. He noticed the security camera, in the corner above the counter. A small monitor showed him in black and white, foreshortened. It exaggerated his little bald patch. He hoped the shopkeeper erased the videotapes overnight.

Outside the shop, he lit a cigarette and walked back to Bob's, as slowly as he could make himself – to allow the temazepam to work, its effects greatly amplified by the alcohol. It was a cold night. He was sweating.

The door was still on the latch. He closed it properly, then walked through, and down to the bedsit.

He walked in and closed the door.

Inside the flat, Bob was on the sofa. The suitcase was open at his feet. He was finishing another drink, and reading the laminated note.

'About time.'

'Sorry.'

Holding the note by the edges, Bob polished it clean of fingerprints then placed it, without ceremony, in the open suitcase.

Then he said, 'Why did you break into the garage?'

'I thought you hadn't left the house.'

'I knew you'd do it.'

'What can I say?'

'How can you be unconvinced? She's here. Right now. In this room.'

'I know she is.'

He threw Bob a cigarette. Bob went to catch it. Missed. He fumbled for it, almost fell from his chair.

'Jesus,' he said. 'What do they put in this stuff?'

'It's fifteen years old.'

Nathan glanced at his watch. It was 7.40. He thought of the cold layer of air that blankets a river at night.

'In a way,' he said. 'I suppose I should be thanking you.'

'For what?'

'For my life.'

Bob's face went sour with derision.

'I'm not joking,' said Nathan. 'I like my life. And it would never have happened, if you hadn't . . .' He couldn't say it. 'If you hadn't done what you did.'

Bob saluted him with the glass. 'Good for you.'

'And I've been thinking. The thing about the afterlife: if there is one, we all end up there, sooner or later. And if there isn't, what's the difference? We'll never know.' He gestured at the volumes in Bob's clammy, swollen library. 'So what's the point of all this? What's the point of wasting your life on death?'

'What's the point of anything?'

'Life is the point.'

Bob was sleepy like a lion. He stared at the glyphs on the floor, into the open suitcase. The laminated note. Nathan watched him for a long time.

Then he said, 'Bob?'

Bob was shocked, as if he'd forgotten Nathan was there. He stared him full in the face for a few moments, as if trying to place him.

He said, 'Right,' and tried to stand.

But he couldn't stand. He fell back, on to the sofa.

Nathan looked at his watch.

Then he took the latex gloves from his pocket. He'd bought them in a box from the chemist. He snapped them on. There were two little puffs of talcum at his wrist. He removed from his pocket a blister pack of temazepam and began to pop the little maroon jelly beans into his palm, one by one.

He walked into the circle. His air of purpose made Bob try to rise. But he fell back again, looking befuddled, as if he'd misplaced something.

Nathan pushed him deep into the sofa.

Bob said, 'What are you doing?'

He sounded disconnected and confused, like one of the voices on his tape.

Nathan put his hands round Bob's throat.

Bob grabbed Nathan's wrists. He wrenched and tore at them.

They struggled for a while. Bob was a powerful man, but the

strength was leaving him. He was breathing through his teeth. He made exerted, snivelling sounds.

Nathan dug a thumb into Bob's eye.

Bob opened his mouth to scream.

Nathan crammed a handful of temazepam into Bob's mouth.

Then locked an elbow around Bob's throat. Bob wouldn't close his mouth. The flexing of his tongue forced a few pills to rain down on the sofa, bouncing on the hexed concrete floor.

Nathan hit Bob's jaw with the heel of his hand. There was a loud click.

There was blood on Bob's lips. But he wouldn't swallow. His face was a deep plum; a broad delta of veins on his forehead.

Nathan pinched Bob's nostrils.

Bob struggled. He bucked and thrashed, but weakly, like someone dreaming.

He made panic noises, whimpers, deep in the back of his throat.

He tried to stand.

Nathan bore down on him. The sharp smell of green tomatoes and cigarettes and stale clothing. Bob's skin and bristles and hair in his face.

Eventually, Bob swallowed.

Then gasped at the ceiling like a drowning man. 'Oh Jesus, what are you doing?'

Nathan picked up the spilled temazepam, as many as he could find, and crammed them again into Bob's mouth. There was a lot of dark blood in there – and something brighter red. Bob had bitten off the tip of his tongue.

Nathan squatted, putting his face close to Bob's. Bob's eyes were hooded and heavy. The hot whisky breath, harsh and slow, like a tranquillized animal.

Nathan glanced into the corner.

Then he stepped outside the circle.

He went to Bob's computers. He removed the tape from the reel-to-reel recorder. It was a fiddly job and his fingers were clumsy. He slipped the tape into his briefcase.

He returned to Bob, taking the empty blister packs from his pocket. He closed them in Bob's fist. Then he opened Bob's fist and removed the blister packs, tossing them in the kitchen drawer.

By now it was 8.15.

He'd told Jacki he planned to meet Bob at 8.30. Fifteen minutes to go, and Bob was still alive. From his throat emanated an unpleasant wheezing.

Nathan couldn't phone Jacki much later than 8.30. She knew him to be a punctual man. It was his salesman's training.

He said 'Fuck' and laid an ear against Bob's chest. It rose and fell, like low tide lapping at a sea wall. Nathan wished he'd done some proper research. Winging it like Justin just wasn't his way.

He held his breath, like a man about to dive, and slipped his hand into Bob's greasy pocket. He fished round. He could feel the soft, firm undulations of Bob's cock and balls.

The keys weren't there. He looked at his watch. He went to the sink and poured a glass of water. He tried not to panic. He counted down from twenty. Then he went to Bob's overcoat, hung behind the door, and searched its pockets. The keys were not there either.

He began to search the flat. In minutes, his determination to be methodical had dissolved. He raced up and down, looking behind books, in kitchen drawers, under the bed. He searched beneath computer keyboards. He searched in the bathroom, in the cistern, the medicine cabinet. He checked the back of the sofas and between the sofa cushions. He re-checked the places he'd already checked. He stopped, infuriated. He looked at his watch.

It was 9.05.

Then he noticed the corner of Bob's briefcase. It was half-hidden by the hastily rolled-up, torn underlay that had been stuffed beneath the lowest bookshelf, the one that ran the length of the longest wall, next to the greying, disordered bed. Nathan ran to it. He waited, made himself calm; it would do him no good to empty the briefcase in haste. He went slowly. There were papers in there; Bic pens and two broken halves of a safety ruler. A pair of leather gloves. Buried in one corner were Bob's keys. The key to the safe, bigger and heavier, hung upon it.

Nathan went to Bob.

Bob wasn't breathing.

Nathan looked at his watch. Then he speed-dialled Jacki's number.

The line rang.

'Nathan?'

'Jacki, something's happened.'

He heard her standing up. She was at home. The television was on in the background.

'Where are you? Are you okay?'

He spoke too fast. He had to pause to catch his breath. He stopped and started again. He looked at his watch.

'I got here. I was late. I just got here. And Bob – I think he's done something stupid.'

The sound of a door being closed. Jacki, at home, moving into the hallway. Her husband was called Martin. Nathan had met him once or twice.

'Nathan, now be calm. This is very important. Be calm. What do you mean?'

'I don't think he's breathing. I think he took something.'

'Do you know what he took?'

'No.'

'Are you able to induce vomiting?'

'I think he's *dead*.'

'Do you know CPR?'

'A bit. I'm the sales floor first-aid supervisor.'

'Then keep calm and remember what you were taught. I'll have an ambulance there as quickly as possible.'

'Okay.'

Nathan gave her the address and hung up.

He walked to the safe. He squatted, put the key in the lock.

On the sofa, Bob snorted.

Nathan nearly pissed himself.

He hurried over to the sofa. He looked into the cold, far corner, where the shadows were deepest. Then he took a greasy pillow and pressed it down on Bob's mouth and nose. There was no struggle. But Nathan pressed down until he could be sure.

His mind drifted.

He was awoken from this stupor by the distant wail of an ambulance.

He wiped the slobber-wet cushion on Bob's chest, propped it beneath his heavy head, then hurried to the safe.

He stooped. He turned the key. The door was three inches thick. It was constructed of cold, solid metal. It swung open with a satisfying weight. Inside the safe was the plastic-wrapped parcel. Through the plastic, Elise's skull showed its teeth to him, missing the lower mandible. Bob had snapped the long bones to make them fit.

Nathan took out the parcel. The safe was empty. He examined the parcel from all angles, rapidly, rotating it in his hands like a basketball.

But nowhere did he find the wrapped-up old carrier bag that contained Elise's rotted clothing, and his rotted DNA.

The sirens were appreciably closer now. Two or three of them. A chorus of emergency.

He stuffed the parcel back into the safe. He locked it. He put the keys in Bob's trouser pocket. He looked round the flat. He remembered that he had searched the bedsit once already. The clothes would not be where he had already looked.

A vehicle drew to the kerb outside. The flashing lights drew patterns on the ceiling. He heard car doors opening, hasty footsteps.

He said, 'Fuck.'

The doorbell rang.

He wondered how long it would be, before they broke down the door.

He called out, 'I'm coming!'

He looked at his drink, on the work surface of the kitchenette.

No ice, Bob had said.

Bob always had ice.

Until Nathan broke into the garage.

He ran to the fridge. He had to force back the rolled-up carpet to open the door, revealing the linoleum beneath, a layer of grease and crumbs. He went to the little freezer compartment. It was frozen shut. He forced it. It opened with a sharp crack. Fragments of dirty ice fell to the floor. He kicked the biggest of them beneath the fridge.

The remnants of Elise's clothing were inside the freezer compartment, still stuffed into a brittle, frozen Sainsbury's carrier bag, itself forced into a Ziploc freezer bag.

He ripped the bag free and forced it into a ball. It crackled like a campfire. He shoved the balled-up bag into the pocket of his raincoat. The bag was cold and wet against his thigh, and it made a bulge in the lining of his coat. Already it was beginning to melt. He looked down at it.

There were hurried footsteps on the stairs. Somebody must have opened the front door, or the police had forced it.

Nathan ran to Bob's side, removing the latex gloves, bundling them up and shoving them, too, into his pocket. He dragged Bob off the sofa – the fall punching the final breath from his lungs.

Nathan climbed on top of him and began to administer what looked like CPR.

The door exploded in its frame. He looked up and over his shoulder. Three paramedics were running in. They carried heavy shoulder bags, a portable defibrillator.

He shouted to them.

'I think I got him *breathing*!'

He was told to stand back. He stood back. He retreated to the far wall and stood there. He said, 'I'm sorry,' and kept repeating it, although he wasn't sure if the paramedics could hear.

But they must have, because one of them directed him to the kitchenette, safely out of the way.

37

Into the bedsit came two uniformed police officers. They were followed by Jacki Hadley. She was in plain clothes.

Nathan had the whisky bottle in his hand. Pretending to ruminate, he was using his thumbnail to pick the tiny bits of solder from the bottom of the cap. He'd almost forgotten about that.

Jacki noticed the wet patch on Nathan's leg – water from the melting carrier bag.

Nathan followed her gaze and half-grinned, sheepish.

'It's the shock,' said Jacki. 'It happens.'

'It happens.'

Nathan set down the whisky bottle and began deliberately to button his raincoat to cover the wet patch.

Jacki led him by the elbow to the far corner of the room. She said, 'Look, Nathan. I know this is a terrible shock. But I need to speak to you before you can go. Just quickly. We'll talk some more in the morning.'

Nathan nodded. 'Appreciate it.'

'The first thing I need to ask is – how did you get in tonight?'

'He left the front door on the latch. I think he wanted me to find him.'

Jacki's face softened. 'He's a troubled man,' she said. 'Don't blame yourself.'

'I'll try not to,' said Nathan.

He looked over Jacki's shoulder at the paramedics, two men and a woman, who were working so industriously to save Bob Morrow's life.

More police had arrived by the time they let Nathan go.

By then, Bob had been taken away. The police would be photographing the place, Nathan supposed; the ranks of books on the supernatural, the chalk circle on the floor. He wondered how long it would be before they found Elise. He was sure it would be tonight.

Not too soon, he hoped. He didn't want to be there when it happened.

Jacki walked upstairs with him. She stopped on the threshold, in earshot of the curious neighbours who'd gathered in the hallway and front garden. She hugged him.

'You did well. You should be proud of yourself.'

Tears came to his eyes. He wiped them away with the back of his hand. He could smell the latex and talcum. 'Thank you.'

She squeezed his hand.

He told her, 'All I have to do now is face Holly.'

'She'll understand.'

'I hope so.'

He gave her a brave soldier smile.

On his way home, he pulled into the kerb. From his pocket he fished out the now-limp freezer bag containing the balled-up vestiges of Elise's clothing. He examined it. They seemed such trivial scraps. What little evidence was on them had surely been destroyed by all those years in the soil.

Now he was alone, and now Bob was gone, that seemed obvious.

He thought about burning the rags somewhere. But that seemed an odd thing to risk being caught doing. So he got out of the car and lit a cigarette. He stood over a drain. He ripped open the bag and stooped down, stuffing the remnants between the rungs. Bits of rotten cloth clung to the wet metal. He eased them away with his fingertips. He poked down what was recognizably the toe shell of an Adidas trainer, perished and withered like a burst balloon.

He didn't think anybody saw him, but didn't think it mattered. For all they could see, he might be looking for something: dropped keys, perhaps. He stuffed the rolled-up gloves down there, helping them with the tip of his pen. The ripped-apart freezer bag followed, and the remains of the Sainsbury's carrier too.

That was it. All gone.

He smoked the cigarette and dropped that down the drain. Then he got behind the wheel of the car, and put the radio on.

38

When Nathan arrived, Holly was sitting in the living room, in darkness.

He stood in the doorway.

She said, 'They found her.'

He went to her. Kneeling, brushing the hair back from her face.

He wanted to look at her.

She did not want to look at him. She turned her head away.

He withdrew, standing.

He said, 'Will you call June and Graham?'

'In the morning. Let them sleep. Just one more night.'

He followed her to the kitchen.

There was too much to explain.

He said, 'We don't know it's her. Not yet.'

'It's her. You know it's her.'

She frowned, knuckling a knot between her eyes. She said, 'You lied.'

'I know.'

'If you hadn't. If you hadn't lied, we might have been spared . . .'
All this.

Holly said, 'Every word. Every word you ever spoke. All of it. Based on a lie.'

She lit one of his cigarettes. Her first for years.

'How could I tell you?'

'How could you not?'

'Because I didn't want this to happen.'

'Well, it's happening.'

'I know. I'm sorry.'

He searched for better words. But they'd passed into a territory where words had no function. So he just said, 'I'm sorry.'

They sat at the table and talked in slow circles until morning.

There was a dawn chorus. Sunrise through the condensation cast pearly drops on their skin.

In the wan light, she went to stare at the photos of Elise. Then she came back into the kitchen to light another of his cigarettes. She ran her hands through her hair. It was frizzy and dry: it needed washing. Her lips were cracked.

She said, 'I can't have you around me.'

'Okay.'

'You should never have lied. You should just never have lied.'

'I know.'

She grabbed his face. Her nails dug into his flesh. Her eyes fluoresced with hatred. And then her eyes welled with tears and she let him go.

At 6.30, she rang her parents. There were long silences at either end of the line. There were no tears. It was like the mumbled declaration of illness. Finding Elise was almost a disappointment. Having her back would change their lives again. Already she was coming between them, breaking up the close unit they had formed.

Holly was sad when she put down the phone. Something was found, something was lost.

He could see into her. She was wondering if it was worth it, and hating herself for thinking that.

Nathan had a headache. All that coffee and all those cigarettes. And no sleep. He was weary beyond measure.

Holly poured herself a glass of water from the tap. She drank it.

She looked at him, the empty glass in her hand. Her eyes were puffy and sore. She looked exhausted and old.

She said, 'When I get home, you need to be gone.'

He drew a long breath. He was so tired. He was almost glad.

'Whatever you think is best.'

She went upstairs and packed her bags. She wasn't very methodical about it. Later, he found the drawers still open: clothes ripped from them apparently at random. She left behind her favourite toiletries, her toothbrush, the book she was reading. She came downstairs lugging a big suitcase in two hands. It was the suitcase she'd taken on honeymoon.

He stood in the hallway, leaning against the stairwell. He rubbed at his bristling jaw.

He said it again: 'I'm sorry.'

She couldn't answer. She looked at him, then hoisted the suitcase and headed for the door, leaning away from the weight of it. She heaved the suitcase into the boot of her car. She sat at the wheel. She sat there for a while, looking at her lap. He watched her from the window. Then she started the engine and drove away.

He thought of her, speeding past the empty grave, the trees that would soon be uprooted.

Then he went inside their home. He went upstairs, to bed, and curled in a circle and slept. The bedclothes smelled of her.

39

It was the doorbell that woke him. Without it, he might have slept all night.

It was Jacki. He let her in. He was wearing the same clothes as the night before. He hadn't washed or shaved. He was in his socks.

He said, 'Coffee?'

She thanked him and followed him down the hallway and into the kitchen. He put the kettle on to boil. The water began to seethe.

'I wanted to see how you were.'

He shrugged and thought, *How do I look?*

'Have you seen her?'

'This afternoon,' said Jacki. 'She'll be all right. It's been a shock. Just give her time.'

'She can have anything she wants.'

Jacki crossed her arms and nodded, looking at the floor.

He said, 'I should've listened to you. All those years ago.'

'What's done is done.'

She took her coffee and blew across it, saying: 'My colleagues will need to ask more questions – as soon as you feel up to it.'

He erupted into goose flesh. He hoped she didn't see. 'What kind of questions? Am I in trouble?'

'Not at all. They'll just want the full picture. There's a bit of bruising around Mr Morrow's throat, for instance. They might want to ask about that.'

'I had to drag him off the sofa. He was so heavy. I hooked my elbow round his neck – like this – and kind of dragged him off.'

'You see. I knew it would be something like that. It's what I told them.'

'You already talked about it? Now you're making me nervous.'

'There's nothing to be nervous about. You just have to think very carefully about what happened last night.'

'Jesus, Jacki. You're freaking me out here.'

'I don't mean to. It's just that, people get a shock, they get confused.'

'I'm thinking pretty clearly.'

'Are you thinking clearly about the second glass of whisky?'

There was a moment. He blinked it away.

'What?'

'There were two glasses of whisky. The one Morrow was drinking from. And a second glass. Almost untouched. Very dilute. Lots of water in it. Lots and lots of water.'

He had spat in it.

Jacki was still waiting.

'I poured myself a glass. After the paramedics arrived. To calm my nerves. Then I thought better of it.'

Jacki nodded. She was not smiling.

'There you are. You see? There's always an explanation. If you're given enough time to think. How are you sleeping?'

'Fine. As well as can be expected. I mean, not so bad. Why do you ask?'

'Holly tells me you haven't been sleeping well.'

'Christ, Jacki. I've been stressed.'

'Did you see a doctor about it?'

'I did, as it happens.'

'Good. And did he give you something to help?'

'He did, yes.'

'It wasn't temazepam, was it?'

'It was, yes.' He waited. Counted three breaths. 'Why?'

'Temazepam is what Bob Morrow used. A massive dose. The whisky amplified its effects.'

'Ah,' said Nathan, scratching now at his inner wrist.

'When did you see your doctor?'

'I don't know. A few days ago.'

'So you've still got the pills?'

He tapped ash into the sink.

'Actually, no I haven't. I never liked taking pills. I flushed them away, the minute I got home.'

'I'd do the same. Horrible things.'

'You can't sleep, it's better to just get through it.'

'Totally. The thing is, you might want to have some temazepam around. You know. For form's sake. Just in case someone mentions it.'

'Will they?'

'Probably not.'

He said, 'I'm not sure I'd know where to get some more, without going back to my doctor.'

'I'm sure you'll find a way. You're not stupid.'

Nathan tugged at an earlobe. 'I don't know what to say.'

'As it happens, Morrow's got a history of drug abuse – and one or two suicide attempts, back when he was younger. He went a bit funny. When his mum died.'

'I didn't know that.'

'I don't suppose he liked to talk about it. He was seventeen. Difficult age to lose your mum.'

Nathan nodded.

'And the glass evidence, if it was evidence, was compromised. In all the rush, someone must have knocked it over. It got broken. It happens.'

'It must.'

'We're only human. So these things might not even come up. They probably won't.'

Nathan wet his lips with the tip of his tongue.

'Okay,' he said.

Jacki set down her mug and began to gather her things. She patted her pockets, looking for car keys. Thus distracted, she said, 'Give her time.'

'All the time she needs.'

Jacki got her coat and checked its pockets for the keys. The coat jingled. There they were.

Nathan said, 'You've always been a good friend to her.'

'Well, I made her a promise.'

She shrugged herself into her coat and said goodnight. She walked down the hallway, swinging the car keys from her index finger.

40

Six weeks later, Elise's remains were released. She was buried in the grounds of Sutton Down church, where Nathan and Holly had married. Some print journalists were there, but there were no cameras.

When it was over, June hugged Nathan and kissed him. Graham clasped both his hands. There was a great distance between them. They had not spoken since the morning Holly left him. They didn't know what to say to each other.

Most of the village seemed to be there, and many of Elise's school friends, older now. One of Elise's old boyfriends was there. He greeted Graham and June diffidently. At first they didn't recognize him. He had put on weight and lost hair. The sight of him made June cry. She touched his face.

Nathan watched them.

The mourners were drifting away. Nathan buttoned his coat and headed for the gates.

There were brisk footsteps behind him.

Holly.

She took his elbow.

He buried his hands deep in his pockets and turned to face her, saying, 'Hi.'

'Hi.'

She'd lost weight: she was thinner in the face. And she'd got her hair cut. It was much shorter now, and it shone red and autumnal in the ancient graveyard. She wore a black coat, black shoes. She carried a little black handbag, patent leather with a brushed-steel clasp.

He looked at his own shoes, shiny black and said, 'How are you?'

'I'm getting there. You?'

'Getting by. Y'know.'

'How's work?'

'Same old, same old. Justin's wife left him.'

Holly grinned.

'How's he taking it?'

'He's fine. Suddenly we've got a lot to talk about. That makes him happy.' He scratched his chin, considering it, then told her, 'We came up with a new line.'

'That's good.'

'We're calling it "Congratulations, You Left Him at Last". Until we can think of something better. The trade's gone mad for it. If it sells like we think it will, we might actually make our bonus this year.'

When he talked about work, she got a little upward turn at the inner corner of her eyebrows. And there it was, right now.

He said, 'People leave people all the time. The trade might as well get to grips with it.'

They stood on the grass verge to let some mourners pass by.

Nobody knew what to say to anybody.

That knot between Holly's eyes.

She said, 'You knew.'

He kicked at a wet tussock.

'Knew what?'

'That it was him.'

He shifted his weight. Looked at the sky and drew in a long breath. 'It did occur to me, yeah.'

'Why didn't you tell me?'

'How could I?'

She narrowed her eyes.

Nathan said, 'I like your hair.'

She touched it. 'It was time for a change. I kept it the same for too long.'

He tugged at a lock of his own hair, just behind the temple. 'I looked in the mirror this morning. I'm going grey.'

'You've been going grey for a long time.'

He took a step back

'Why didn't you tell me?'

'How could I?'

He laughed, sudden and hard; it shocked a murder of crows from the bare trees. They launched into the low sky and described a slow, outraged spiral.

He said, 'You always made me laugh.'

She leaned on a grave. It was eight hundred years old, worn smooth with time.

She said, 'I have something else to tell you.'

Six months later, their daughter was born.

Nathan held her, still bloody, and looked into her black eyes. He put his nose to the warm suede of her scalp. He breathed in the rich, fungal smell of her and had to sit for the headiness of it. She held his finger and he wept. He cradled her. He passed her to her mother, who bundled her in a crocheted blanket.

He stood at the bedside, looking on.

Bob didn't die. But his brain had been starved of oxygen; it lost its higher functions. Bob was in a persistent vegetative state. The vehicle of his consciousness had been destroyed.

Bob's library was put into storage. The reels of tape were examined and found to contain nothing but Bob's voice, asking questions to an empty room.

Information retrieved from the hard drives of his computers included the first fifty pages of a PhD thesis that had been discontinued in 1988, when the university rejected his proposal.

1988 was five years before Bob met Nathan, in the days when Nathan lived in the shared house at the end of Maple Road.

Nathan visited him sometimes. He never told Holly. He'd drive all the way to the hospital and sit at the bedside and just look at him. Sometimes Bob made noises. He howled or whooped or snarled. And sometimes he opened his mouth or tried to roll over. Sometimes he opened his sightless eyes. Nathan watched them spin in the sockets. But whatever had made this body Bob was gone.

Nathan wondered.

Once, he brought along a tape recorder. He set it down and let it record the stillness next to Bob's bed. He played the tape several times. But he never heard Bob's voice, or any other. There was just the hiss of silence and the random, distant clattering of the hospital.

He threw the tape away. From beneath the spare tyre in the boot of his car, he removed the reel-to-reel tape he'd taken from Bob's flat. He thought about playing it. But he knew it would be blank. So he unspooled the tape, cut it up with a pair of scissors and burned it.

Then he went inside, to his wife and his daughter.

Neil Cross is the author of the UK-published *Christendom, Mr. In-Between, Holloway Falls, Always the Sun*, which was short-listed for the Man Booker Prize, *Heartland*, and *Natural History*. He is the lead writer for the BBC's hit series *Spooks*, known as *MI-5* on BBC America. *Burial* is his first work published in the United States. He lives in New Zealand with his wife and two children.